An Angel Among Dogs

Charli Mac

Dreamsphere Books
Winnipeg, Canada

Published February 2023 by Dreamsphere Books, an imprint of Story Perfect Inc.

Dreamsphere Books
PO Box 51053 Tyndall Park
Winnipeg, Manitoba R2X 3B0
Canada

Visit http://www.dreamspherebooks.com to find out more.

An Angel
Among Dogs

1

I floated in a warm haze.

The world around me was a cushion of black velvet, stars winking like tiny jewels. I could almost feel my arms and legs stretch out as I luxuriated in the feeling of weightlessness. All was calm; all was well.

For the six days I was held captive. I lived in utter fear of death. But then it came, in a rush of pain, and...I was still here.

Still thinking, still being.

The world was gone, my body was gone, but not me.

I cried. I cried for what I'd gone through, and all the ways they'd hurt me before my body finally decided it could take no more, but mostly I cried for my husband, who might never know what happened to me, and my babies, who might not remember my face, who'd know me only through photographs and a few short video clips.

I had no eyes to shed tears, and no lungs to shudder as I wept, but I cried.

Then, eventually, I stopped. And there was nothing to do but exist. To dream.

And to wait.

2

First Hound Kai Strand was sweating.

The South Marshlands were living up to their name. The air was heavy with moisture and the sun beat down on his unprotected head. Next to him, General Mult Tuill sat on his mount like a statue. He hadn't uttered a single complaint in the three hours they'd been lined up, waiting for orders, and wouldn't if they stood there for a half dozen more, but he had to be suffering beneath the heavy padding he wore and the shining metal helmet that covered most of his bald pate.

Sometimes, just sometimes, it was good to be a Hound.

"Fucking hot," he complained.

The general just grunted.

"Think they'll fight? Or did we get all dressed up for nothing?"

The general opened his mouth as if he might answer, but nothing came out. Instead, a snide, clipped voice spoke from Kai's other side.

"Dogs don't need to think, Strand. Just keep your claws sharp and be ready to do the only thing it is your kind is good for."

Kai turned towards the voice, belonging to Lord Kath III, heir to the Xyron province and all-around pampered prick. His lordship was bedecked in all his finery, practically glistening in scarlet and green satin in the blinding sunlight. He could afford to be dressed like the rich man's son that he was, he wouldn't be getting involved in the action no matter what happened.

"I'm a Hound, your lordship, not a fucking dog. There's a difference."

"Is there?" Kath asked spuriously. "You don't have a tail, but that's about the only difference I can see."

Already on edge from the scent of violence in the air, Kai peeled back his lips and flashed his canines, fully extended and ready to taste blood, at the lord. A low, guttural snarl rumbled up his throat. Lord Kath paled, his mount fidgeting beneath him.

"I'll have you flogged," he warned, proving that he was as stupid as he looked.

"Shut up, Kath," General Tuill said mildly. "Without Kai and his boys, the odds would be heavily in the Badari's favor. Don't bite the hand that saves your arse."

"I'm the one that bites," Kai quipped.

General Tuill didn't rise to the joke. He just jerked his chin further down the line of mounted soldiers.

"Go and find out what the fuck's happening, would you? My balls are cooking, and if we're going to fight, I want to get it done before half my men drop dead of heat exhaustion."

"Sir."

Kai spared Lord Kath one more, menace-filled look, enjoying the way the man squirmed beneath his light-gold gaze, then kicked his horse forwards, heading for the royal pennant in the center of the line.

The man who sat astride the royal white stallion, dressed in the king's royal blue colors, with the king's banner fluttering above his head, possessed as much royal blood as Kai did, and a lot less than the self-important shit, Lord Kath. Janis had been the king's representative in battle since Kai was wet behind the ears, and he knew what he was about, wringing victories where they seemed nigh on impossible, so he had earned Kai's respect.

"General Tuill would like to know the king's plan," he enquired, when the older man nodded at him to speak.

A small smile escaped Janis' grim facade.

"Him and everyone else, Strand. Tell him to be patient but keep his sword sharp. We'll have at it before the sun sets."

Kai glanced quickly at the sky. The sun hovered high overhead, a long, long way from setting. When he looked back at Janis, hard grey eyes dared him to comment. He could, he knew, and he'd get away with it - today. But punishment would come along later, one way or another, and the price wouldn't be worth paying.

"I'll pass that along to the general, sir."

To his surprise, Janis let loose with a bark of laughter. "It only took you twenty years to learn to hold your tongue, Hound."

Proving he had, indeed, learned his lesson, Kai wheeled his horse about and galloped back to where Tuill waited without another word.

"Well?" the general demanded, his patience finally snapping.

"By sunset, sir."

General Tuill looked up to judge the sky for himself and let out a long, vicious stream of profanity.

"We are fighting then?" Lord Kath asked, his voice high and tight.

General Tuill threw him a scathing look. "*We* are, Kath. You'll not want to get your fancy togs dirty."

"My father—" Kath stammered.

"Is aware of what a weak son he's sired," Tuill finished for him. "I know full well what the orders are regarding you, *My Lord.*"

Kath spluttered, a hundred and fifty pounds of semi-royal indignation, and Tuill turned his back on him.

"You'll need to go and settle your dogs," he told Kai. Unlike when Lord Kath used the phrase, there was no malice in General Tuill's words, and Kai didn't take offense. "They'll never last the afternoon without killing someone, and we'll need every man we've got."

Kai tried not to look too relieved as he slid off his horse and tossed the reins to General Tuill's squire. It was useful, being in the lineup with the men in charge, but it wasn't where he belonged. When blood started staining the ground red, scenting the air with copper, he needed to be with his own kind. Leading them, protecting them, and sharing the euphoria of the kill with them. He was what he was, and Kai had learned a long time ago that it was better to embrace it, because no amount of wishing was ever going to make him a man.

There were over three thousand of the king's men lined up in mostly well-organized regiments across the wide plain Janis had chosen to challenge the Barari for this, their own land, but it was no problem for Kai to find the group of two hundred Hounds he commanded for the king. Though they were less than ten percent of the gathered army, they'd be responsible for at least a third of the enemy kills to come. They were feared by the rest of the soldiers—though not respected—and as large a gap as would be tolerated by the regiment sergeants had been established around where the Hounds stood, at the front and center of the field, where they'd be in the most danger, and able to inflict the most damage.

Though he approached silently and from behind, the rear-most Hounds turned to register his presence before he emerged from the depths of the King's Gold Shields, his best and most skilled fighters—after the Hounds, of course.

"First," the Hounds muttered quietly, dropping their gaze and angling their necks in respect of their leader.

Acknowledging them with a glance, he shouldered his way to the front so that he could gaze out at the open plain, verdant green and shimmering with moisture. As soon as he took his place there, he felt the restlessness and tension that he'd sensed emanating from the Hounds a half field away, dissolve into a keen, bloodthirsty readiness. They had their First; they were ready to unleash their beasts.

Air stirred to Kai's left and the earthy scent of his Second, Brannon, told him he'd taken his place by his leader. He could smell Brannon's excitement, his thirst for the kill, and he dropped a hand on the Hound's shoulder, reining him in.

"Not yet," he told him. "Soon."

He understood Brannon's eagerness. He felt it himself: the urge to run, hunt. To find the enemy and render flesh from bone. To taste blood, let it flow so fast he could paint himself with it. To bask in fear and pain until the beast inside him was satiated.

It was what Hounds were good for. It was what they did, why they were tolerated instead of being persecuted into extinction.

Beside him, Brannon whined eagerly. He leaned in toward Kai as the First lifted a hand to his shock of reddish-brown hair and gripped it firmly.

"Soon," he repeated.

Letting go of Brannon, Kai dropped to a crouch and reached down to the thick grass covering the ground. With a bare thought, thick, razor-sharp nails slid out and pierced the water-logged soil, anchoring him to the land. He let its cool solidness soothe the fire in his blood and hone his killing instinct to lethal sharpness. He hung his head for a moment, then lifted it to focus his gaze across the vast expanse of empty marshland. The Badari forces were just visible, a black smudge along the heat shimmer of the horizon. If he closed his eyes and inhaled deeply, he would smell it, their fear.

Soon he would taste it.

Kai stood, feeling the Hounds' focus. It wasn't across the field; on the enemy they'd soon be facing. It was on him, only on him. They watched and waited, the eagerness pushing on Kai. It was nearly overwhelming, but he swallowed back the instinct to throw himself forward into the fray. He had to hang onto his human mind for just a little longer…

It began with a howl.

Kai threw his head back and allowed the sound to

saturate the air around him. Two hundred throats answered it in unison. It was enough to make the fine hairs on his neck stand to attention and tremble, and he knew it would do the same and worse to the men who waited on the other side of the battlefield.

Now they knew what was coming for them.

He felt it come over him, the change. It was subtle; the Hounds did not transform into dogs, no matter the crude insults nobles like Kath flung at him. His pupils retracted to pinpoints as the yellow of his eyes shined brighter. His nails extended and his canines descended, becoming fangs ready to tear at flesh. Blood rushed to his muscles, making him bigger, more intimidating. Stronger.

The barked order to advance had come from somewhere far behind Kai, but not a single Hound moved until he echoed it in a throat almost incapable of speech. Then it truly started.

Long legs ate up the ground. There were faster Hounds than Kai in the group, but none of them placed a foot ahead of their First. He was the leader of this hunt. He ran upright, his long legs eating up the ground, but around him, several Hounds dropped down to gallop on all fours, their bodies made to adapt to uneven and sodden terrain.

Behind the Hounds, the men scrambled to catch up, but not too hard. They knew their best chance of survival was to allow the Hounds to tear the heart out of the enemy, then they would charge in to cut off its limbs and chop off its head. To steal the victory.

Were Kai thinking with the head of a man, he'd be infuriated by their actions, but the scent of battle was in his nose and his every thought was consumed by the need to kill. To destroy.

Kai ignored the pull of the mud and the chill of water soaking his trousers. An eternity counted in the racing beats of his heart, but finally the Badari were there, before him, ripe for the taking.

There was no trace of fear on their painted faces, but it hung in the air around them, exciting Kai and his Hounds even beyond the fervor of the fight that had them in its grip. Then the last few meters were closed, and the Hounds fell upon their prey, and fed.

"Strand."

Kai blinked and brought the face of General Tuill into focus in front of him. He had no idea how long the man had been standing there, or if he'd said anything beyond his name.

"What?" he asked.

He could form words, which was good. It meant he was coming back to himself, regaining whatever humanity it was he possessed.

"I said, well done," Tuill repeated. He went to drop a hand on Kai's shoulder, then thought better of it, letting the hand drift down to rest on the pummel of the sword he'd re-sheathed at his hip. "We took them with minimal damage. Less than a third of the army has fallen, and more than half are still on their feet."

"I lost eleven Hounds," Kai told him thickly. The pain of each was a dagger to his chest. He felt it, every time one of them slipped away. It fueled his rage in the heat of the fight, but now he felt only a terrible cold. They were so few, and now they were fewer.

General Tuill didn't offer platitudes or false words of consolation, but simply dropped his head in respect for a moment, acknowledging the loss. Kai appreciated the gesture; it was just one more reason why he liked the general.

"Janis wants to see you," Tuill told him. "They've taken over the Badari command tent."

He pointed behind Kai to where a large tent stood on a slight knoll. It was circular in shape and crafted from leather. Whatever flag might have been flying from the flagpole staked into the earth alongside it had been torn down and replaced with the royal blue of the House of Carvell. Kai started at it, stunned. He must have been held in the grip of his beast for longer than he realized. That was…worrying.

"I'll go," he told Tuill.

Though Janis wasn't a man to be kept waiting, Kai paused long enough to speak with Brannon and make sure his Second was grounded and able to take the responsibility of the pack without him, then he made his way to the blood-spattered patch of earth where each of his eleven Hounds had fought to their last breath, and, one by one, placed a hand upon their forehead. He didn't pray—it had been beaten into him more than once that the Hounds were not God's children—but he wished for peace for each of them and thanked them for giving their life for the king's cause.

Though he knew they hadn't, not really. They'd given their lives for him, and that was a heavy weight to bear.

His steps weary more from the pain in his heart than the ache in his muscles, Kai made his way to the tent where Janis waited. As soon as he stepped inside the cool, dim interior, Kai realized Janis wasn't alone. Dropping to one knee onto the rugs covering the floor, he waited to be acknowledged.

"Rise, First Hound," a warm voice commanded.

Lifting his head before he shifted to his feet, Kai took in the smiling, unlined face of Prince Faron as he came towards him.

"Your Highness."

The prince was young and had yet to prove himself in politics or war, but he had always been kind to Kai, to all the Hounds, and that was a rarity among the kingdom's nobles. He also showed a willingness to listen to his elders, and the two things combined gave Kai hope for the future.

"Another battle won because of you and your Hounds," the prince commended, clapping both hands on Kai's shoulders. Kai flinched, his senses still razor-sharp from battle, but he willed his body to stillness, quieted the beast who was still set to react to any touch with violence.

"You honor us," he replied.

"No, you honor us," the prince contradicted, "and you will have your reward."

There was a stirring of movement from the line of nobles who stood in the darkness at the rear of the tent, but Kai kept his gaze on the prince.

"Your Highness?"

"Next month is a blood moon."

"It is," Kai confirmed. It would be a wild night for the Hounds, the moon singing to them with her strongest voice. It came around only once every four years, and Kai had still not worked out if he craved or dreaded it.

"Father's head priest has also confirmed that it is a Solar Convexion." Prince Faron paused for a beat. "The first for a hundred and fifty years."

"That is…fortuitous," Kai said cautiously.

There was more movement from the shadows, a rush of urgent whispers.

"Sire!" one of the nobles gathered in the background called out. "You cannot mean to—"

Prince Faron waved his complaint into silence. His gaze was steady and serious as it bored into Kai.

"On the blood moon, when the Solar Convexion reaches its height, the gate in the temple sanctum will open. You may approach with your sacrifice and see if the spirits bless you, Kai Strand, First Hound. That is the reward my father offers for the service you have performed for his kingdom."

Kai could only stand there and stare at his prince, utterly speechless.

3

"I still can't believe this."

"I don't believe it."

Kai stood and listened to his son Dane's awe and his Second Brannon's suspicion as he stared up at the White Mountain Temple, the Kingdom's oldest and most glorious shrine to the Ether. He couldn't decide which of them he agreed with. Brannon likely had the right of it, but the small child inside him dared to dream that it was real. That something like this could happen to something like him. It gave him hope that maybe the world was changing enough that his son wouldn't have the youthful optimism that allowed him to believe in the truth of this day, beaten out of him.

He turned to Dane now, but his son was staring up at the temple, eyes wide and drinking it in. Hounds were usually not even allowed in the grounds of the place, never mind inside. In fact, this was the closest even Kai had ever been, he'd only ever glimpsed it from patrols of the surrounding hills before. Now, at the base of the narrow path that had been hacked into solid rock, Kai craned his neck to look up at the narrow towers of ornately carved stone, and the high arching roof of the main sanctum. He had to admit, it was impressive.

"Strand." The voice calling his name was as familiar as it was welcome. Kai turned to see General Tuill dismounting slowly from his horse, his stiff movements exposing his age. The lingering doubts he'd harbored, even before Brannon's words, began to slowly dissolve. The general would not involve himself in some elaborate scheme to humiliate him.

Tuill smiled as he approached, his steps smoothing out as he walked off the stiffness of a long, uncomfortable ride. The temple was a long way from the capital city. It had been built deep in the mountainous countryside, out of sight of even a hamlet or croft. The general gave a nod to the two Hounds standing at Kai's shoulder, then turned to Kai.

"You'll not be allowed to take any others in with you." Tuill's mouth pursed with distaste, eyes darting over Dane's long-limbed, lanky, youthful build. "It's not something the young one should see, anyway."

Tuill's final comment didn't make sense to Kai, but he was unsurprised by the rest of it. There were many places barred to the Hounds. Catching Dane's look of disappointment, he realized he should have prepared his son for the eventuality. He wasn't long out of the commune and hadn't had time to adjust to the shock of being considered a second-class citizen.

"It's for the best," he told him, before Dane could put voice to his unhappiness. "I don't want the nobles to know who you are. They'll use you to get to me, if they can."

Dane still looked dissatisfied, but he nodded bleakly. His eyes flickered towards General Tuill.

"I'm not a noble," the general supplied helpfully.

"And he's not an asshole, either," Kai finished.

"I'm glad you've got such a high estimation of my character, Strand," General Tuill shot back dryly. Kai flashed him a grin full of razor-sharp teeth and the general laughed.

"Come on, let's get on with it."

"You sound like you're going to an execution rather than about to receive the highest honor of your life," Kai remarked, patting Brannon on the back as he stepped forward. His Second would keep an eye on Dane, still any reckless urges the boy might come up with. The area at the base of the temple grounds wasn't spacious, and it was tightly packed with the entourages of all the important people already inside. Given that the noble's personal attendants tended to be as stuck-up and superior as their masters, there were likely to be all sorts of opportunities for trouble.

"Well—" General Tuill grimaced and gave a half-shrug. A military man through and through, *he* had come with nothing more than a dusty, tired-looking squire. "You'll see soon enough. It'll not be any easier with advance warning."

Kai would have pressed the general, but they had begun up the path and the final approach to the temple doors wasn't a long one; they were already within hearing distance of the tiny, wrinkled priest who stood in the open entryway to greet them. At least, he welcomed General Tuill. Kai, he looked at like a piss stain on the front of his robes.

"This way," he said, before turning on his heel and disappearing into the darkness.

Kai let General Tuill precede him into the temple, taking a moment to glance back down the hill to where Dane and Brannon waited. In the tight confines of the space, the two Hounds were given a wide berth. They were dangerous, even Dane who was full of the joy of youth, and who was yet to fill out the tall frame he'd inherited from Kai. Dane lifted a hand to wave, and Kai returned the gesture. When he returned—*if* he returned—he'd be irrevocably changed, one way or another. He'd read the accounts of the previous openings of the gate—even if everyone gathered inside, General Tuill aside, would be incredulous that he *could* read—and he knew something of what was about to befall him.

He'd either be one of the Bound or one of the barren. Blessed or cursed.

No Hound had ever been Bound before, but then, as far as Kai knew, no Hound had ever been allowed inside the temple. Perhaps he'd be the first. He hoped so, because Kai had had about all he could take of being cursed.

The heat hadn't been intense outside, the sun already down and taking her fire with her, but Kai still felt the relief of the temple's cooler air kissing his skin. Even his eyes needed a moment to adjust to the gloom, and as his boots echoed on the stone floor, following the footsteps of the priest and Tuill, he glanced around, drawn to drink everything in despite himself. It was stark, but beautiful. The walls were painted with images of the Ether: tiny glints of silver and gold inlaid into the frescoes. The pillars supporting the soaring roof were marble, and jewels winked from the leaded glass windows.

They crossed the large room and then moved through

a small, unadorned door that was propped open. The passageway beyond was narrow and low-ceilinged. It began to descend almost immediately; the steps were uneven and irregular, awkward in the dark, and Kai saw the general stumble. He righted himself before Kai could reach to steady him, and Kai heard him grunt at the priest's murmured admonishment to be careful.

Voices reached Kai long before the tunnel ended. He caught the youthful timbre of Prince Faron and the harsh, grating rasp of Lord Kenwick, who'd been almost strangled the year before by assassins who'd managed to sneak past his entire guard, into the Lord's bedchamber. If he hadn't been in bed with two girls instead of one, there would have been no one to scream and alert the guards posted just outside the room. At least, that was what Kai had heard he'd told his wife when she arrived back from visiting her father's coastal estate. Having met the Lady Kenwick, Kai wasn't sure she hadn't been the one to send in the assassins in the first place, and having also a more than passing knowledge of Lord Kenwick, he didn't even blame her.

There were others, but before Kai could register who else had been invited to receive the Ether's gift, the light changed and then General Tuill stepped forward and to the side, and Kai found himself in a claustrophobic bowl of a room, facing a lineup of the kingdom's richest and most privileged, most of whom he knew by sight, almost none of whom he liked. Given the way they were staring back at him, the feeling was mutual.

"General. Strand." Prince Faron greeted both Kai and Tuill as if they were the same, equals. Kai nodded back tightly. His every instinct was clamoring at him to extend his claws and allow his canines to descend—not helped by the imminent appearance of the blood moon, high, high above—but he fought it. The nobles in front of him may not see him as a man, but he'd be damned if he'd let them dismiss him as a beast.

"Your Highness."

Kai was bottom-ranked of everyone in the room, by a considerable margin. He'd no place being there, everyone except Tuill and Prince Faron knew it—and wanted to make sure he knew it, too. They needn't have worried. Kai knew where his place was, but he'd been granted the reward by the king, and he'd be fucked if he was going to let them piss all over this for him. Lifting his chin, Kai glowered at each and every one of the nobles who sneered at him, eyes glowing enough to be clearly discernible in the torch-lit room. Not a one of them could hold his gaze.

They were fools, because there was no surer way to incite the killer within a Hound than to show him weak prey, there for the taking. Kai's heart started thundering, the muscles in his legs twitching, preparing to leap.

Only Tuill sensed the danger, stepping in front of Kai and blocking the rest from view. He caught Kai's gaze and held it, no fear in his eyes.

"Stand down," he said, too low for any other to hear; too low for Kai to hear, had he been a man. "You'll have your chance for death in a moment."

There was no satisfaction in his words, and their somberness broke through Kai's focus. He fixed his gaze on the older man, trying to read what he wasn't saying on his face, since Tuill seemed determined not to give it away with his tongue.

"That's it," Tuill said, seeing his words had had the desired effect. "Settle down."

"What—"

Tuill's raised hand stopped him from questioning any further, and when the general turned his head towards the rear of the room, he followed his gaze. The same priest had emerged again, from a doorway Kai was disturbed to realize even he hadn't noticed. The priest's expression, if possible, was even more stern and unsmiling than before.

"You Highness, my Lords—" His gaze hit Kai and he tailed off. The pause lasted only for a beat, then he recovered. "It is time."

They traveled down again. A great chasm of rock hung above their heads, and it made Kai shudder to think of the vast weight dropping down on them all. He expected the tunnel to open out into another tight, airless room. Instead, they moved forwards into a great cavern that put the main sanctum above ground to shame. A trickle to the left told Kai there was running water somewhere, but he paid that no mind, his attention wavering between the cluster of wretched souls squatting in the center of the room beneath the angry gaze of a whip-wielding soldier, their fear so thick on the air Kai all but choked with it, and the rear wall of the great room, where a huge archway had been carved into the rock, the space beneath the arches an ebony stone that gleamed like polished glass.

The terrified unfortunates began whimpering and

keening at the appearance of Kai and the others, until one of the nobles, Lord Yule, snarled, "Shut them up."

It only took three indiscriminate lashes to quiet the group, though the soldier might have kept going, if the small smile on his face was anything to go by, had his arm not been halted by the vicious snarl that erupted from Kai's throat without his permission. He wouldn't have tried to stop it anyway; the beast might salivate at the thought of easy prey, but neither the Hound nor the man in Kai liked to see mindless cruelty. He'd been at the hands of it too many times himself.

Lord Yule turned on Kai, but the priest cleared his throat before he could do anything stupid like open his mouth. He'd positioned himself in front of the glistening black rock, the archway dwarfing him. He looked both eager and frightened, the hunch of his shoulders telling Kai he did not like having the strange surface at his back.

"The gate will open shortly," he told them, his hands twisting together in giddy readiness. "You will approach one at a time, with your chosen—" a darting glance at the group of sitting men and women who, Kai was just realizing, looked to be a sad mix of beggars, whores, and servants. His stomach twisted trying to work out what they were doing there. "You must make sure the blood touches the surface. When it does, well..." A smile small, fervor winning out over fear, "you will know."

Bonded or barren. Kai swallowed hard. He was here now; what would be would be.

"Time is of the essence; the blood moon appears only fleetingly. Our window of opportunity is small." He glanced around the group. "You will approach in order of your rank. Prince Faron, Your Highness, if you would make your choice."

Kai had known Prince Faron a long time. They weren't friends, but he knew him. Well. He thought he'd seen the man's every mood, but watching the prince approach the mewling, terror-stinking cluster, he saw something new. Resolve; at the cost of something very dear.

The soldier kicked out at a woman who was edging away from the prince, growling something Kai should have been able to hear but for the sudden thunder of his pulse pounding in his ears. Almost deaf from the noise of it, he watched Prince Faron deliberately step over the woman and grasp the arm of an old man so thin, it was nothing for the prince to pull him away from the others, practically dragging him across the floor towards the archway. The man made no attempt to move under his own steam, but he didn't fight, either. He seemed resigned to whatever was going to happen.

Low chanting broke out around the room, priests stepping forwards from shadows that had hidden them from even Kai's keen senses. He glanced at each of them, on alert and uneasy at being surrounded, even if it was by a bunch of old men in ugly grey robes, but they couldn't hold his attention for long. With their words, they'd unlocked something at the archway. The black rock was emitting a low light and was changing, subtly rippling like eels were swimming just beneath its surface.

Prince Faron's steps faltered as he saw the effect, but only for a moment. His grip on the man firmed, as did the resolve on his face. Closing the last few feet, he hauled the man higher, quickly shifted his hand from the man's arm to his lank, filthy hair, and jerked his head back. As soon as his neck was extended, Prince Faron slashed across with his free hand, the knife he'd discreetly palmed there slicing through skin and sinew and muscle, letting blood spurt free. It arced forwards, splattering onto the black rock, which—Kai could think of no other way to describe it—seemed to swallow it, to drink it down. Prince Faron dropped the now limp and lifeless body to the floor as the archway blazed with a sudden light and pulsed, a throbbing base that caused the floor to shake and small debris to drop from the ceiling.

Horrified and awe-struck, Kai waited.

Bound or barren. Bound or barren. Bound or barren.

Prince Faron ignored his audience and the dead man at his feet, his attention fixed on the wall in front of him.

Bound or barren. Bound or barren.

The liquid black mass swirled and rippled, and an answer came a moment later.

Bound.

4

The pulse woke me.

I wasn't asleep, just drifting. Being without thinking. It was what I did when I couldn't bear to be alone with my thoughts anymore. A way to let the time slide by, in the hope that, eventually, there would be something.

This was something.

I waited, alert and tense with anticipation, and then it came again.

What was astonishing, more so even than the appearance of the pulse itself, was the fact that it came from behind me. With that realization came the awareness of front and back, up and down. I'd been disembodied, floating weightlessly, for so long that the comprehension came with a rush of vertigo. The violent sensation of nausea whipped through me after so long not feeling anything at all. Bodily, at least.

I turned—another weird sensation—and then relearned the art of looking, focusing on something now that there actually was something to focus *on*.

My world had been an endless sea of nothingness, of inky black with tiny starlit sparkles. Now, that featureless night-time canvas was reborn. An oddly shaped blob of light, like an oversized Gothic church window, appeared, hanging impossibly in the air. As I watched, it rippled twice, and with each ripple, I felt another of those pulses. They reverberated in my center, rocking the heart of me.

The light itself wasn't that strong, like an open door to a room lit only by the beam of a small torch, but to me, after so long in darkness, it glared with all the brightness and vitality of the sun.

I willed myself to move towards it and found that I could. Relief made me giddy. Closer and closer, I drifted forwards. I had the curious sense, the nearer I got, that I wasn't alone. I couldn't see or hear or smell anyone or anything else, but I *felt* them, lingering by my side. That might have been enough to frighten me away, but I was near enough now to see that there was something beyond the light. That it was, in fact, some sort of window.

That there were *people*.

People!

Demons from hell couldn't have swayed me from my path.

A man stood in front of the strange archway, staring out at us. He was dressed oddly, in something that looked both expensive but ancient, like an outfit from a medieval play. His face was unlined, hair a dark chestnut and long, pulled back into a ponytail. He was looking right at me but his gaze, though determined, was unfocused. He couldn't see me, I was sure. He had someone else with him, a ragged-looking old man dressed in what seemed to be layers of scruffy sacking. He was holding on to him and, as I watched, he hoisted him up…then slit his throat.

I jerked, rearing backward as best I could with no body to move me, but still, it felt like the old man's blood sprayed across my face. I could feel it, touching me, even though there was nothing of me to touch. I might have made a noise. I would have if I'd had any control over my voice. I certainly screamed inside my mind.

That noise was abruptly cut off when something moved past me, close enough to brush against me, the feeling both tangible and intangible, and seriously disturbing. I couldn't see it, not until it hit the window and then...passed through. I saw the change in the surface, like water breaking slowly, or oil, and then I saw some*thing* on the other side.

I don't know how to describe it. It was both solid and not; real, but transparent and slightly glowing, like a ghost in a film. It was a creature, about the size and shape of a dog, though it looked more like a great cat, and its appearance seemed to have astonished the murdering man through the window as much as it did me, maybe even more so. He gaped at it, then reached forward and touched it with one, trembling finger. I saw the moment he made contact; he shuddered, and a little of the creature's strange glow rolled over him, like a flash of current. The man smiled then, though he was still visibly shaken, and a voice called from behind him. I couldn't hear what was said, it was muffled, as if underwater, but it caused the man to move back, out of sight. The creature went with him.

Another man moved forward to stand before me. This one had a young girl with him, though she was writhing and twisting and turning, doing everything she could to get away. Her open mouth told me she was screaming, too, though I could hardly hear it.

I knew what was coming next, I just knew. I wanted to close my eyes, but I couldn't look away. The man stabbed her, pushing through her back until the knifepoint broke out from her bony rib cage, tearing through her dress. She stiffened, then sagged down. He let her fall, just dropped her carelessly on the stone floor. Then he gazed straight ahead, the look on his face expectant.

Everything in me drew away from the man. I waited, expecting another of the presences surrounding me to move forward like before, but it seemed they, too, were repulsed. Nothing happened over long, painful seconds, until the man's expression changed from certain arrogance, to confusion, to rage. He had to be pulled away. Before he went, he aimed a kick at the lifeless young girl, glowering down at her like whatever had happened—or not happened—was all her fault.

One after another, men stepped forwards. One or two were youthful, but most were old. To a one, they were finely dressed. And each and every one of them brought forward some unfortunate wretch to murder. Some looked sickened, others grimly determined. One or two obviously took pleasure in the act. But all of them did it. The blood splashed through the window. Sometimes I felt it hit me with a tingle like a static charge, other times, I felt nothing. Except horror, and a morbid fascination that wouldn't let me move away.

At least eight times, I watched death happen right in front of my eyes. Then, whoever stood before us would wait. Sometimes, nothing happened at all. And sometimes, I'd feel a stir of air and then the window would ripple as whatever had responded to the call of the blood passing through, and a creature of some sort would appear. Small, tall, timid looking or terrifying, they were all different. But none of them were human, not even close.

Surrounded by life for the first time since I died, and I wasn't sure if I'd ever felt more alone.

Just when I thought I could take no more, when everything in me was screaming to turn away, begging my eyes to close, another man stepped forward. He was different from the rest. He wasn't so fancily dressed, for one thing, and his eyes were a strange color, a light shade of amber that glowed brightly from the shadow of his face. The main difference, however, was that he was empty-handed.

Well, not quite. He held a knife in his hand, but his other was free to clench into a tense fist. He stared in towards us, in our inky prison, though his head was cocked to the side, as if he was listening to something. I watched him shake his head and respond with something terse, then he opened his clenched fist and, without hesitating, drew the knife across his palm, slicing deep. Blood ran down his fingers, dripping onto the stone floor, but nothing penetrated the window. Bizarrely, I found myself pushing forward, reaching for it. When he lifted his hand and pressed it to the window, I was right there, inches from him. So close, I should have been able to feel the gentle puff of his breath against my face.

Though I couldn't have told you I could do it until that second, I lifted my hand in return, and pressed it against his. I felt a moment's heat, then a full-body frisson as that static charge washed over every nerve.

Then I fell through the window.

5

I don't know who was more shocked, me, or the man who caught me.

And he did have to catch me. Finding myself in a body for the first time in what seemed like an age, I crumpled, my legs folding beneath me. He didn't let me hit the ground and the horrifying pool of blood that waited there. He reached out, reflexes amazingly fast, and wrapped one arm around my back, his other hand gripping my upper arm. We stared at each other for a brief moment, both of us wide-eyed.

As I gazed at him, I registered the fact that his arm was pressed firmly against the bare skin of my back. I'd come through unclothed.

He recovered before I did, and he lifted me back to my feet. As soon as he was sure I wouldn't drop again, he let me go and tore his tunic off. In another swift, economical movement, he had it over my head. It was warm from being on his body, and long enough to hit me at my knees, like an oversized dress. Then, before I had a chance to thank him, to my astonishment—as if I could get any more astonished—he dropped to one knee, not seeming to care about the grisly remains on the floor. He bowed his head and muttered something in a low and reverent voice. It sounded like a prayer.

I didn't know what to do. There were other people in the room, I could hear them, see them out of the corner of my eye, but my attention remained fixed on the man in front of me. Tentatively, feeling like I was about to touch a live wire, I reached out and placed a hand on the top of his head. He had shorter hair than the rest, and it was thicker, coarser, more like a horse's than a man's.

He shuddered when I touched him, then he looked up, the movement making my hand fall away. Those eyes. They were not normal. If I thought they were glowing before, it was nothing compared to now. He slowly got to his feet, gazing at me the whole time, and as he reached his full height, I had to tilt back my head to look at him. He was tall and broad, consuming my attention so I didn't notice the hand reaching in from the side. It shackled my wrist in a bone-crushingly tight hold, pulling me from the spell I'd been gripped by, and suddenly I was aware of all the shouting in the room.

"—cannot be allowed! He's not even a man!"

"Get some soldiers in here!"

"Your Highness, step forward! We can still perform the binding if we—"

The hand holding me squeezed impossibly harder, pulling at me, and I cried out. It was painful, but it also released a flash of memory: being tied down, pain a fire across my belly, yanking and tugging and pulling at my wrists, but the restraints shackling them only tightening even more. One of the creatures from before must still have been in the room, because I heard growling and snarling, like an enormous dog preparing to attack, but I couldn't focus on anything, trapped in the grip of a panic attack. My breath wouldn't come, and I couldn't move. The terror inside me swelled up and up my throat, until I thought I'd choke on it.

There was a flash, a rush of heat like a fireball unfurling in the room. Everything went white for a heart-stopping, disorienting instant, then I could breathe again, the air whistling into my starved lungs. Dizzily, I registered that I was being held by someone, their strength behind me propping me up. It was the man whose blood had called to me through the archway.

There was no more shouting; in fact, the room was deathly quiet.

As soon as I thought that, I remembered the bodies of the murdered men and women, and immediately regretted the turn of phrase. They were just lying there, discarded and forgotten. And they weren't the only things on the ground. All of the ones I'd seen stand before the gate and kill, were, to a man, lifting themselves up off the stone floor, along with a handful of men in ugly grey robes. I didn't see the creatures that had made their way through the gate before me, just a tell-tale glow peeking out from the shadows of some of the men. Who were all looking at me, though I didn't understand why.

There was a caution that hadn't been there before, perhaps even some fear in their faces.

The man closest to us, though I would have pegged him as the oldest in the group, got to his feet first and approached us, each step deliberate, his eyes watching me carefully. He spoke, his voice gruff and authoritative, "And that would be why you do not step between a Celestial and her Bound. What in the hell were you thinking, Kenwick?"

The question didn't sound particularly rhetorical, but whoever Kenwick was, he didn't answer. The man turned to the one holding me. "Go, Strand, take her. Quickly. I'll deal with this."

Strand let me go and stepped to the side. He held out a hand and I reached for him. I didn't know him, not at all, but he'd drawn me as soon as I saw him, and if it was a choice between going with him or staying with the rest, the creepy-looking priests and the band of murderers—including the man who'd just told us to leave—I was definitely going with him.

I thought he'd take my hand and lead me away, but instead, he bent down and lifted me up into his arms. As soon as he had a firm grip on me, we started moving. Fast. His arms were an uncomfortable cage around my back and beneath my knees, but I didn't fight his hold, I clung to it. I felt weak and my head was throbbing, and more than anything I wanted out of the dark, cavernous room that had become a tomb. I leaned my head against his chest, suddenly weary to the depth of my bones.

Strand glanced down at me, worry etched across his features, but then he focused once more on the path ahead. He quickened his pace until we were jogging, heading up a passage so narrow the stone scraped my bare feet and snagged swinging tresses of my hair.

The tunnel ended and we spilled out into a large room, the man's footsteps echoing loudly in the space. I barely had time to register a high ceiling and fancy marble columns before we were outside. It was night-time, but it was warmer, the air soft and balmy. The darkness was kept at bay by a series of torches, but it hadn't gone far. The world beyond the patches of light remained a mystery. Strand, clearly not feeling we were going fast enough, started running again. I clutched at him, terrified he'd drop me, and he murmured something soft at me, rubbing his jaw against my head in a comforting gesture.

I was comforted, but that didn't mean I wasn't relieved when we stopped. Strand put me down and took a solicitous step back. I wobbled, but I kept my feet. We'd halted beside two other men, but there was a small crowd standing around, watching us curiously.

"Kai, what the fuck is going on? Who's she?"

I turned towards the voice and the man who'd spoken took a closer look at me and paled. He swallowed, the movement visible in the column of his throat, then looked over my shoulder towards the building we'd just exited. When his eyes flicked back to me, he was so wan he looked as though he might faint. He dropped fluidly to one knee; head bowed so low I couldn't have reached out to touch it even if I hadn't been too stunned to move.

"Get on your fucking knees, Dane," he hissed and tugged the second man, who looked much younger, down beside him.

I turned towards my rescuer, Strand—Kai?—looking for an explanation, but he just gazed back, eyes running across my face time and again, as if he couldn't believe what he was seeing.

"My lady," the older of the kneeling men murmured, "we are blessed."

"I—" I had no idea what to say. "Please, stand up."

Both men rose fluidly. They stared at me for a heartbeat longer, then looked at Strand.

"I don't know," he said, in answer to an unspoken question. "But we need to leave. Now."

He glanced back up the way we'd come once more, and both men took the hint, jumping into action. I stood numbly, dumbly, while they bustled about me. Strand remained by my side, a silent watchdog, and none of the men—for they were all men, I noticed—standing paying witness to the scene, spoke to us or made any move to approach.

They weren't silent, though; a dozen furiously whispered conversations echoed around us, hissing like a breeze in the claustrophobic circle of light.

Thankfully it wasn't long before the two men with Strand were ready to go. They led over three horses and the youngest vaulted on board one while the other man came to stand by Strand's side.

"You'll run?" Strand asked him.

The man nodded and Kai turned to me, holding out his hand.

"My lady," he said.

"My name is Bethany," I blurted, because I felt ridiculous being referred to as a lady, and establishing names seemed quite important if I was, as it appeared, going to be riding off into the night with these men.

Strand took a deep breath, as if I had gifted him with something momentous, rather than just my name. He put a hand on his chest and gave me a short bow.

"I am First Hound Kai Strand. This is my second,

Brannon Valden." He nodded towards the man not on horseback, then looked up to the younger male. "And my son, Dane." He paused. "It is an honor to be your Bound."

Bound. That was the second time someone had mentioned that word. I had absolutely no idea what to say in response, so I turned to the two other men and offered a small smile.

"It's nice to meet you."

They were ridiculous words, given the circumstances, but it steadied me to say something so normal.

"Please, Lady Bethany," Kai urged. "It would be best if we left quickly."

So much for just being plain old Bethany.

I allowed him to lead me over to a horse. He lifted me up with gentle hands and, from the way he positioned me, I think he expected me to sit side saddle, but I'd never done that before and I didn't fancy having my first try right now. Deciding he'd just have to be horrified at my blatant lack of ladylike comportment, I swung my leg over and tried to feel as secure as I could on a horse for the first time since I was a teenager.

Kai stared at me for a moment, but obviously decided discretion was the better part of valor, because he got on his own horse without saying anything and the man called Brannon moved forwards to wind a short length of rope through my horse's bridle.

"Brannon—"

"Her life before mine," Brannon replied quickly.

"And her life before mine." Kai looked to Dane, then

back towards me. His eyes were flames. "Her life before all of ours."

Brannon nodded, acquiescing. I swallowed, feeling sick.

"I don't want anyone to put themselves in danger for me," I said.

Kai smiled thinly at my words, but the serious look he leveled at Brannon told me he paid them no heed.

"Let's go," he said.

A soft click had his horse moving, and mine followed docilely behind. We walked a few choppy steps before breaking into a trot, Brannon jogging beside me. In less than a minute, we'd left the rest of the men behind, along with the light. The sky was heavy with cloud, and I could see nothing. Lost and frightened, I clutched my reins uselessly and hoped I was doing the right thing, trusting three strangers.

6

"How, in the name of the Ether, did you call a Celestial?"

Kai didn't reply, focusing on his fingers as he wound a protective leather strap around the wound in his palm. He'd sliced deeply. Puffy and red now, the gash would be sealed by the time the dawn rose. In another week, there would be no trace of the injury. That didn't mean it didn't bloody hurt.

"Kai, seriously. She's a fucking angel!"

"Did you think I hadn't noticed?" Kai asked quietly. "And keep your voice down, you'll wake her up."

He glanced over at the angel in question, the Lady Bethany, letting himself drink in the sight of her. Like he had every five seconds since she'd fallen through the gateway, straight into his arms.

He was Kai Strand, a Hound, a damned dog. A nothing. And he'd called an angel.

It didn't make any more sense now than it had the last dozen times he'd thought it.

"I thought they were a myth," Dane murmured, his voice tinged with awe. "I mean, an angel hasn't walked the land for—"

"More than a thousand years," Brannon finished for him. "They won't let you keep her," he added quietly to Kai.

Kai knew that. It didn't stop the surge of possessive anger from streaking through him.

"She's mine," he growled.

"We won't let them take her!" Dane declared.

Brannon ignored Dane; his gaze fixed on Kai.

"They'll kill you. They'll kill all of us, to get to her."

"If they kill me, they lose her anyway. I'm her Bound."

The spirits that came through the gate could only remain so long as their Bounds' hearts beat. As soon as a Bound died, the spirit winked out of existence, returning to the Ether.

Brannon shook his head. "I've heard there's a spell, that the priests can do a rebinding, so long as the spirit is willing. They'll cut her ties with you and bind her to the king, or Prince Faron."

"Prince Faron wouldn't—"

"For eternal life? Endless power? Of course he would! Don't be stupid, Kai!"

Kai's snarl ripped through the clearing where they'd set up a temporary camp. Brannon ducked his head, his shoulders tight, but he clenched his jaw, refusing to take the words back.

Long seconds of silence ticked by. The air was thick with aggression, Kai's instinctive response to being challenged. He beat back the need to reinforce his will with violence; Brannon was his friend as well as his Second. And despite his anger, Kai knew he was right.

If he tried to hold onto the Lady Bethany, he risked not just his own life, but all of the Hounds. Because the king's closest advisors would know exactly how to hurt him.

He turned his head to look at her, lying in a pallet of all the blankets they'd been able to scrounge together, and still it was a poor excuse for a bed. She squirmed in her sleep, trying to get comfortable on the hard ground, and Kai felt his heart thump hard in his chest. He'd kill for her already, there was no question. He'd die for her, too, and consider it just payment for the honor she had given him, choosing him above others.

Would he allow all of his kind to die to hold on to her?

Gods help him, he thought. He would.

"Kai," Dane said quietly. "Eternal life?"

Kai gave a grim smile. "It's not eternal life."

"Oh." Dane looked disappointed. "But Brannon said—"

"A man Bound to an angel doesn't age," Brannon confirmed.

"Then how—"

"Just because a man doesn't age, doesn't mean he doesn't die," Kai said grimly. "How many Hounds do you know who've died before their time? How many died just days ago, when we faced the Badari? And a man Bound to an angel has unfathomable power at his disposal. It makes him dangerous, makes him a threat. To anyone and everyone. No," he shook his head. "A man Bound to an angel has a short lifespan."

Dane considered that, gazing over at Lady Bethany.

"She doesn't look all that dangerous," the younger man said finally. "She just looks like…a woman."

"I'm not sure she even knows what she is," Kai murmured. He gave a small smile. "But she's powerful, I promise you that."

The explosion of energy she'd unleashed in the cavern had been enough to send every man there to their knees.

Sheer luck had kept Kai out of its path, but he'd felt the force of it rip past him. He'd seen her face when it happened; he was sure she hadn't understood what she'd done, or even that it had come from her.

"Where are we going to go?" Brannon asked. "What are we going to do? If we disappear, they'll just target the females and the young. They'll publicly execute them one at a time, until we slink out of hiding."

"They don't know where the commune is," Kai argued.

"They'll find it. They'll tear through the whole kingdom inch by inch if that's what it takes. You know they will. Kai…," Brannon broke off, his voice choked with emotion.

Kai knew what was on his mind. His son. He'd be four summers old now, and Brannon hadn't seen him since he was a baby, since he took the child from his human mother and snuck him away to the commune. He wouldn't see him now until the boy returned as a man, ready to take his place with the Hounds. The price every male paid for the promise the females and children would be allowed to live in peace. Even so, even with the treaty signed by the king, males didn't travel to the commune unless it was to deliver a child. There was too much risk the location would be discovered.

Kai sighed. He tried to stare into the flames, but his gaze was drawn beyond, to where Lady Bethany slept. She looked completely harmless, lying there. It was hard to believe what she really was.

She was the greatest gift Kai had ever been given in his life, more than he could ever have dreamed of, but the cost to keep her?

How could he look Brannon in the eye and know that his selfishness had cost the man his son?

"I'll take her back to the temple," he said quietly.

Dane gave an unhappy exclamation, but Brannon's shoulders dropped in relief, the breath releasing from him in a shudder.

"That," a voice growled from the dark, "would be a spectacularly bad idea."

Kai had scented the man just a moment before his voice pierced the night. Brannon, too, had known he was there, but Dane jumped to his feet in alarm.

General Tuill entered the circle of firelight alone, and from the opposite side to where Lady Bethany lay. On his shoulder, sat his Bound. Cold-blooded, with thick, leathery skin and razor-sharp claws, Gryts could be vicious when the need arose, but it was the wings folded tight against the creature's back that made it valuable – a Gryt could deliver a message faster than anything else in the Kingdom. The gods had favored Tuill.

There were no others with him, or else Kai would never have allowed him this close. Still, as he approached, Kai stood and positioned himself protectively in front of the angel.

Brannon, too, shifted to cover both his First and Lady Bethany. No matter his opinion, he would follow Kai's lead.

"It's all right, Strand." Tuill held his hands up. "I'm not here to take her from you."

"As if you could," Dane sneered.

Kai twisted to fix his son with a quelling look, then

turned back to the general. He waited, every muscle tense. He trusted this man, but the stakes had changed.

"Well, this has been a hell of a night," Tuill said at last, breaking the tension. He rubbed his face and let his shoulders sag; he looked exhausted. Still, Kai didn't retreat from his state of quiet watchfulness. "Can I sit?" the general asked.

Kai considered for a beat, then gave a nod. He stepped around the flames, keeping his protective position and leaving the far side of the fire for Tuill to seat himself. The older man levered himself down onto the rotting branch they'd been using as a bench. He saw the way the three Hounds remained standing, body language radiating threat, and grimaced. On his shoulder, the Gryt shifted uneasily, feeling the tension too. Tuill reached up and rested a hand on the creature's claws for a moment, stilling it. It was tough, but it wouldn't survive a fight against three Hounds.

"You're right to be wary," Tuill said, sighing. "There's a half dozen nobles out there ready to cut off your head. Of course, given that that would send the cause of all this trouble right back where she came from, I've managed to convince them that wouldn't be the best idea."

"You're trying to tell me they're going to accept this?" Kai didn't believe it for a minute.

"Well, no." Tuill's lips twisted wryly. "I wouldn't say that."

"What *are* you saying then?" Brannon asked.

"They want to keep her," Tuill said simply. "They don't give a shit about you, Strand, and if they could kill you, they would, but after her little stunt in the cavern, well," he spread his hands. "They've decided asking might be better than taking. You've Prince Faron to thank for that. The boy's a smart head on his shoulders; he's not rash, like the rest of those fools."

"You've a message for me." Kai was soldier enough to understand why they sent Tuill to deliver it, and not to resent him for it.

"I do." Tuill nodded, making no pretense. "Prince Faron and his nobles respectfully request you bring the Celestial to the palace. You are First Hound, sworn to protect the king. So long as you pledge your continued loyalty, and promise you will only use the power available to you through your Celestial to the benefit of the kingdom, they will not try to take her from you."

"Bullshit."

Tuill pressed his lips together, his expression unreadable. "That is the message I was sent to deliver."

Kai snorted. He believed it of Prince Faron, maybe, but as for the rest of them… They were a nest of snakes.

What choice did he have, though? If he declined, he'd have every soldier the king could command after him. He'd take the Hounds back a hundred years, when they were persecuted and hunted, this time until they were wiped out of existence.

"I will come," he confirmed.

Tuill didn't even bother to try to hide his relief. What he did try to hide was his disquiet.

"Now?" he asked.

Now? When he'd be alone but for his Second and his son, a fledgling soldier? No.

"Ten days," he said. Tuill shifted uneasily. "My life and the lives of all of the Hounds forfeit if I fail," he promised.

The general clearly wasn't much happier with Kai's vow, but he nodded. Message imparted and promise extracted, he got up as slowly and painfully as he'd sat. He paused when he'd straightened, looking for the first time toward Kai's angel.

"She looks so innocent, doesn't she?" he sighed. "It's hard to believe a little thing like that could be the cause of so much trouble."

7

The sun rose in a wash of oranges and pinks. High, high up, a small flock of birds flew across the lightening sky.

I lay on my back, drinking it in like a woman dying of thirst.

Color. Life.

God, how I'd missed it. The beautiful scene blurred as tears misted my eyes. I had no idea where I was, or who the men were that I was traveling with, but after so long floating aimlessly in the dark, I was *somewhere*, and even terrified as I was, that was a relief.

I sat up to find three sets of eyes watching me. There was a reverence there that really unnerved me. That, along with all this Lady Bethany business, made me fear there'd been a case of mistaken identities of epic proportion.

"Hi," I said weakly, when no one spoke.

"Good morning," Kai said. He sat closest to me; the other two had taken positions on the other side of the campfire that had burned out long enough ago that it wasn't even smoking anymore. "Are you well rested?"

"I—" I'd slept fitfully, but well rested? Maybe it was being in a body for the first time in...I had no idea how long, but after a night of sleeping on the ground, even with a couple of blankets beneath me as a makeshift bed, my every muscle was stiff and sore. Of course, some of that was likely the horse ride from yesterday. I eventually settled on a smile and a quiet, "I'm fine."

Kai nodded. "We need to set off soon, but you have a little time to eat."

He held something out to me, and I took it automatically, realizing when I had it in my hand that it was some sort of dried meat, a kind of jerky. It looked tough and unappealing, but I was hungry enough—another sensation I'd forgotten—to give it a try. Murmuring my thanks, I started gnawing on it, trying to rip a piece off. It tasted gamey, but mainly of salt. Yuck.

"I'm sorry," Kai said, catching my expression. "We did not bring proper provisions on this trip. I didn't think—" he broke off, clearing his throat uncomfortably. "Never in my wildest dreams did I think I would call a Celestial from the Ether."

And there it was.

"I don't think I am what you think I am," I offered softly. "I'm not...I don't really know what a Celestial is, but I'm fairly certain I'm not one."

"An angel," Brannon offered from across the circle. "You're an angel."

He ducked his head after he spoke, as if he was embarrassed to address me directly.

"I'm not," I corrected, as gently as I could. "I'm just a woman."

I was on dangerous ground here. They'd taken me with them on the assumption that I was one of these Celestials— an angel, ha!—and I didn't know what I might do if they abandoned me when it became clear I wasn't. I had no idea where I was, and I'd nothing to wear but the tunic Kai had given me. I didn't even know how to find water.

And I definitely didn't want to go back to the temple where I'd witnessed mass murder.

But still, if I pretended, and they found out later on that it was all a charade…

Better to just get the truth out up front, I decided. Then I'd deal with whatever the consequences were.

I took a deep breath, trying to work out what else I could say to convince them, when I realized they were all smirking at me, amused.

"I'm not an angel," I repeated stubbornly, a scowl edging onto my face despite the precariousness of my situation. I'd never dealt well with being the butt of the joke.

"Forgive us, my lady," Kai said apologetically, "It's just…you are."

"I'm not—"

"You are," he insisted. "There is no doubt in my mind. Look at you, you are glowing."

"I'm—" I looked down and the words I was going to say died in my throat. I was, I was glowing. The rising anger I felt gave way to astonishment, and then, before my very eyes, the glow dimmed.

I looked at Kai, and he was staring back at me as if it was as miraculous to him as it was to me.

"You're a Celestial," he told me. "An angel."

"I don't understand what that means," I whispered, unable to deny anymore that there was *something* different about me. "I don't understand any of this."

Kai looked troubled. "I didn't think when I came to the temple that the creatures that came through to be Bound…that they weren't aware of what was happening."

He shifted towards me, his eyes pleading. "You chose me," he said. "You chose to be my Bound."

I wanted to shake my head at him, to tell him I hadn't chosen anything at all, but I couldn't. Firstly, because even strong as he was, he looked like that answer would crush him, and secondly, because I had chosen him, hadn't I? He'd drawn me to the very edge of the window, and when I'd felt that static charge roll over my body, I hadn't even thought about it. I'd had to lift my hand and touch him.

"I did," I said, "I chose you, but I didn't understand what I was choosing. I don't know what it means to be your Bound."

"Kai." Brannon's low voice cut across our conversation, but Kai didn't tear his eyes away from mine. "Kai, we have to go."

Kai nodded, acknowledging the words, but he kept his gaze on me. "All right." He stood suddenly, and held a hand out to me. I took it, and he pulled me up in one fluid movement, not letting go of my hand even when he had me on my feet. "I'll explain on the way."

I was able to take stock of the land a bit more as we traveled, the horses going at a slow canter that still seemed much too fast for the poor man reduced to running as he towed me along on a rope. He didn't complain, though, or even seem particularly out of breath, and so after the third time my suggestion that the horse could probably survive with the two of us on was met with a head shake and a curt but polite, "No, my lady", I shut my mouth and concentrated on looking around me.

It was hot, first of all. Before the sun had even climbed

midway into the sky, I felt its punishing heat turning my very pale skin an ugly shade of red. The sky was a wicked blue, the land a clay red. There wasn't a lot of green, the shrubs and grasses that dotted the ground burned to muted shades of yellow and brown. We seemed to be following a creek, though its bed was filled with nothing but sand and stones. A series of mesas rode alongside us far off to my left, but to my right, there was nothing but plains stretching as far as the eye could see. It was a brutal, unforgiving land, and my sweating fingers clutched tight to the reins.

We pulled to a stop at no signal from either man that I could see, and Kai handed me a waterskin. There wasn't much left in it. I took a hesitant sip, frighteningly aware that there didn't seem to be anywhere close by to refill it. The water was hot and had a brackish aftertaste but still, my body craved more. I ignored the urge to gulp it all down and passed it back. Well, I tried to. Kai just stared at me, with that unnerving yellowish gaze, until I took another sip, and then another. Only then did he indicate that I should pass it over to Dane, who'd halted his mount on my other side.

"She's burning," Brannon commented from below me. I looked down to see him running his gaze over my exposed skin, his mouth turned down in an unhappy frown.

"I'm fine," I commented quietly, though in truth the back of my neck prickled like fire ants were running riot across it. My companions all had darkly tanned skin which was holding up much better to the sun's rays.

"We could wrap her in one of the blankets?" Dane suggested.

"No," I said quickly. I'd suffocate, and the breeze

created by our forward momentum was the only thing making the ride bearable. We'd been stopped for only a minute or so, and already I could feel the baking heat closing in on me from all sides. I was also becoming uncomfortably aware of the inside of my thighs, which were chaffed raw and stinging like blazes as sweat sprang up all over my body.

"It would be best, Lady Bethany," Kai chided. "Your skin is so fair—"

"I'll get heat stroke," I told him firmly, trying to sound like I knew what I was talking about. He didn't look convinced, his eyes on the wad of fabric rolled up and tied to the back of Dane's saddle. It hadn't felt all that thick when it was between me and the hard ground now wrapped around me.

I hauled in a deep breath, already feeling its smothering embrace.

"Please," I added quietly.

That did it, somehow. Kai's mouth pressed into a line, but he gave in with a quick nod. "You'll drink, then," he instructed.

Without prompting, Dane thrust the waterskin back under my nose. I took it, weighing it in my hand and noticing again just how light it was.

"Brannon needs it more," I argued. "He's running in this heat!"

"He's fine." Kai dismissed my concerns with a slash of his hand, and Brannon himself looked thoroughly insulted, though sweat stuck his hair to his forehead and darkened the sleeveless tunic he wore. "Drink, my lady."

"Bethany," I muttered.

Kai allowed his lips to twitch up in a tiny smile of acknowledgment, but he made no move to use my name, instead frowning at me until I took a small swill, then, conscious that he was still watching, another, deeper one. He didn't release me from his unwavering gaze until I'd drained the thing and handed it back to him.

"We'll walk a bit," he said, as he tucked it back into his saddle bag where, I was praying, he had another, fuller one. "Rest the horses."

I nodded, grateful for the reprieve both for my thighs and for Brannon, who'd worked so much harder than the rest of us and whose water I'd just drunk. I'd have offered to swap with him for a while, to let him rest while I stretched my legs, but I could guess how the offer would be received, and I didn't have any shoes to protect my feet from the ground. As the horse started to move and the saddle shifted beneath me, scraping the tender skin on my thighs, I thought I might be willing to put up with the sharp stones and burning sand, but I doubted anyone would let me.

"You promised to explain to me," I said to Kai, searching for a distraction from my small miseries. "You said you'd tell me why you think I'm an angel."

I tripped a little over the word because it still seemed so absurd. Perhaps angels weren't the same to these people as they were to me—no one had commented on my lack of wings or shining halo—but it was clear by the respect with which they were treating me that an angel was someone of importance, someone special.

Which was...not me.

Kai was silent for a moment, and I thought he was going to renege on his previous offer, but then he sighed quietly.

"How much do you understand of what happened back there, at the temple?" he asked.

"None of it!"

He grimaced, and I felt an unexpected stab of guilt. I remembered the pain in his eyes earlier, remembered the pleading in his voice when he claimed that I'd chosen him. I felt like I was stealing something away from him, something precious, and everything in me rebelled against the idea.

"I saw the window appear," I told him, trying to explain, to make it better somehow. "I was curious about it, so I came closer, and then I saw—"

My voice tailed off. All those people. I'd never seen anybody killed before—except for me, which didn't really count. I'd never even been to a funeral. Seeing them die, right before my eyes, and being helpless to do anything about it...I shivered, despite the heat.

"The window you speak of is the doorway between our world and the Ether," Kai told me quietly. "On the very rare occasion, when a blood moon occurs in conjunction with a Solar Convexion, the gateway opens."

I didn't know what a Solar Convexion was, and I was scared to ask about the blood moon. It didn't really matter; they opened a gateway, and that was all that was important.

"When this happens, those who are favored are invited into the temple to stand before the Ether and make a sacrifice. If they are deemed worthy, a spirit will choose to come through the Ether, binding itself to them, and bestowing its gifts on them. Usually, the spirits are minor powers. They take the form of small creatures and have limited abilities, perhaps to manipulate flame or...or—"

"Or to fly," Brannon supplied helpfully.

Kai nodded. "Very rarely," he went on, "a sacrifice may bring forth a stronger spirit. A Celestial. These always take the form of a person, most often a man, but sometimes a woman, and they are powerful. Immensely so." A sly look at me out of the side of his eye.

"No Celestial has walked this world in a millennium," Brannon added. "To be Bound to one...it is a blessing a man can only dream of."

"Of course," Kai finished darkly, his gaze fixed straight ahead, "that blessing means nothing if the Celestial comes through not knowing what is happening."

The sound of the horses' hooves scratching on the gravelly earth somehow magnified the silence that fell between us. I swallowed past the lump in my throat, desperate to say something to take away the stiff, straight-backed way Kai sat in the saddle, proud and devastated all at once.

"You didn't kill anyone," I said. The words were strangled as they came out, but I knew he heard me. His shoulders lifted and fell in a faint shrug.

"I was not prepared to hurt an innocent, no matter how great the gift."

"You sacrificed yourself," I went on, a little stronger now. "You were different, that's why I was drawn to you."

I had his complete attention now, though he didn't

betray it by so much as a flicker of an eyelash. Brannon and Dane, too, were hanging on my every word, but I ignored them.

"I wasn't compelled. I didn't fall through by accident. All right, I didn't know what was happening, but when you put your hand up to the Ether, I…I couldn't resist. I felt the pull, and when I reached for you, when I touched the blood sacrifice, I felt—" I broke off, gritting my teeth. I wasn't explaining this right. "I chose you," I repeated stubbornly

It sounded lame to my ears, but when Kai turned to look at me, some strong emotion was glittering in his eyes.

"Thank you, my lady." He gave me a solemn nod, but I could tell he was pleased.

"Bethany," I pushed, still uncomfortable with all this 'my lady' business.

"My Lady Bethany," he agreed readily.

I narrowed my eyes at him, and he turned away, though not before I caught a glimpse of a smirk on his lips.

"Brannon," he called, "are you recovered enough to run once more?"

Brannon gave a grunt that managed to convey assent and disdain all at once, then without another word picked up the pace, beginning the fluid run that I now knew he could keep up for hours on end. I sighed and held on tight, trying to ignore my aches and pains since I, at least, was sitting astride.

What had I learned? Nothing much that I hadn't known before. At least now, though, I understood why those poor people had been murdered.

And I understood that, if I had been going to choose any of the men at all, I had definitely picked the right one.

8

The sun set, and darkness was quick to shroud the plains. Kai didn't call for a stop, though. They'd no food or water for another night's camp and besides, the rendezvous point was not far ahead. He couldn't see any signs of the camp— his men were too well-trained for that, the spot they'd picked hidden from almost all sides by a ragged outcropping of rocks—but he knew it was there.

Still, every horse's footfall of the last mile chafed, because Kai was painfully aware of how much Lady Bethany was struggling. She sat hunched forward, tensing against the pain she was clearly feeling after a full day in the saddle. He couldn't see the angry red of her skin anymore, but he knew that if he dared reach over and press his palm to any of the exposed patches, he'd feel the heat radiating off her.

He'd had a Celestial in his possession for less than a day, and already he'd all but crippled her.

"We are almost there," he told her.

He imagined she'd be pleased, relieved at the chance to get off the horse if nothing more, but she just clenched her jaw and gave him a tight nod. Her posture, if possible, became more rigid, and even in the gloom, he could see her white-knuckle grip on the horse's reins.

"And where is there?" she asked quietly.

A spear of shame shot through Kai's chest. She was afraid. Afraid because he'd neglected to tell her where they were going, who they were going to see.

"There is an encampment just up ahead. We'll meet up with the rest of my Hounds."

"Your...Hounds?"

Her question was softly spoken, but it hit Kai with the force of a thunderclap. She didn't know. What he was...and what he wasn't.

"You thought I was a man?" he asked quietly.

He kept his eyes on Lady Bethany, but he was keenly aware of Brannon's sudden tension, Dane's wide-eyed stare.

"Are you not?" she asked. "You look like a man."

Brannon growled harshly, twisting his head to the side to spit at the unintentional insult. Lady Bethany obviously didn't understand what she'd said wrong, but she flinched and curled her shoulders in, as if she'd try to make herself smaller in the saddle.

Kai's answering snarl ripped from his throat in an instant, but Lady Bethany, not understanding that the sound was for Brannon, sunk lower.

"I'm sorry," she said quickly. "I didn't mean to offend."

"Forgive me, my lady," Brannon answered. "My reaction was not for you."

Lady Bethany looked even more confused at this, and she turned to Kai, searching for an explanation.

"We are not men," he told her. "Though, at first glance, perhaps we look that way. It is something that is easier to show than to explain. With your permission, we'll wait until we reach camp?"

"Hounds," she repeated. Then a funny look crossed her face. "You don't...you don't turn into dogs, do you?"

Brannon snorted. "We don't turn into hounds, my lady. We *are* Hounds."

Whatever Lady Bethany was going to say to that was halted by the low whistle of one of the camp scouts. Kai held up a hand and all three horses stopped.

"What?" Lady Bethany asked. "What's happening?"

"First." The voice came out of the darkness. Kai knew the scout was there, but only because he was supposed to be. He didn't give himself away by sight or scent.

"All's well?" Kai asked.

"Aye."

"Good." With a soft click, Kai started his horse forward.

"First?" Kai paused, the other two horses halting their progress in tandem. "The ceremony?"

He thought his First was returning as one of the barren, Kai realized. It was a fair assumption—he'd no spirit creature perched on his shoulder nor following on his heels. He'd returned with naught but a woman so exhausted she gave no hint of what she truly was, and the scout was too well-trained to betray his curiosity over her.

"You'll see," was all he said as he nudged his mount back into a walk.

As soon as they rounded the high wall of rock, the camp was impossible to miss. There were few tents—they made the Hounds vulnerable and were a burden to be carried when they moved from place to place—but fires dotted the open space, lighting up the faces of his Hounds as they sat to eat and, for those not on duty, to relax. Bar the eyes—amber yellow or icy blue—they could easily be mistaken for a group of men, untransformed like this, Kai conceded to himself. Of course, they were better trained than any camp of men, and were a threat to befall the temporary settlement, their true selves would erupt between one blink of the eye and the next.

His trained eye didn't miss the air of tension floating about the camp, though. They were all on edge, waiting for him. Waiting to see if such a blessing could truly happen to one of them. They weren't going to believe it when they saw just how fucking blessed they'd been.

A shout went up before the small group breached the warm glow of the first of the fires. It spread like the scent of cooking meat that was already making Kai's mouth water, and in the space of a moment he was aware of all eyes on them.

So was Lady Bethany. He saw her realize the fact, saw apprehension, even a flicker of fear, cross her face, and slid from his horse to take her hand. She dropped from her conspicuous height immediately, curling into him, trusting him to protect her.

A fierce satisfaction filled him, one he felt right down to his bones. Her words earlier had moved him, and quieted some of the pain he'd felt at thinking their bonding was nothing more than an act of ignorance and accident. But words could be false; actions always spoke true.

"Come, my lady," he said. "We'll get you food, something to drink."

"And a place to sit down," she mumbled into his chest. "Somewhere cushioned."

He laughed, a supporting arm winding around her waist.

He intended to lead her through the camp to the very center, where his command tent would be set up and waiting for him, but her legs threatened to collapse with the first step. By the second, he had her up in his arms, safely nestled against his chest.

"I have you, my lady."

He was taking liberties, he knew. He was her Bound; he was hers to command, not the other way around. It was his duty as her Bound to care for her, though, and right now, Celestial or not, she was a woman at the end of her strength.

Had she shown any discomfort, had she made her displeasure known in any way, he'd have put her down at once and fallen to his knees to beg her forgiveness. Instead, she tucked her head into his shoulder and allowed him to take her into the midst of his Hounds, his family.

It didn't take long for him to settle her by the fire, a blanket around her shoulder to ward off the chill brought down by the starlit sky. Brannon, wonder that he was, had already magicked up a skin of wine and a bowl of stew before Kai could turn to ask for it. Quick as they were, though, the Hounds had already gathered. They were a hardened bunch, made tough by a world that saw them as less but demanded their savagery even as they scorned them for it, but as Kai looked around, the main emotion he saw was hope. One of their own had been chosen for a great honor by men. What they wanted to know now, was whether the gods deemed them worthy too, or whether they truly were the cursed creatures they'd always branded.

"Well?" asked Kert, one of his most dominant males, the one he left in charge of the Hounds when he and Brannon both had to be away from the group. "What happened? Were you blessed?" He shifted his head to the side, and tried to see around Kai where he stood, shielding Lady Bethany from view. "Who's she?"

"Pretty piece," Flinn, Kert's constant shadow, commented. "What, did the Prince give you a woman as recompense when the gods left you barren?"

Brannon was in Flinn's face in an instant, his hand around the Hound's throat. "Watch your mouth," he spat. "That is the First's Bound you speak of!"

"A woman?" Hanu, the oldest of their group, croaked. His eyes widened in sudden understanding. "You are Bound to a Celestial?"

"A what?" Flinn asked, his confusion at odds with the hushed whispers that ran around the group like a fall breeze as understanding rippled through them.

"A fucking angel," Brannon hissed in his face. "So, you disrespect her again, and I'll gut you, Hound or no."

He let Flinn go, and tossed the Hound down so that he fell to the ground. The violent movement seemed to break the paralysis that had settled over the Hounds, and they followed suit, dropping to one knee and bowing their heads in respect. Kai stared out at the sea of lowered heads and felt a clench in his chest and his gut that was both the heavy weight of responsibility and the heady thrill of hope.

Drawing the sweet night air in to fill his lungs, he let out a howl from the depths of his soul, and felt it magnify until it threatened to reach the heavens as every Hound echoed it back.

Whatever fresh hells the nobles thought up for him, they would not steal this moment. Looking back, he saw the Celestial, his Lady Bethany, sitting stock straight as she took in the sight, saw his Hounds, his dogs, honor her and the incredible blessing that she was.

An angel among dogs; perhaps there was hope for them, after all.

9

The noise was loud enough to wake the dead, but I didn't cover my ears. I also didn't scuttle backward and hide behind the log I was sitting on, like the raised hairs on the back of my neck were encouraging me to do. I was pretty sure the howl was for me, that I was being honored, so I sat, and I smiled, and I tried not to show how the eerie, primal sound had me quaking in my non-existent boots. That smile threatened to die a death a few moments later when the noise stopped, and they all lifted their heads and looked at me.

Their eyes, they were glowing.

They weren't all amber-eyed, like Kai. There were shades of blue and green and icy grey in the faces that gazed my way, but no matter the shade, those eyes…they were not normal. Kai had said they were Hounds rather than men, and I assumed I was getting my first lesson in those differences.

I stood up, feeling too vulnerable sitting down, even though none of the men had lifted from their crouch.

That was another thing—they were all men. I didn't see a woman anywhere. Just me.

My small movement drew Kai's attention, and he turned to look at me. His eyes, too, were brighter than they'd been before. A reaction to the darkness? Maybe, but I didn't remember noticing them like that when we were riding, the light seeping out from the world around us.

"Are you all right?" he asked me quietly.

We were standing several feet apart, but I'd no problem hearing him. Though there had to be almost two hundred men waiting just beyond, they were deathly quiet, not even seeming to breathe.

"Should I... Am I supposed to say something?"

"Do you want to?"

I shook my head quickly. What I really wanted to do—what all my instincts were telling me to do—was to run away, but that was stupid. I'd seen enough nature documentaries to know running just incited predators.

That's what these men were, I understood suddenly. Predators. The longer I looked at them, the longer I was around Kai, and Brannon, and Kai's son Dane, the more that thin veneer that'd made me think them nothing but ordinary men was slipping away and revealing the truth beneath. They were something else. Something different.

They were Hounds. They were something *more*.

"No one will hurt you here," Kai promised me, his voice low enough to carry to my ears alone—I hoped. "You do not understand what you are to them, what you mean. Not yet. But know that every single one of them would die for you. You are theirs."

"I thought it was you I was Bound to," I said, trying to inject a little levity into the moment.

It didn't work. Kai's face lost the edge of concern and became razor-sharp in its intensity. "You are mine," he promised.

I couldn't hold his eyes for more than a second; I had to look away to be able to breathe.

"What now?" I asked. Though, truthfully, I wasn't sure how much more I could take.

"Now you rest," Kai told me. "Eat, then sleep. Tomorrow will be soon enough for everything else."

Tomorrow came before I was ready for it.

I awoke before dawn and lay staring up at the roof of the tent I'd been given to sleep in. I was still tired—I felt the grit in my eyes every time I blinked—but no matter how I tried, I couldn't will myself back into unconsciousness. I was in another world. I was surrounded by people who looked like men but weren't. Hounds. Who thought I was an angel—I *really* couldn't wrap my head around that one.

But mostly...

I was alive.

I felt the air as it whistled into my lungs; I heard the million tiny noises of the night as sleepers tossed and turned and grunted and snored, as small creatures swooped about hunting for a meal before dawn. I saw the silhouette of the Hound sitting by the campfire just outside my tent, guarding me as he'd been all night. And I *definitely* felt the hard earth beneath me, even with the many layers of blanket that had been volunteered to make up my bed.

I was alive, a part of the—*a*—world again, and while I was terrified out of my wits by the number of unknowns before me, I was also indescribably happy.

I sat up, giving up on sleep, and instantly the guard outside twitched, turning his head in my direction. I held still, trying to quiet even my breathing. I didn't know who was out there, but I didn't want to make conversation with anyone. Not right now.

He held his alert position longer than I could hold my breath, but eventually, he gave me his back once more. I relaxed into a slump, relieved. It wasn't that I was afraid of him or anything—well, not much—but I needed a little time alone. Some space to process.

And there was something I wanted to try.

Blowing out a long breath, I stared down at my hands. An angel, they'd said. I'd laughed at the idea, but when Kai had smiled at me and told me I was glowing, I looked down and…I was. I'd been glowing. I didn't know how I did it, or what it meant, but I was curious to see if I could make it happen again—on purpose, this time.

My hands weren't glowing. They were just there, in my lap, looking like hands. I snorted, feeling stupid, then froze when my guard twitched again.

"My lady?" his soft call came through the leather wall of the tent.

"I'm fine," I said. "Just thinking."

I waited until he went back to face the fire, then tried again. Flexing my hands did nothing, nor did concentrating all of my attention on the very tips of my fingers. I even tried rubbing my hands together. No glow.

Frustrated—and more than a little concerned, because I could all but feel the weight of the Hounds' expectations pressing in on me and what if I never managed to do it again?—I closed my eyes and tried to just breathe. In, and out. In, and out. What had I been doing before? How had I managed it?

I hadn't, at least not intentionally. I'd just been scared and in shock, and full of disbelief. It had been overwhelming, and the only reason I'd been able to keep functioning had been to bottle it up and push it down. I could feel it still, the panic and fear, waiting to take me over.

With nothing else to try, I lifted the lid and let it. My breath came out in a shudder and tears pricked my eyes. What the hell was I going to do? I was lost, and alone among strangers who expected me to be able to do things that I just *couldn't*.

I opened my eyes, ready to give up pretending to be strong and just cry- and stopped short. The whole tent was aglow.

"My lady?" The voice of my guard came again, a little more urgently this time. "I- Is everything all right?"

I didn't answer him. I was afraid to move or even open my mouth in case it went away.

I took a quick breath, then another. The glow stayed, and my surprise faded enough that I could feel it, like a tingle all over my skin. A warmth. It pulsed slightly, like my heartbeat. Or maybe it was my heartbeat?

My guard stood up, calling something across the camp, but I was too absorbed to hear what he said. I closed my eyes, concentrating on the sensations buzzing over every inch of me, and realized that was only the tip of the iceberg. The glow was really coming from the heart of me, my very center, and when I concentrated on that...

Jesus.

I sucked in a gasp as sensation exploded, like the

roaring waves of an orgasm that takes you over until your eyes roll back in their sockets and your toes curl.

It was almost like being back in the nothingness of before, the Ether, Kai had called it. I felt disconnected from my body, floating, like I was everything and nothing. I could feel my heart beating—I could feel *everyone's* heart beating. I could feel anger and concern and laughter and tiredness. Each Hound was like a tiny star, flickering on the edge of my subconscious. I had the feeling, if I turned towards any one of them, I could draw it to me and unlock its secrets, but then I caught on one, burning so much brighter than all the rest, like my own personal sun. A sun that was barreling towards me at speed.

I opened my eyes, already knowing it would be Kai before he swept the opening to the tent out of his way and stepped inside. He went to his knees before me, and his heartbeat was a drum pounding in my ears. I could see the concern on his face, but more, I could *feel* it, clenching in his chest.

"Lady Bethany," he rasped. "What is wrong?"

"I feel you," I told him, too startled by my discovery to pay attention to his question. I reached out and placed my hand over the spot where I knew his heart was racing. "I can feel your worry."

Kai stared at me for a heartbeat longer, then I felt a burst of relief as he allowed the tension to seep out of his muscles. He covered my hand with his own; his skin was warm, but it wasn't a patch on the heat pulsing out of his core.

"Just me?" he asked. "Or can you feel the others too?"

"A little. They're...it's hard to concentrate on them, you're so bright."

He liked that. A smirk crossed his face, and a blaze of satisfaction ran up my arm. I tore my hand away, shocked by the intensity of it.

Instantly his face clouded, the joy morphing into concern. I felt his emotions change even as I watched his expression change, though it wasn't the searing jolt I'd felt before, when I'd been touching him. It was more of an echo than a thunderclap.

"Did I hurt you?" he asked.

"No," I said, shaking my head. "I just...it's strange, that's all." I tried to gather my scattered wits. "I didn't believe you, but—"

"But seeing is believing?" He smiled at me, and I did my best to smile back.

"Something like that."

A beat of silence fell between us, and I looked away. The tent was very small, and as big as he was, he took up most of the space. As if he realized how tight, how intimate it was, the two of us squeezed in there, he shifted back until his shoulders nudged the entrance flaps.

"You gave my Hounds quite a scare," he joked. "They've never seen anything like the tent bursting into light like that." He paused, and quirked a grin. "No one's ever seen anything like that."

That gave me pause.

"Aren't there others like me?"

"There have been, in the past. But right now? You are the only Celestial in existence."

I gaped at him, astonished. I mean, he'd told me I was special, but I didn't realize quite *how* special.

"I'm the only one."

He nodded, his expression unexpectedly solemn. "The only one for a long time."

"How long?"

"A thousand years."

A thousand *years*?

I knew I was in a different world, but the only frame of reference I had for that amount of time was taking me back to the Vikings. A long time, indeed!

"Is that…" I took in the troubled look on his face. "Is that a bad thing?"

"It is a wondrous thing," he replied immediately.

"But?"

He sighed. Rubbed his jaw. That wasn't a good sign.

"You are the only Celestial in existence—" he began.

"You said that," I reminded him. I was getting a very uncomfortable feeling in my stomach. It was darker in the tent, too, because the glow on my skin had extinguished with the cold atmosphere slowly sliding inside.

Kai grimaced, which didn't make me feel better.

"You are the only Celestial in existence," he repeated, "and though we don't know yet the full extent of your powers, it's obvious you *are* powerful."

It wasn't that obvious to me, given that all I'd done so far was light up a tent and feel emotions I could just as easily have read on his face, but I didn't argue. I didn't want to interrupt when he was hopefully getting to the crux of the matter.

"You are a treasure beyond value. You are a treasure men will kill for."

I stared at him. "You don't mean that literally."

"I mean that very literally, my lady."

"But…you said I was *your* Bound. How can—"

"Kill me, and you return to the Ether," Kai confirmed. "So long as you remain Bound to me. There are…ways, apparently, to transfer the binding. I don't know the details, I doubt any but the priests do, but I have been told it is possible."

"I don't want to be Bound to anyone else," I said quickly. I had not forgotten the carpet of blood in that dark cavern below the temple.

A bloom of joy; it took me a moment to realize that it hadn't come from me.

"It warms my heart to hear you say that," he told me, "but there are those who would not give you a choice. Your strength is in your mind, in your soul; it is not in your muscles. Were you to be taken right now, before you have had a chance to learn what you are and what you can do, I do not know that you would be able to stop them." A muscle clenched in his jaw as he forced the rest through gritted teeth. "The ceremony would be performed, I would be dead, and you would be Bound to another. I cannot vouch that they would have any concern for your happiness."

No, I bet he couldn't. Someone who would steal me away and force me to be Bound to them, wouldn't give a shit about little things like if I was happy. Or fed, or warm, or even not in pain.

I hauled in a deep breath.

"I would like for that not to happen."

My words—though heartfelt—had the effect I hoped for. He barked out a laugh at the understatement, and the tension in the tent lessened somewhat.

"I would like that also," he promised. "I have the word of a man I trust that Prince Faron, first in line to the throne, has no plans to steal you from me, that he will accept my pledge as your Bound to use your powers to serve him and the kingdom."

"Okay." I waited, because it was clear from Kai's face that there was more.

"Prince Faron is a trustworthy man, I would stake my life on it." He smiled. "I *am* staking my life on it. But he is not his father, and the king can be ruthless. He is honest with it, though. I would expect any attack from him to come head-on. The nobles, however—"

"Not honest?" I guessed.

"They are a nest of scheming bastards," he confirmed. Then he flushed. "Forgive my language, my lady."

I waved away his apology. He'd already seen how unladylike I was in my horse riding; my language was likely to send him into a faint.

"So, we should avoid them, then?" I suggested.

The unhappy grimace twisting his features told me that wasn't an option. "Would that we could," he said, confirming my fears. "But, as I said, I have pledged us to serve the prince. You are a powerful weapon, and it was the only way that I could—" he broke off. "I will not lie and say it was the only way to keep you safe, although I believe you are safest with me. It was the only way to keep you."

I didn't know how to respond to that, so I focused on the other thing he'd said. "I'm not a weapon."

"You will be," he said. "Already you are able to sense the emotions of others. Imagine how the king could use that. You could weed out treachery and dishonesty. Corruption." He nodded as surprise, then understanding washed over me. "You begin to see your value. And that is only the smallest facet of what you will eventually be able to do."

"I don't want to be a weapon," I corrected.

"Nor do I," he responded. "I do not want to have to give my Hounds as attack dogs to the kingdom, but I do it, because it is the best way to keep them safe."

I wrapped my arms around my middle, feeling childish. And small, and scared.

"I have frightened you," he said softly.

I nodded, because there was no point denying it.

"I wish that I did not have to, but I will not lie to you. And if you understand the danger, you will be prepared. When we go to the palace—"

"The palace?" I squeaked. "Where the king is?"

"The king, Prince Faron, the royal advisors, and every noble who wants something from the crown." He snorted. "So, all of them."

"But...why?" After what Kai had just told me, that seemed like a terrible idea. A much *better* idea surely would be to stay far, far away.

"I pledged our service," he reminded me. "I had to promise to present you at the palace within ten days or fight for the right to keep you then and there. I would not have won, not outnumbered and with an untutored Celestial to try and protect."

"So, we're going there now?"

Kai nodded. "It is four days away at full marching pace, so we have a little leeway, but yes. It is not a long time to acclimatize you to your new powers, to me, and I am sorry for that. As I said, there was no choice."

"Right," I agreed. "Right."

It was terrifying, and overwhelming, and a hell of a shock after drifting in a void for I had no idea how long, but as Kai said, I didn't have a choice.

I stitched a brave smile together and plastered it on my face. Kai surprised me by reaching for my hand, grasping it tightly in both of his.

"Don't be afraid," he said. "I am with you. I will keep you safe. I swear it."

10

After my little chat with Kai, there was no chance of any more sleep, so I allowed him to lead me out of the tent for breakfast. It was still dark out, dawn lightening the sky far out on the horizon but not touching us yet. Despite that, it seemed I was the only one not up. Hounds sat scattered around, doing whatever it was soldiers did when they were in a camp.

That all stopped the moment I appeared, of course. Every head turned in my direction, every hand stilled.

I froze, but gentle pressure from Kai's hand at my elbow got me moving again, and he directed me to sit at the fire just outside my tent. Someone gave me some sludgy-looking porridge and I clutched it gratefully. The bowl was small and narrow, thin enough to have been warmed by the mixture inside; if I closed my eyes, I could just about pretend I was holding a cup of tea. Imagining I was sitting at my kitchen table was a stretch too far, though; not when I was cross-legged on the hard ground, a breeze was sneaking around the crevices of my borrowed tunic, and the air around me rumbled with the sounds of two hundred men.

"Please eat, my lady," Kai urged me quietly. "It's simple fare, but filling."

I took a spoonful. It tasted all right, but it sat like glue in my mouth. With supreme effort, I swallowed and forced it down my throat.

"What's going to happen today?" I asked. "Are we leaving?"

A quick glance around confirmed that there wasn't any packing up going on, but Kai had said we needed to present ourselves to the palace.

"Not today," Kai replied, confirming what my eyes were telling me. "Tomorrow, most likely. Today, I wanted to give you the chance to grow used to us." A small pause. "To grow used to me. There is also the matter of your guard to settle."

"My...guard?" I looked up at him, holding my little bowl of porridge to my chest like a shield.

Kai jerked his head in a short nod, his eyes sweeping over the camp as if he was choosing them right there and then. "You must be protected at all times. Even in the camp, though I trust all these Hounds with my life. I am your Bound, and I will always be with you, but there may be times when we are overwhelmed." A grim smile. "I cannot fight off the whole world. Your guard will know your patterns and behaviors, and you must know their faces well, so that, should anything happen, you know who to look to."

I nodded mutely. "Are you going to ask for volunteers?"

I couldn't imagine anyone would be too thrilled to be stuck babysitting me.

"I already have," Kai said grimly.

Oh dear. "Nobody wanted the job?" I guessed.

He gave a short bark of laughter. "They *all* wanted the job."

"Oh." I hung on to my porridge a little tighter and looked out towards the camp again. No one was looking my way, and yet I could tell they were all watching me. A hundred surreptitious glances, dozens of twitching ears. "So how…how will you pick?"

Kai's face closed over, and he folded his arms over his chest. The answer came from behind me, startling me into slopping barely cooled porridge over my hand.

"The same way we settle competition for all coveted duties: we compete."

Brannon moved around me to stand beside Kai, bowing low to me. "Good morning, my lady. Are you well rested?"

No, not at all. But I curved my mouth into a smile and nodded at him. "Yes, thank you."

To prove it, I took another mouthful of food. It didn't go down any easier, especially when Kai frowned hard at Brannon, his eyes cold enough to freeze the sun.

"I don't like this, I think it's a piss-poor idea." Kai threw a guilty glance for his language my way, then returned his laser focus to Brannon. "We should just pick. I know who I want."

"You'd have dissent within the camp?" Brannon asked, seemingly unperturbed by the icy chill of Kai's anger. "This is always how we have settled things. You change things, you risk the peace. Right now, they cannot believe this is real. Take away their chance to fight for a place to be close to her, you kill their hope, their joy. Let them compete and lose, fair and square, and they'll respect it. They'll be a second guard, working from a distance, knowing the best Hounds earned the honor to watch over her." Brannon shrugged, stuffing a mouthful of something that looked like flatbread into his mouth. I stirred my porridge without enthusiasm; where did he get *that*? "You know the ones you'd pick are likely to win anyway."

Kai remained tight-lipped and rigid, apparently unconvinced.

"She belongs to them; let them fight for her," Brannon urged.

"She belongs to *me*!" Kai erupted, loud enough to be heard by those sitting closest. "She is my Bound!"

"Not for long if you fail to protect her."

That seemed to be the clincher for Kai. I was allowed to finish my breakfast and wash up with a bucket of water behind a hastily erected screen. The water was warm, and someone had rustled up some soap from somewhere; it had a weird, waxy texture and it smelled strongly of pine—not my favorite—but I figured this passed for luxury bathing in a camp like this. The tunic I'd been wearing was replaced with one that looked slightly newer. It fit me better, too, hanging mid-thigh but not gaping quite so badly around the chest and shoulders. I wondered if it belonged to Kai's gangly son, Dane. There were trousers, too, which were far too long but stayed around my waist when I cinched the belt tight. Kai knelt in front of me and sliced the extra length off at the bottom with a small knife that glinted wickedly sharp in the early morning sunlight, allowing my bare toes to peep out. No shoes, unfortunately, but the day was heating rapidly so at least I wouldn't be cold.

So long as I didn't have to do any running across the hard-packed earth, deviously studded with tiny sharp stones, I'd be fine.

As decent as I was going to get—my hair I'd braided

out of the way since washing it seemed a step too far—I followed Kai to where a circle had been cleared in the middle of the camp. There was a single seat around the edge where I was deposited, everyone else sprawled on the floor. I'd have felt silly, sitting perched above them all, but Kai loomed over me, casting a shadow as gloomy as his unhappy aura. I was grateful for the shade, less so for the tension and doubt I could feel pressing in on me.

Surprised by my own daring, I reached out and grabbed his hand.

"If you don't want this, I will happily accept whoever you think should guard me," I told him. "I can feel your unhappiness."

The words were barely out of my mouth before I felt a lifting of that grim edginess, replaced with shock, then understanding, and finally shame.

"Forgive me," he said, looking abashed. "I did not mean to upset you."

"It's you I'm concerned about," I told him.

It wasn't fun to feel negative emotions that weren't mine wrap themselves around me in a claustrophobic grip, but I also didn't like that those emotions were coming from *Kai*. It moved something in me, made me want to fix it, to soothe him. I could only assume it was an effect of the binding between us.

More shame.

"I'm fine," he promised me. "Brannon is right, this is the way." His lips quirked. "Even if I do not like it."

All right. I pasted a smile on my face, agreeing with

him, then looked out to the circle, where a dozen or so men were limbering up, eyeing each other warily.

"So, what happens now?"

"They fight. Hand-to-hand combat, no weapons. Any Hound who successfully executes a move that would lead to a killing blow, wins. They move forward to the next round. The best four win a place in your personal guard, the four below them become your reserve guard. They will watch over you when your primary guard must sleep."

"Well, that seems simple enough."

It was. It was also quite brutal. Brannon gave the word, and the Hounds started hammering each other viciously. It was hard to watch; there were punches and kicks, bodies flying through the air. Teeth flashed, trying to sink into flesh.

I'd seen violence before, lots of it—all from the safety of my armchair, eating popcorn as I stared at the screen. And those were all actors playing a role, they weren't really being pounded to a bloody pulp. This was actually happening. Every bone that popped out of joint was real. Every trail of blood spoke of pain. I wanted to close my eyes and hide until it was all over, but these men—Hounds, I reminded myself—were fighting for me, for the chance to be in my guard; I owed it to them to stick it out.

The porridge I'd eaten churned uneasily in my stomach. I'd say it was harder to watch than to take part, but those who weren't competing in this round watched from the sidelines and hollered support and insults at their comrades.

I survived the first round, and then the second. The

number of Hounds in the circle and the frenetic pace of their movements meant that, if I relaxed my eyes, the scene before me became a blur of bronzed limbs moving at lightning speed, with the occasional shocking smear of bright red that I tried, mostly unsuccessfully, to pretend wasn't blood. As Hounds were defeated, though, and retreated to join the other losers on the sidelines, the fights became more clearly a competition between two people and, impossibly, somehow more intense.

"We are down to the last sixteen," Kai murmured above me. "All those who win this round will be rewarded with a place in your secondary guard at a minimum."

He hadn't stopped hovering since the carnage started, as if he was ready to spring into action to defend me should it somehow spill out of the circle and envelop me. Given that they were fighting for the privilege of defending me, I found that quite ironic. I didn't point this out to Kai, though, because he was still wound tighter than a spring.

I shifted on my seat, trying to ease the tension turning my shoulders into knots. The last sixteen were all standing in a line, waiting for Kai's command to continue the competition. I went from face to face, taking in square jaws and determined eyes. It was impossible to have a preference. They all looked strong and capable and, well, scary. I was pleased to see Dane in the lineup. From the twitching of his lips and slight restlessness I could detect only because his older compatriots were standing with a predator's alert stillness, he was pleased, too, if surprised. Brannon wasn't among the contenders. When the fighting had first started, he'd sidled up to Kai and complained about not being in the midst.

"I need you," Kai said simply. "I will not leave my Bound, not ever. There will be times I'll need someone to act in my stead, and there's no other I'd trust to do that."

Brannon had accepted that—he'd looked honored, even—but he continued to watch the "entertainment" with unconcealed envy.

"We go in twos now," Kai called to the waiting men. "You know what is at stake." Sixteen eyes fixed on me with unnerving intensity. "Begin."

I didn't know how they decided who was fighting who, or in what order, but in the space of a handful of seconds, the circle emptied of all but two opponents and the whole atmosphere changed.

Before my untimely death, I never went to a boxing match; I never wanted to. This was exactly what I imagined it would be like, and I'd been right—I didn't like it. Now that there were only two Hounds in the ring, the watching audience divided itself into factions, cheering on their favorite and booing and jeering the opposition. There was a fervor to it, an eagerness for every thud of fist against flesh, for every drop of blood spilled. I'd been trying not to react to anything, trying not to show my distaste for the violence, but as one of the fighters grabbed a flailing arm and held it tight before kicking at the exposed forearm, making the bone snap, I couldn't contain my shudder.

"Kai!" I protested.

Kai had been watching the fight with the same excitement as the rest. He turned at my exclamation, balanced on the balls of his feet, exhilarated and ready to engage in his own battle. I watched his eyes scan the area around me, searching for the non-existent danger, before dropping to me.

"What is it, my lady?"

"They're hurting themselves!" I said, my eyes pleading.

All right, they'd been hurting themselves since the whole contest started, but the way the defeated Hound's forearm was kinked in the middle, he'd broken both his radius and ulna, and there wasn't exactly an Emergency Room we could wheel him off to. I didn't want anyone to sustain lasting injuries just to get to watch over me.

Kai looked back to the circle, then again at me. He was surprised by my concern, I could see, even amused by it.

"Don't fret, Lady Bethany. He is a Hound, we heal quickly. He will be fine."

I didn't appreciate being patted on the head like a dim-witted girl. I didn't feel quite sure enough of myself to tell Kai that, but I tried to infuse it in my glare. Unfortunately, he wasn't looking at me, he was watching the ring. The victorious Hound, grinning hugely, jogged off to the left to stand and wait. The loser limped off to the right, clutching his arm, while two new opponents took center stage. Kai's gaze was immediately drawn to the fight that was about to begin, but I couldn't look away from the poor loser. His face was white with pain, but rather than be concerned with his arm, he was looking wistfully back to the ring, clearly distraught at being disqualified. At least, that was, until his friend took a firm grip on his arm and ruthlessly straightened it.

I blanched then, my stomach heaving, but I'd been the cause of his pain—willingly or not—and I felt I owed it to him to watch as the bone was wrestled into place and wrapped tightly in leather, a splint against the skin to keep the limb straight. All through it, the Hound betrayed no hint of pain other than the bloodlessness of his face and the tight clench of his jaw. Once it was done, he looked over towards me and our eyes locked for the blazing heat of a moment. He lost his paleness then, his face flooding with red before he directed his eyes down to the ground in shame.

I wanted to do something then, maybe go over and speak to him, tell him he'd fought well and that I was impressed with how he'd handled the pain, but I didn't know if that would make him feel better or worse, to be singled out like that after his defeat, and I felt pinned in my seat, the guest of honor, unable to move until the whole grisly spectacle was over.

Grimly, I looked back to the fight just as an enormous cheer went up. A Hound stood in the center of the circle, head thrown back in triumph, whilst his adversary lay flat on his back in the dust, hands on his head. He didn't look hurt, just defeated—and exhausted if the rapid rise and fall of his enormous chest was any indication.

As I watched, he hauled himself up and patted the victor on the arm, shaking his head ruefully at something the other Hound said.

"That's a shame," Kai said to Brannon, who'd been moving around the circle but had now returned to stand with us. "I'd been hoping Gyn would make it all the way through."

"He was stupid," Brannon replied, sounding unimpressed. "Too confident by far. You don't want complacency when there's a Celestial's life at stake."

I sat through another six fights until there were eight Hounds gathered in the impromptu victors' area. And then we had to do it all over again. These fights were even longer. Not only had we whittled down to the best fighters, but each of them seemed absolutely determined to make it to my primary guard, almost to the point that they were willing to die in the attempt. I tried to feel proud or honored as I watched them pounding each other into oblivion just feet in front of me; what I really felt was a faint sense of nausea and a whole load of guilt for the injuries being inflicted.

Finally, *finally*, the final four stood before us. None of them were grinning now. Instead they looked deathly serious, as if their sentry duties had started already. I hoped that wasn't the case, because at least two of them had broken bones, and a third could barely see out of one swollen shut eye. They looked like they'd spent the day getting the hell beaten out of them—which they had—and if I'd been in their shoes, I doubted I'd be standing.

Although, let's face it, I wouldn't have volunteered in the first place.

"My Lady," Kai said, moving to stand beside his champions and looking back at me with a rush of pride. "Here are our winners: Tor, Conlon, Ferris, and Rye. I present your guard."

Right. My guard. Men—sorry, *Hounds*—with whom I

was going to be spending an inordinate amount of time with, according to Kai. I stood somewhat awkwardly and stared at them. I had absolutely no idea what to say, but they were gazing at me, waiting, so I knew I had to come up with something. And it had better be good, because they'd gone through hell for the dubious honor of being between me and danger.

They wanted my approval, I realized with a sudden rush of astonishment. They wanted me to show that I was happy for each of them to protect me. With that understanding, my impression of them as soldiers, as terrifying fighting machines, faded a little. I took in each of their faces in turn, trying to see the individual beneath the warrior façade.

Tor was the oldest, I thought. Scarred and with grey hair starting to bleed into his temples, he looked formidable. Beside him, Conlon looked almost friendly, with auburn hair. He stood inches taller and broader, and looked too big to move as fast as he had. In comparison, the third in the lineup, Ferris, looked nothing so much as an assassin. He was dark-haired and sallow-skinned, whippet-thin. He looked designed to meld in with the shadows. He didn't have a smile for me. Instead, he eyed me with an odd mixture of reverence and calculation, like I was a priceless trinket, and he was considering all the ways someone might try to steal me. It took all my courage to smile at him, and almost none at all to return the wide grin of the last man in the line. Rye had been blessed with a very handsome mix of glossy brown hair and green eyes. I could only see one of those at the moment—the other one had fully closed over now—when he blinked, it looked almost like he was winking at me. He had a roguish charm, I thought, that had probably gotten him into trouble more than once.

"Thank you for volunteering to be my guard," I told them, feeling like an utter imposter. The thought that I was important enough to have four deadly warriors devote themselves to my protection was laughable. Of course, I wasn't just Bethany Gunn, wife, mother, and English teacher, anymore. I was a Celestial. The *only* bloody Celestial in existence. I tried to breathe through the unease and apprehension that idea filled me with and concentrate on what I was saying. "It's an honor that you would give yourselves to protect me, and I know that you'll keep me safe."

I looked at Kai, then, seeking rescue. I didn't know what the hell else to say.

He nodded approvingly at me, so I apparently hadn't done too disastrously. I gave him a small, relieved smile and then tried to melt into the background as Kai took over, addressing his men.

"Well done, my lady," Brannon said quietly, coming to stand beside me. "You handled that well." He looked over at the final four and gave a solemn nod. "I'm pleased with your guard, Kai will be, too. These men will protect you with their lives."

"Let's hope it doesn't come to that," I said, my voice tight.

"It will, my lady. More than once, it will."

Great.

11

"I don't need to explain to you what a great honor has been bestowed upon you." Kai put his hands on his hips and stared at each man in turn. Tor, Conlon, Ferris, and Rye in Lady Bethany's primary guard, and Jay, Miller, Bex, and Dane in her secondary. He spared the extra moment to nod at his son, pride swelling his chest. He'd not expected Dane to make it so far, and if he'd not faced Ferris in the final round, he might well have made it into the primary.

Dane's slight scowl told Kai he knew that, too.

"Lady Bethany is a gift from the gods, and a lot of people are going to be pissed that such a gift has been handed to the fucking Hounds."

A chorus of growls rumbled in the air.

"They think we're worthless. They think we're savages, going for nothing but bloodshed on demand. They think we're stupid, and they will try to take her from us." Kai felt his own blood start to heat at his words—all of which were true—and his fingers itched, ready to unsheathe his claws and rent imaginary enemies. They weren't here to kill, though, and when they did, the fight would come from the shadows. He didn't intend to let his guard down, not for a second, but he was just one person. "This is a special duty. You all knew what you were signing up for but let me say it one more time so that we're clear. There are no free days on this assignment. There is no downtime. The only time you're off is when you're sleeping. You disappear on duty, you're out. You get drunk on duty, you're out. You give me any reason to think you are not one hundred percent alert and committed to keeping the Celestial safe, you're out. If anyone wants to give up their place, now's the time."

Kai waited, letting the moment draw out. There were no complaints, no withdrawals. The four selected to be Lady Bethany's personal guard were lucky fuckers and they knew it. They weren't going to be restricted to gazing at the Celestial from afar; they were going to be up close and personal with her, every day.

Jealousy spiked in Kai's gut, but he pushed it aside. He was her Bound, he was her tether to the world. He let her words run through his head one more time: *it's hard to concentrate on them, you're so bright.*

Forget her guard; *he* was a lucky fucker.

"We've been handed a treasure from the gods," he finished softly. "We need to prove that we are worthy of it." He paused, letting that sink in. "We move out in ten. Tor, Ferris, you're on horseback. Conlon and Rye, I want you on the ground. Get yourselves ready."

His Hounds dismissed; Kai turned back to Lady Bethany. She was standing talking to Brannon, the wary look that seemed almost permanently etched onto her face softened slightly as she smiled at something his Second said. For a moment he allowed himself to stand and just look at her. If he tried to be objective, he supposed she looked like an ordinary female. Her hair was scraped back and her face was unadorned by makeup or jewels. The clothes he'd cobbled together hung loose on her and hid the womanly curves he knew she possessed. Put together, these facts made her sound mediocre, unimpressive.

They didn't take into account the energy, swirling so close under skin that she seemed to pulse with it, or the glow that caused her skin to shimmer a beautiful silver when her power coalesced inside her. Or the jolt to Kai's core she caused when she turned her pale green eyes his way, the heat she burned him with when she put her hands on him.

Kai didn't know if she affected the other Hounds this way, or if he saw her true nature only because she was Bound to him. They'd all seen her set the tent alight yesterday when she'd been practicing drawing forth her power, but when she was like this, quiet and contained, could they still see the wonder of what she was?

It was something Kai needed to know—it would be important when they moved into more populated areas—but he couldn't quite bring himself to ask just yet. He wanted to hold tight to the idea that only he could see her true self a little longer.

"My lady," he said, interrupting them and feeling a punch of satisfaction when she turned to him immediately, a smile lightening her face, even though Brannon was still in the middle of speaking. "We are all but ready to go."

The first rays of the morning were just beginning to peer over the horizon, but his Hounds had been up for hours, dismantling the camp and doing their best to make it look as if they'd never been there. The ground was disturbed, of course, and there were small, scorched circles where they'd lit fires, but nothing would be left behind to identify them, and when they moved out, the tracks wouldn't reveal their number.

They might be a sanctioned part of the king's army, but secrecy and stealth were part of their very nature, and it never hurt to be cautious, now more than ever. Kai wasn't fool enough to think news of his incredible acquisition hadn't circulated beyond the tight-knit group of over-privileged pricks (General Tuill and the prince aside) who'd been at the temple. They'd want the word spread so that the public would be on the lookout for Lady Bethany, keen to get a gawp at the first Celestial in a millennium. They wouldn't be able to pass through a small, backwoods hamlet without somebody hearing about it.

"Let me help you onto your mount," Brannon offered.

It was an innocuous offer, but Kai felt adrenaline surge his system, his canines descending and a feral growl rolling out of his throat as his body prepared to defend against this threat to his mate.

No, not his mate.

She was his Bound. A Celestial, and so far above him it was an insult to her to even think such a thing.

Kai tried to remind his body of that simple fact, but it wasn't listening. Brannon was. He dropped to his knees immediately, his head tilted forwards and to the side, exposing his neck.

Fuck.

Kai hauled a breath in through his nose and tried to get a grip on himself. It didn't help that Lady Bethany had no clue what was going on and was leaning over Brannon, her hand on his god-damned shoulder.

"Are you okay?" he heard her ask.

Brannon wouldn't disrespect her by flinching away from her touch, so he remained where he was, every muscle tense, waiting for Kai to kill him.

"Get off your knees, Brannon," Kai ground out. "Help Lady Bethany on her horse."

Then he turned his back on them so he wouldn't see his second put his hands all over his Bound. He couldn't kill Brannon; he needed him.

Ten minutes later and Lady Bethany was on her horse—a colossal gelding who wouldn't spook if a cannon went off in his ear—Brannon had made himself scarce, and Kai had gotten his rogue body under control. Somewhat. Already astride his own mount, a gleaming black stallion with more testosterone than sense, he trotted over to her. Tor and Ferris were already in evidence on horseback on either side of her, while Rye stood by her horse's head, one hand on the reins. Conlon lingered a little way off, his back to the group, watching everything else that was going on.

Good.

"Are you comfortable, Lady Bethany?" Kai asked.

She grimaced at him, glancing down over her horse's shoulder.

"I feel high," she said. "Really high. It's a long way to go if he chucks me off."

"He will not throw you," Kai promised. "He has excellent manners."

Lady Bethany smiled and gave the horse's neck a timid pat.

"It'll be an all-day ride, my lady. My Hounds will be

shifting in their own patterns, but all you need to worry about is staying in between Ferris and Tor."

The two men nodded at Lady Bethany, and she gave them shy smiles in return. Kai had introduced her to them the previous evening, but he could see that she was still a little uncomfortable.

"I'll be with you as much as I am able," he went on.

"I'm sure you've lots to organize," she replied. "Please don't worry about me."

"I will be with you," he repeated, and the smile she gave him warmed him right down to his toes—and a couple of other places. "We'll pause to rest a couple of times, but we do so as a unit. There can be no unscheduled stops. I'm sorry, but it is for your safety, you understand?"

"Of course." She nodded, but he could sense her apprehension.

"Should you need to take any additional breaks, just let me know and I will call a halt," he found himself saying. "But it is important that we reach our destination by nightfall."

"I'll do my best to keep up," she promised.

Kai nodded, then gave her guard one final, meaningful look before he rode away. They returned it steadily: they knew what the stakes were. They wouldn't let him down.

Brannon was waiting for him at the front of the group. His Hounds didn't run in rigid formation like the rest of the King's army; they moved more like a pack, hunting, watching, always aware of their surroundings. Normally Kai led them, but not today. He'd be riding with Lady Bethany, at her side, where he should be, but he'd miss running with the pack, his feet connected to the earth and his soul connected to the Hounds as they moved in coordination with him.

He trusted Brannon to do the job, though—and he trusted no one else to protect his Bound.

"I reckon we can make it through the pass by the end of the day," Brannon said, shielding his eyes against the sun as he looked up at Kai. "Then, if we take the northern road—"

"We're not taking the northern road," Kai disagreed.

"We're not?"

"I want to go through Cleavestown. We can make it there by the end of today if we move it."

"What?"

He understood Brannon's confusion. Cleavestown was a busy market town. It had grown in fits and spurts, so the streets were narrow, twisting and turning like a briar bush and always jam-packed with people. It was not a safe place to take a Celestial, not least because most of the Hounds would have to make camp outside the town limits.

"I refuse to disgrace Lady Bethany by presenting her at the palace looking like a pauper. We'll stop at the town for a day or two and get some provisions for her. For fuck sake, she's wearing Dane's cast-off clothes."

Of course, it was better to be dressed in cast-offs than be captured, or worse, but if Kai couldn't protect her in Cleavestown then he couldn't hope to keep her safe when they reached the palace. This was as good a test as any.

12

Cleavestown was the only sizable town this side of the northern road. Mountains bracketed it at the back, but the ground before the town was good, fertile land. Every inch of it had been divided into neatly farmed fields, forcing the Hounds to approach down the single road. It chaffed at Kai after the openness of the plains, and he could see from the rigid tension in the shoulders of his Hounds as they jogged two abreast ahead of him that they felt it, too.

At least his Hounds could spread out as they made camp. Kai eyed the narrow streets of the town with disdain. It was like a warren, tight and constricting. His every instinct told him that taking the Celestial in there was a mistake, but he would not present her at the palace in rags, and if he could give her the softness of a bed to rest in, he would. When he thought of the luxuries every other man at the temple would have been able to shower her with from the moment she appeared, he burned with shame.

But the Ether had given her to *him*.

"You sure about this?" Brannon asked, voicing Kai's own doubts.

"No," he replied honestly. "But we're going to do it anyway. I expect the ten of us to be a match for a townful of peasants, don't you?"

Only he, his second, and Lady Bethany's two guards would enter the town. Much more, and they'd attract attention. Or worse, fear. And a frightened populace did stupid things.

Brannon grunted, giving the comment the contempt it deserved.

"Hopefully we can get in and out without making too much noise. I guess it depends on whether word's gotten out about your binding yet."

"This town pays tithes to Kenwick," Kai said. "He'll have stopped here on his way home to be groveled over, and to show off his Bound."

"What was it?" Brannon asked.

"Living flame."

Brannon whistled and Kai nodded. A fire spirit was a dangerous weapon in the wrong hands. And Kenwick was definitely the wrong hands.

"You think he'll have spread the word about you calling an angel?"

"I don't know." Kai frowned. "He'll have left watchers, I bet. Spies. He'll know we were here, I'd stake my life on that. But I doubt he'll have made it public knowledge."

"He'll not want to admit that you called a Celestial and all he got was a fire spirit." Brannon grinned. "Well, so long as you can keep her from glowing, or, you know, exploding, hopefully no one will guess what she is."

"Tell me how I'm supposed to keep her from glowing?" Kai asked, his eyes on his angel as she stretched away the stiffness of the long ride, her primary guard a tight circle around her.

"Well, she's not doing it now, is she?" Brannon commented.

Kai smiled, he couldn't help it. So, no one but him could see the subtle energy swirling under her skin? No one but him could see how special she was. As he stared, she looked over and caught his eye and smiled back. The energy within her pulsed gently, and Kai felt something tighten in response. The binding. He didn't fully understand it yet, but he couldn't deny that it was real.

They rode into the town just as the sun was setting. It was bad timing, the streets were crowded with people heading home from work, but if they waited until dark, the town sentries would be sure to challenge eleven strangers. The idea was to keep as low a profile as possible. Lady Bethany wore a scarf over her head, hiding her hair and part of her face. She'd blanched when Kai had suggested the idea, and had accepted the woolen shawl timidly, draping it over herself at once, but as they entered the town proper and the first few streets gave way to the slightly wider main avenue filled with shops and inns, her head was twisting this way and that as she tried to see everything. Her obvious curiosity drew more attention than her bare head would have, but Kai couldn't bring himself to chastise her for it.

"We'll stop at Friends Inn," he told Brannon, bending low on his horse as he spoke so his voice wouldn't travel far.

Brannon nodded and shifted direction, using his broad shoulders to cut a path through the crowded street.

Friends Inn wasn't the fanciest place in town—Kai wouldn't have set foot in it if it was, that was exactly the clientele he was trying to avoid—but it was a cut above most places. It had a large, spotlessly clean stabling area, and a proper dining room that separated the inn's lodging guests from the locals making use of the bar. The innkeeper met them in the stables, his hands practically rubbing together as he took in the number in their party.

Kai was about to disappoint him.

"Two rooms," he told him, "and stabling for four horses. I'll pay a silver coin a head for my men to sleep in the barn. Your best two rooms," he added, and the man's eyes, which had begun to dim from their initial eagerness, brightened perceptibly.

"Absolutely, sir. This way."

He led them inside after assuring Kai their horses would be well looked after by their stable lad. As Kai followed him in, he looked back and saw the boy—who couldn't have been more than fourteen—hanging on with grim determination as Kai's own mount attempted to trample him.

The best rooms had a view over a small square. They sat side by side with an adjoining door, something which pleased Kai. If her guard had to get to her, they were seconds closer. Kai, of course, would already be in the room. This penned in, surrounded by so many strangers, he planned to be even more diligent in the protection of his Bound.

And he liked to look at her, to remind himself constantly that she was *his* Celestial; might as well be honest about that.

"Are the rooms to your liking, sir?" The innkeeper asked, hovering in the doorway. He was still smiling, delighted to renting out sigh pricey rooms. Kai bet he wouldn't be quite so happy if he realized it was a Hound he was giving it to. He'd probably be worried about one of them lifting a leg on the fancy fainting couch, or licking their own balls on the enormous, ornately carved wooden bed.

Well, so long as he didn't piss any of them off, he'd never have to find out. Kai could pass for human if he had to.

For a little while.

"This'll be fine," Kai replied. "We'll take dinner here."

"Of course."

He waited until the innkeeper closed the door, his sharp ears catching the fact that the obsequious little prick loitered for several long seconds, ear probably pressed to the door, before approaching Lady Bethany.

"We'll stay here tonight and get provisions in the morning. Depending how it takes, we may be able to head out of town tomorrow, but we have time to stay an extra night."

"You don't like being here," she said.

"No, it's not that—"

"Yes." She smiled to take the sting out of her words and lifted her hand to her chest. "I feel it. Here."

Kai took a deep breath and tried to quell the cloying sense of panic that always gripped him when he found himself surrounded by the world of man.

"It's not safe," he told her, which was true enough. If the whole town turned against them, they'd be overrun. True, but extremely unlikely. Lady Bethany watched him with calm green eyes, waiting for the rest. "I don't like being hemmed in," he found himself saying. "It feels like I'm surrounded, like there's no room to breathe."

"You feel vulnerable," she said.

Kai scowled, not liking the weakness she'd pulled out of him with nothing more than a look. He directed the glare at Brannon and her four primary guards, daring them to say a word. They, intelligent beasts that they were, had their gazes directly firmly at the floor and walls.

"You need to understand," he said to Lady Bethany, "We were hunted almost to extinction. Before I made the agreement to bring the Hounds into the King's army, we were hanging on by a thread, scavenging to survive, afraid to go near humans in case we found ourselves at the wrong end of torches and pitchforks. Things are different now, but—"

"But scars take a long time to heal," she finished for him.

"They do."

He dared a look at her and was startled to realize that he'd missed the soft patter of her feet crossing the carpeted floor. She was glowing slightly—a quick glance at the riveted expressions of the other Hounds in the room told him they could see it too—and as he watched she reached out and rested her fingers lightly on the back of his hand.

"We don't have to stay here. Let's go back to where everyone else is camping. I can sleep on the ground, Kai."

His whole hand tingled, and he could feel the emotion she was projecting pierce the very core of his chest: sympathy, understanding. And shy hesitation; she wasn't sure it was okay to touch him.

Which was a joke. She could touch Kai in any damned place she liked.

"You are grace personified, my lady, but we will stay here. There is security provided by the walls of the inn that a leather tent cannot compare to. And while you *can* sleep on the ground, I will not have it unless there is no other choice." Kai took a deep breath, trying to flush out the negative emotions she was reading. "When we get to the palace, we will not only be surrounded by people, but by enemies. I need to learn to handle it."

"All right." Lady Bethany looked dubious, but she didn't argue any further.

The innkeeper brought them a decent meal—certainly better than anything Kai's men had been able to produce in the camp—but Lady Bethany didn't do more than pick at it, pushing the stew around her plate. Kai didn't have to guess what was troubling her: she kept looking over at the big bed, then throwing quick little glances over toward Kai, glances he wasn't supposed to see if the way she tore her gaze away every time he caught her eye was any indication.

She thought he planned to share the bed with her.

A bolt of lust shot through Kai as another thought came to him: did she want him to?

Fuck, wasn't that an idea? That power, that energy, tingling along the length of him as they lay skin to skin.

Lady Bethany threw him another look, this one longer, her eyes startled, and he remembered she was able to feel strong emotions from him even when they weren't touching. He was *Bound*, and he needed to remember that.

He needed to stop thinking with his dick.

By the Gods, if the nobles even had a hint of a suggestion that he was so much as thinking about touching a Celestial that way, they'd forget centuries of distrust, betrayal, and bad blood that existed between them, and band together to take her away from him. Even the prince and General Tuill—and they'd be right. It would be a desecration.

"I'll sleep on the floor," he said.

"What?" Lady Bethany fumbled her fork and it clattered to the floor, gravy splattering the deep red carpet.

"Tonight," Kai clarified. "Brannon and your primary will stay in the room next door, and your secondary will patrol the inn. Discreetly. I'll make sure there's someone outside the door, but only you and I will be in this room, and I will sleep on the floor."

"There's plenty of room in the bed," Lady Bethany said faintly.

There was. And if Kai had been a man maybe he'd be thinking about sharing it, but he wasn't.

"I'll sleep on the floor," he repeated.

"All right." Was that disappointment in her tone? Maybe, maybe not. It didn't matter. Kai needed to keep his dick in his pants, his body away from hers, and his filthy fucking mind out of the gutter.

She was an angel; he was a Hound. He wouldn't defile the gift he'd inexplicably been given by reaching for more.

A quiet knock at the door interrupted the awkward moment. Lady Bethany jerked, taken by surprise, but Kai, Brannon, and her primary guard had all heard the tread come up the stairs, and caught the familiar scent.

Brannon went over to the door and opened it cautiously, even though he would be as sure as the rest of them that there was no one but a Hound on the other side of it.

Kai approved; caution was good. Caution would keep them alive.

Dane stood there, his cheeks red and his eyes on the ground. Kai eyed his son. He'd known he was there, but not why. The secondary guard were meant to be getting enough sleep to see them through a night of making sure no one tried to sneak up on them.

"I brought this for Lady Bethany," he stuttered, holding up a handful of white fabric.

Before any of them could stop her, Lady Bethany had crossed the room and stood in the doorway, reaching for it. Even Brannon, who was standing right there, was too slow to shift his body and prevent her from exposing herself to an enemy just waiting for an opportunity to get to her.

Of course, there wasn't anyone lying in wait in the darkened hallway, just Dane, holding a fucking nightgown of all things, Kai saw when Lady Bethany took it from him and let the long billows of fabric unfurl, but she hadn't known that.

"Thank you, Dane. That's so thoughtful of you."

She beamed at the Hound, who looked thunderstruck by the attention—and the fact she knew his name, had taken the time to memorize it.

"Dane." Kai wasn't going to give away the fact that he was delighted, too, that his Bound would care about his Hounds. "Go get some sleep."

Lady Bethany turned limpid eyes on him when Brannon shut the door without further niceties, the nightgown Dane had had the thoughtfulness to procure for her held tight to her chest. The frustration and anger Kai had felt at the careless way she'd endangered herself died a death in the face of her quiet reproach, but he forced himself to chastise her anyway.

"My lady, you should not have done that. What if there had been someone behind Dane, someone waiting for a chance to grab you? We cannot protect you if you do not help us by protecting yourself."

Lady Bethany blinked, then looked stricken.

"I didn't think." Her eyes went to the door and then back to Kai before dropping to the floor. His sharp eyes took in the way she clutched her gift a little tighter.

"This is a new situation for us all," he allowed. "We need to learn together. We'll leave you so you can get dressed. Rye," he jerked his head towards the door to the hallway. "I want you out there until the secondary comes to take over."

He waited a moment for Rye to position himself on sentry, then herded Brannon and the rest of the primary into the adjoining room before he could ruin his admonishment entirely by begging forgiveness for daring to say anything to put that wounded look on her face.

Of course, nothing got by his second.

"You're going soft," he said, as soon as the door was closed behind him. "If any of us had made a mistake like that, you'd have had our balls."

Kai rounded on him.

"You did make a fucking mistake. What the hell were you doing, letting her get by you at the door like that?"

Brannon paled and the beast inside Kai smelled blood. Brannon, Kai found, he could castigate no problem.

13

I floated in a haze.

I was comfortable and warm, rolling over in the bed and plumping the pillow slightly. It was still and dark, so I let myself sink back down into oblivion.

And fell into a room. It was stark and bare, the light too bright and the air too cold. As I took in my surroundings, I became aware of the pinch of leather around my wrists—wrists which were held tight above my head. I tried to bring my legs up, to cover some of my naked body, and found I couldn't. A face appeared above me, one that was sickeningly familiar. A knife came into view, held up beside the face—

Which started to smile.

Then worse: the knife disappeared. I screamed as pain bloomed along my left-hand side…

I sat bolt upright, the echoes of my scream still ringing in my ear. The inn bedroom was light, now, and as I looked around me in a panicked daze, I saw Kai immediately beside my bed, my primary all fighting each other as they tried to get in through the adjoining door. One of my secondary guard—I couldn't remember his name in the heat of the moment—loitered in the doorway to the hall, torn between wanting to come in and remaining at his post.

"Lady Bethany!" Kai's voice was rough and urgent, and I had the feeling it wasn't the first time he'd called to me.

I turned to him, stunned, and tried to remember where I was, what was happening.

I was not back in that room.

I was not trapped under those lights, those cruel, cruel hands.

I yanked a breath in, then another. Willed my heart to stop racing.

"I'm all right," I said, looking from face to face, trying to ground myself back into my new reality. The words hurt coming out and I winced. Just how loud had I screamed?

Plenty loud, if the worried looks on the faces around me were anything to judge by.

"I'm sorry," I croaked. "I had a nightmare."

"A nightmare," Kai asked softly, "or a memory?"

"Do Celestial's have memories?" someone muttered quietly, followed by the distinct slap of a hand on flesh.

"I do," I said, looking over towards my guard. I wasn't sure which one it was who had spoken, Rye maybe. "I had a life…before. Not here, it was a different world. Then I was in the Ether, I don't know how long for." I gave a helpless little shrug.

"What happened?" Kai asked.

I hunched my shoulders and gave a short, sharp of my head. "I was murdered," I said.

"What?" Kai hissed. He shifted position, as if he was preparing to attack, death in his eyes. Well, he'd have to fight ghosts, then.

"I was out jogging. I took a route I'd run dozens of times, a quiet road that ran along the back of my neighborhood. I was just about to head back when I noticed a van was following me. I stopped, and I was going to ask them what was wrong—I thought they were lost or something—but when I saw the driver and the man sitting beside him, I just...I don't know. I felt it, this premonition. I tried to run, to get back into my neighborhood, but they were faster than me. They threw me into the back of the van and took me somewhere. I don't know where, some ranch. I barely got a glimpse of it when they dragged me inside. And then—" I drew in a deep breath. "It wasn't a nice death, let's leave it at that."

It took Kai a while to get himself together enough to speak.

"I'm sorry," he said. Simple words, but they were heartfelt. Tears pushed at my eyes.

"I had a family," I blurted, my nose burning and my throat clogging up. "I don't even know if they know what happened to me. Or if they think I just...ran away."

That was my worst fear. That my children might think I had abandoned them. And I had no way to tell them otherwise. I hoped my body was never found, that they never discovered what went on in my final hours, but I wanted them to know that I'd be taken. That I hadn't—that I never would have—left them.

Kai didn't know what to say to that. He reached out and took my hand, and I felt his sympathy, his sorrow for all I'd suffered, but most importantly for my loss. I gripped his hand tight in mine, grateful he wasn't trying to fill the air with platitudes. His comfort was silent, but it was genuine and soul deep.

There was no chance of anyone getting more sleep after

my explosive alarm call, so Kai sent Jay, the member of my secondary who was stationed outside the door, to wake the innkeeper and rustle up breakfast and hot water for washing. I had no choice but to put my borrowed clothes back on, though they were decidedly grubby after two days of wear.

"We'll have you in something more befitting your station by the time the morning's out," Kai promised.

I grimaced. Hopefully the Hounds didn't have super-sensitive noses, too, because I was pretty sure I didn't smell particularly angelic.

"Something simple will be fine," I assured him. "I don't want to put you to any trouble." Or expense. I didn't want to be a burden.

Kai's face set in a manner I was beginning to realize was typical to the Hounds—an obstinate, mulish expression that said he was preparing to dig his heels in.

"I won't shame you by taking you to the palace in tatters," he said.

I looked at his stiff, defensive posture and decided this was not the hill I wanted to die on.

"As you wish."

Leaving the inn was an exercise in patience. First, Kai spent ten minutes drilling the four Hounds in my primary guard about how he expected them to watch me, which, given the looks on their faces—there was that obstinate frown again—they knew very well. Then he sent my secondary guard out into the town, ordering them to specific watch points to look out for trouble. Lastly, it was my turn to be lectured.

"You will be safe," he assured me, which, ironically, instantly made me feel a lot less safe. "Your guard know what they are about, and I will be by your side. Should anything happen, stay close to me, and listen to my instructions. I will not allow you to be hurt."

"I trust you," I said. I felt a rush of pride which quickly ebbed to be replaced with the worry I'd been feeling all morning. Worry that wasn't mine, I realized suddenly. "It will be all right," I told him, smiling gently.

I felt his start, then embarrassment that I'd picked up on how anxious he was. Which in turn made him more anxious. Taking a deep breath, I tried to sweep the feeling aside and replace it with calm. As soon as I felt I had a firm grip on my composure, I pushed it outwards.

I visibly watched as Kai relaxed, the tension seeping out of his shoulders, the tightness easing from his mouth. Unfortunately, it only lasted long enough for him to realize the serenity was coming from outside himself, and then he gaped at me, astonished.

"You are manipulating my feelings, Lady Bethany," he murmured. "I didn't know you could do that."

"I didn't either," I replied, a little smugly.

He watched me intently, interest taking over as his dominant emotion.

"Can you only do it to me, or can you extend it to others? Could you manipulate the emotions of everyone in this room?"

I had no idea. I turned to eye my primary guard and Brannon, who were by the door, ready to go. What could I make them feel? Not anger. They were too big, too primal already. And not fear, though it was an emotion I thought I could call forward readily enough.

I pulled a deep breath in through my nose and tried to blank my mind. I thought about waking up, and seeing the four huge Hounds trying to wedge themselves in through the door. It was like something out of a Loony Tunes cartoon, so I added some exaggerated facial expressions, feeling sliding on the polished wood floor. My mouth threatened to twitch, a laugh bubbling up in my throat, but I held it back. I didn't want to give them any clues about what I was up to.

A snort from Conlon was my first hint that it was working. I opened my eyes briefly and saw humor flashing in his eyes. I worked a little harder at my image, dressing them in ridiculous nightclothes with Wee Willy Winky style hats. Brannon, I dressed in the nightgown Dane found for me.

Definite laughter now. Rye's sharp teeth flashed in his grin as he shoved at Brannon's shoulder. "It suits you," he said.

"What?" My grip on the humor slipped as I stared at Rye. "Can you see that? Can you all see that?"

"If you're talking about Brannon in a dress, my lady, I saw it," Tor replied. His craggy façade hadn't cracked, but his light grey eyes were twinkling.

"I'm sorry," I said to Brannon, who looked the least amused. "I didn't realize I was doing that."

"I take no offense, my lady," he replied stiffly. I bit my lip, he certainly looked offended. He turned to Kai. "We should go."

In a heartbeat, all my good work was ruined. My primary guard took on grim, stoic expressions and Kai went right back to worrying. I sighed out a breath and accepted inevitability. At least I had learned something about myself.

Kai was right, I was beginning to see the value in what I could do. If I could alter the emotional state of a handful of people, could I do the same to a mass gathering? Calm a group of angry protestors? Whip an army up into a violent frenzy? Or turn an opposing force jelly-legged with terror? I was tempted to practice on the inn staff we passed as we left our rooms, or the small clusters of townspeople out on the street, but I wouldn't be able to measure my success.

It didn't occur to me until we'd reached a shop, obviously a clothes store by the mannequins in the window, just how wrong that would have been. I stopped dead, thinking about the sad young man leaning against the wall that I'd wanted to cheer up; the argument between the angry, buxom woman and the market vendor I'd thought about defusing. Strangers, caught up in their own lives, doing their own thing. Not puppets for me to play with.

"My lady," Kai prompted, his concerned face in front of mine the moment I stopped. "Are you well?"

"Fine," I managed. "Just...thinking."

"Perhaps you could continue thinking inside?" he suggested, his smile strained. "We are exposed here on the street."

I let him lead me through the door to the shop's cool interior. Conlon and Tor came inside with us, Brannon, Rye, and Ferris taking up positions outside. There weren't any other customers in the store, and it looked like the

Hounds intended to keep it that way. When the shopkeeper came bustling through from the backroom, her irritated expression told me she realized it, too, and she wasn't happy about it.

"Can I help you, sir?" she asked, addressing Kai who'd got in front of me as soon as she materialized. "Is there a reason your men are barricading my door? I've customers who need to get in."

"I have a customer for you," Kai replied smoothly. "I promise you it will be well worth your time."

He stood aside, revealing me, and the woman started. "Madam," she said, dropping into a bob of a curtsey. "Forgive me, I didn't see you there." If she had any opinion on my current state of dress, she was smart enough to keep her mouth closed. "What is it that you need."

It was Kai who replied. "Everything."

Getting me suited and booted took time. The shopkeeper took me through to a private, screened-off area at the back of the store, something that Kai allowed only after he scoped it out and proclaimed it free of bad guys. He still insisted on standing just out of sight, something that flustered the matronly-looking seamstress no end. Only the amount of money she stood to make from us held her tongue, and she clucked as she measured me through my clothes.

"Not even decent under things," she mumbled under her breath. "Whatever has happened to you?"

I treated it as a rhetorical question, smiling sweetly when she paused and looked up at me from her diminutive height, as if waiting for an answer.

Since we didn't have time to hang around the town for a week while the seamstress knocked me up a made-to-measure outfit, she dressed me with what she had in stock, making hasty adjustments with quick, practiced hands. The dresses she brought through for me to try on made me think I must be a bit more solidly built than the average woman here, but that was before she laced me into a sort of vest top that felt less restrictive than what I imagined a corset to be like, but pulled me in with much more rigor than the camisoles and bras I was accustomed to wearing. The underwear, thankfully, was just a slightly frillier version of a French knicker with thin stockings that tied at the knee.

What wasn't as reassuring—though I was expecting it from the glimpses I'd got of what women were wearing so far—was the distinct lack of trousers in every outfit she brought me to see. Women wore dresses. Period. I could count on one hand the number of times I'd worn a dress in the last ten years, and the only floor-length dress I'd ever worn was my wedding dress. I tried to push that memory away as soon as I thought it. Keeping my past locked up tight was the only way I could manage to deal with my present.

The future I was leaving well alone.

"Well?" the seamstress asked after she'd shoe-horned me into another concoction. "What do you think?"

I looked in the full-length mirror and tried to take a deep breath securely tied into my new basque. I looked ridiculous, the fabric billowing out in layers of ruffle, the florid pink at odds with my sun-burned face.

"It's beautifully made," I said tactfully. "But do you have anything…less ostentatious?"

"This is the current fashion!" the woman complained.

"But it isn't *my* fashion," I replied, gently but firmly.

She harrumphed, then disappeared. When she came back in, she had a thankfully much smaller bundle flung over one arm.

"My apprentice has been working on some things," she said, unfolding a relatively simple shift dress with asymmetric shapes stitched down the front. "She has some," her mouth pursed in disapproval, "unusual ideas about the future of women's clothing."

"I'll try it on," I said.

Even with the under-bodice I was wearing, it was a tight fit, and I guessed the apprentice had imagined her creation on someone young and nubile. I got it on, though, and when I looked at myself in the mirror, the silhouette was flattering. The skirt didn't flair in the same way as the rest of the seamstresses' dresses, but it was cut a bit like a wraparound, a hint of thigh flashing when I kicked my leg out just right, so I thought I could manage to get on and off a horse okay.

"I like it," I told the woman. "Do you have anything else like this?"

"You're sure?" she said dubiously. "You'll stand out."

Kai probably wouldn't like that idea, but I did.

I ended up with four outfits, all in the same figure-hugging style, the cut actually making movement easier than the voluminous, more traditional dresses. Better yet, one was a jumpsuit, the trousers cleverly formed to look like a skirt. I was disappointed when the seamstress told me the apprentice had only made one of those.

"I could get her to sew you some more," she said cannily, coins flashing behind her eyes.

"We're leaving town," I told her regretfully.

Besides, once we'd added a second set of underwear and a pair of pretty but sturdy boots, the cost was enough to have the seamstress practically giddy as she stood with palm outstretched, watching Kai count coins into it. I held my tongue in the shop, but as soon as we were outside, I rounded on Kai, tripping out apologies.

He halted my words with a whisper touch of his fingers to my lips. "You are a prize beyond measure," he said. "I am grateful that I can give you such a small thing."

It was a short walk back to the inn, where Kai intended we eat before heading back to the camp where the rest of the Hounds were waiting. The press of townspeople in the street had thinned somewhat as the heat of the day started to build. Perhaps that was why my guard relaxed just a fraction, their watchfulness losing the razor edge, or maybe it would have happened regardless. All I knew was that one minute we were walking along, undisturbed, and the next the street was filled with noise and activity and confusion.

At first, I didn't understand what was happening. A warning shout went up from one of my guard, and then Tor was hand-to-hand with a boy who couldn't have been more than fifteen. A thief, I realized, as Tor yanked one of my bags out of his grasp. The boy was wriggling and twisting and turning, trying to get away, but Tor had a firm grasp, Conlon moving into help. The thief's friend appeared out of nowhere, shoving into Tor and knocking him off-balance. The Hound snarled, hands immediately reaching out to recapture the original thief, but he was gone, moving like lightning as he disappeared down an alleyway. His friend made to dart after him, but Conlon was too fast, reaching out to grab at a flailing arm.

The youngster—a girl, I realized, noting her long hair and dirty, elfin features—twisted round, her free arm flying at speed. The glint of the knife buried in her fist registered a heartbeat before she thrust it into Conlon's side. He grunted and might have held on if I hadn't intervened, gasping and reaching for him. Torn between holding onto the girl and protecting me from her knife, ripped free and covered in blood, he chose me, and she was off before I could blink.

"Conlon!" I screeched, my hand going straight to the wound. It came away wet and painted with red. Conlon's mouth worked furiously, but no words came out. He collapsed to the dirt floor, blood already pooling beneath him.

14

The next few minutes were a chaos of movement. Someone picked me up and sprinted with me back to the inn, their broad shoulders hiding my view of Conlon, sprawled motionless on the road.

"Wait!" I gasped. "Stop! Is he all right?"

"Get her inside," Kai growled, confirming that he wasn't the one who held me. I twisted in the hold of whoever it was and saw that it was Rye, face set in a determined mask, his mouth pulled back in a snarl that showed off razor-sharp teeth, the incisors elongated and pressing down into his bottom lip. He was growling, the sound rumbling up through his chest.

He burst through the inn door, ignoring the startled yelp of the innkeeper, and sprinted up the stairs, not stopping until he reached our rooms. There he deposited me on the floor and began patting me all over.

"Are you all right?" he asked. "Are you hurt?"

"I'm fine," I said, trying to back away from his over-enthusiastic assessment.

He didn't take the hint, continuing to touch my arms, my sides, until a harsh snarl from the door had him freezing, hands outstretched. A moment later he was all the way across the room, pressed against the wall with his head angled oddly, his neck stretched out.

I didn't have long to puzzle it, because the next instant, Kai was in my face.

"My lady," he growled. "Are you all right?"

"I'm fine," I told him. "Where's Conlon?"

As soon as the words were out of my mouth, he appeared, carried by Tor and Rye with Brannon covering their backs. I looked around for Ferris and was surprised to discover he was already in the room, his body somehow soaking up a shadow that rendered him all but invisible. His chosen spot allowed him to cover both me and the door.

Tor and Rye deposited Conlon on the bed with care and then stood back, Brannon moving forwards to cut away his tunic and reveal the deep wound gouged into his side. I stared at it with horror, noting the little bubbles of blood that seeped out with every exhale. The knife had punctured his lung. It took only a moment for Brannon to make the same assessment, and the look he threw Kai was tortured, his diagnosis evident in the small shake of his head.

It was hard to meet Conlon's gaze knowing he'd been injured protecting me, even if it had just been a couple of street urchins, picking on too-big prey. He'd never have been there, in that street, at that moment, if it hadn't been for me. It was even worse to see that he wasn't looking at me with regret or judgment; instead, he was drinking me in as if he was staring at God. As if my life was worth such a sacrifice.

I sobbed, utterly distraught, and fell across the room towards him.

"My lady, no!" I heard Kai shout, but I ignored him, as I ignored Brannon's hand, reaching out to stop me. I batted him away and crashed to my knees beside Conlon.

"I'm sorry," I cried. "I'm so, so sorry."

I put one hand on his forehead, the other going to his injury. It was hot and slick with blood, the tiny bubbles popping against my palm with every breath he took. I had first-hand knowledge of the sort of pain he must be in, and I closed my eyes, willing him peace. He relaxed under me, and I first I was terrified that he might have gone already, but when I opened my eyes again, he was watching me with those strange eyes, agony no longer twisting his features.

Peace, calm. That was what I felt emanating from him. I tried to smile, my pulse thundering through my veins in response to the slow fading of his. It got so loud it was throbbing in my ears, blurring my vision with each pounding beat. By the time I understood something was wrong, I couldn't pull my hands away, wicked hot fire blazing through both palms.

"Kai," I dimly heard someone whisper, I think it was Brannon. "Are you seeing this? Are you seeing what she's doing?"

I didn't see what I was doing, not until the violent throbbing stopped and I could draw my hands away. Then I stared down at Conlon in disbelief. His side was still coated in blood, but the ugly slashing wound was gone, the skin as unblemished as if there'd never been an injury.

Astonished, I looked to Conlon, who was staring at me as if I'd just performed a miracle. Which I suppose I had. Without warning, he rolled off the bed and onto his knees in front of me, crouching low so that his head was level with my belly, hair draping down to brush my knees.

"You blessed me," he gasped. "I'm not worthy, my lady, but you blessed me."

I didn't know what to do. I looked over to Kai, but he was just standing there, speechless. Conlon's shoulders were shaking now, fine tremors running down his back. I lifted a hand and stroked through his sweat-soaked hair, leaving my hand on his nape. I could feel his disbelief and astonishment, but overriding every other feeling was awe. Worship.

I didn't know how comfortable I was with that.

"It's okay," I murmured softly. "You're okay."

I'd healed him. It was taking a little while for that to sink in, but as it did, I felt a strange sort of strength seep into my limbs, despite the fact I felt light-headed and wobbly. I felt, well, powerful. Finally, I'd discovered something I could do that was indisputably good. That was a heady feeling.

"Let's get him up on the bed, look him over," Brannon suggested.

Conlon resisted when they attempted to prize him from my lap, but eventually, he allowed them to lift him up onto the bed and Tor slapped a wet rag across his side, cleaning off the blood. It was as I'd thought; he was completely healed.

I got to my feet slowly, eyes glued to what I'd done. Kai came up beside me, his hand reaching out to touch the unblemished skin on Conlon's side before he twisted and dropped down to a knee in front of me.

"Thank you," he said, "for the life of my Hound."

It took me two attempts to speak, my mouth dry and my throat too tight to swallow.

"I don't know how I did it, but you're welcome."

When he stood up, his arms twitched like he wanted to hug me. I desperately wanted to be hugged, the whole scene out in the street having ripped my equilibrium away from me, so I moved forward into his chest, pressing against him. It took a moment, but his arms wrapped around me, warm and comforting.

"Are you all right?" he murmured into my hair.

I wanted to nod, to be brave, but instead, I shook my head. "I was scared," I confessed.

"It was nothing," Kai murmured. "Just an ambitious pickpocket, a little street skirmish."

Right. The little I'd gleaned of the Hound's lives told me violence was an integral part of it. Fighting and war were their bread and butter. I'd never so much as been in a catfight at school. Still, I thought Kai was underplaying it.

"Conlon could have died," I pointed out.

"But he didn't. And if you asked him if he wanted to give up his place in your primary guard over what just happened, what do you think he'd say?"

"Please." Conlon sat up; his usual good-natured expression wiped from his face. "Don't take me off her guard." He stared at Kai; his eyes fixed on Kai's chin. I'd noticed that, that most of the Hounds avoided direct eye contact with him. I assumed it was a dominance thing, another Hound trait. "I know I made a mistake—"

"*I* made a mistake." Tor stepped forwards; head angled away to expose his neck. "I let a couple of street thieves get the better of me. My place should be forfeited."

Wide-eyed, I looked at Kai. His expression was serious as he considered Tor, the rest of my guard watching warily.

I had the feeling something quite important was going on, but I didn't know what. The tension was thick in the air, my skin all but tingling with it. I didn't like the feeling; it made me want to fling open the windows to let untainted air in. Or better yet, let me out.

"You see," I said quietly, hoping to dispel the strained atmosphere with humor. "Five minutes of babysitting me and they're already trying to get out of it. I mean, Conlon attempted to get himself killed, which seems a bit extreme, but..." I tailed off and shrugged, a smile quirking at the corner of my mouth.

None of them smiled back at me.

"The guard remains the same for now," Kai said, settling the matter. "If there's another incident like today, I'll bring in members of her secondary guard. I don't have to tell you they're keen to take your place."

Nods all round, somber faces.

Brannon rustled up some food for us and I listened as he and Kai debated staying another day in Cleavestown versus getting the hell out of there. I was all for the latter, my confidence in the small market town shattered by the events in the street. Thankfully, Kai seemed to be of the same mind.

"Are you finished, Lady Bethany?" he asked, approaching me where I sat eating at the only table in the room. "Half the day is gone already. If we wish to move on, time is of the essence."

"I'm done," I confirmed, setting my bowl down. I stood, ready to get out of there, but the world spun crazily, making me pitch. I would have hit the floor, but of course, Kai was there to catch me.

"My lady?" he asked, his voice full of concern, the hands gripping my waist sending the emotion through me in blasting waves.

"I'm okay," I insisted, patting his arm. "I just…stood up too fast."

Though the dizziness wasn't really fading, neither was the weak feeling in my legs.

"You used too much energy healing Conlon," Kai growled, disapproval hardening his face. "I thought you looked less vibrant."

"Less vibrant?" I asked, the low-level queasiness I was feeling taking a back step to Kai's unusual choice of words. To my surprise, he reddened.

"I can see your energy, swirling under your skin," he told me. "Even when you aren't glowing. It flared brightly when you healed Conlon, but afterward, it was dim, barely noticeable. I thought perhaps it was the light in the room, but it's more than that. You've drained yourself."

I glanced over to Conlon, who looked appalled. I could feel it from him, too, his shame eclipsing even Kai's displeasure.

"I'm fine," I said, pushing away from Kai and proving it by staying upright. It took effort, though, my vision slightly tunneled as if I was drunk. "It's nothing."

"You won't heal again," Kai announced.

I turned to look at him, swallowing back saliva as the sharp movement made my stomach roil, my lunch threatening to make a reappearance.

"What?"

"The gift you gave Conlon has weakened you. We don't even know how long it will last. My Hounds are not worth that, and none of them will ask it of you."

He glowered at my primary guard, at Brannon, as if any of them had uttered even a word of protest. In fact, the opposite was true. All of them were nodding, and Conlon looked utterly distraught.

"Forgive me," he begged me.

"I'm not agreeing to that," I said.

"My lady—"

"No." I cut across Kai, ignoring the unhappy frown on his face. In the periphery of my vision, I was dimly aware of the subtle light infusing my skin. I was glowing again. "I won't be told I can't help people. If any of you are hurt because of me, I will make it right."

Kai set his teeth, his eyes glowing a brighter shade of amber. Around me, every single Hound dropped their gaze. I felt the need to do the same, so I held his stare, though it made my heart thunder in my chest.

"I can order them not to accept your aid," he ground out.

I lifted my chin, anger flowing through my veins like electricity. "Do that, and I won't accept a guard at all."

He glowered at me, furious, and I glared right back. I refused to back down on this, though pushing back against the force of his will was almost a physical pain.

When he shut his eyes suddenly, I almost fell forward, such was the power of the release. He pulled in a deep breath and blew it out, and when he opened his eyes again, they'd lost the fiery glow and the aggression.

"Apologies, my lady," he rumbled, his voice low and slightly distorted. "You are a Celestial, and I forget my place. I beg your forgiveness."

I thought for a horrible moment he was going to get on his knees again, but he remained tall and proud, waiting to see if I was going to grant absolution.

"There's nothing to forgive," I promised. "Just let me use my gifts if there are any who need them."

I took his silence for assent.

At least one good thing had come out of our altercation, I thought, as we headed out of the inn to where the horses were waiting, saddled and held by my secondary guard. I didn't feel weak anymore. If anything, the confrontation had infused me with a jittery kind of energy, like I was a glass that had been overfilled. My skin was pulsing ever so softly, but I hoped it wasn't all that noticeable in the bright mid-afternoon sun, because we'd already drawn enough attention to ourselves.

"We're going to the palace now?" I asked as Kai came to my side to help lift me up onto my horse.

He nodded. "I promised to present you within ten days, we can't delay anymore."

"How long will it take us to get there?"

Kai glanced up at the sky and took in the angle of the sun.

"By sunset, I hope to make it to the pass." He gave a small smile. "It's a beautiful sight, watching the day fade behind the mountains. It is a three-day trip through to the other side."

"The palace is on the other side?"

"Yes."

"And what will happen once we get there?"

His face hardened between one moment and the next. "That depends on the king. But I swear to you, my lady, I will protect you with my life. And if I can't, I will return you to the Ether."

15

The whispers were buzzing round the camp. How she'd brought Conlon back from the dead, how she could take fear and turn it into bravery. Worse: how she'd faced down the First Hound and made him bend to her will. Kai sat on his horse, jaw clenched so hard he thought he might crack a tooth, and watched as his Hounds tripped over each other, fucking up a simple job like packing up a temporary camp, because they were all trying to get a peek at Lady Bethany, sitting on a fallen log and looking for all the world like she was nothing but a woman, smiling and benign.

Kai had just had a first-hand lesson in the fact she was anything but.

His muscles tightened, remembering how she'd stared him down, the bond between them setting his every nerve alight until his bones felt like they'd melt under the fiery weigh of her conviction. That she felt that strongly, that passionately, about exhausting her essence just to help his band of mongrels, that humbled Kai until he wanted to present himself prostrate in a puddle at her feet. He wasn't the only one; every Hound inside that room felt the same, and the bastards apparently had flapping tongues, which was why his pack was currently acting like such a group of nannies rather than the hardened soldiers that they were.

If they were in awe of her before, now they saw her as a goddess.

Kai didn't know why that irked him so much. All right,

he fucking did. She was smiling at them, every Hound brave enough to catch her eye, and Kai didn't like to share.

"Get her up on her horse," he snarled at Brannon. "Any Hound not set to go by the time she's ready to ride out can fucking stay here."

"Yes, First," Brannon replied, his unusual formality telling Kai he was picking up on his aggression.

It didn't take long for Brannon to get Lady Bethany's horse saddled and her up on it. Her primary guard appeared out of nowhere, Ferris and Tor on horseback once more and Conlon and Rye ready to run beside her. Kai wanted to kick his horse forward and muscle his way in between her and Tor, but he forced himself to hang back. She was smiling at Ferris, saying something to the Hound, and Ferris, who had never cracked a smile in his life, was grinning widely at her, making some response that had a laugh ringing out across the camp.

It was the first time Kai had ever heard her laugh, and that another Hound had drawn the sound from her had jealous fury boiling in his blood, but he had to let her connect with her guard. She needed to trust them with her life, and she wouldn't do that with strangers. He was gratified when she started to look around for him, her expression troubled until they locked eyes, but the satisfaction faded quickly when he realized it was likely because she could feel his anger—worse, his possessiveness. She offered him an uncertain smile, a shadow of the one she'd bestowed on Ferris, and he made himself give it back, blanking his mind so she wouldn't feel his muddled emotions.

He was saved from having to ride over and respond to the question in her eyes by the sudden appearance of Brannon, horseless since he'd be taking Kai's usual role of leading the pack on the run. "We're all set. We go on your command."

"Now, then," Kai replied. "Let's get the hell out of here."

Brannon gave a respectful nod then turned away and headed for the road that would lead them away from the town towards the distant mountains. He gave a whooping call that was answered by the pack, all of them somehow having got their act together and got ready to go in the last few minutes. Kai saw Lady Bethany jump at the sound and Tor reassure her. She gathered her reins and adjusted her seat on the saddle, looking around for Kai once more.

Fuck it. He wasn't going to deny himself the pleasure of her company. Who knew how much longer he'd have it for? He nudged his mount forwards until he could move alongside her.

"You're ready to ride, my lady?" he asked.

"As ready as I'll ever be," she replied ruefully.

"This won't be as taxing as yesterday's ride," he promised. "We're going no further than the base of the mountains. We'll have to stop before we begin to climb the pass."

"The pass?"

He nodded. "There are only a few routes to the capital that can accommodate groups in our number. The northern pass would have been the quickest, but we'll be taking

Hogan's Pass. It's an easier road, though it takes a little longer."

"But we'll still be there within the ten days?"

"Easily."

Her eyes flashed with a spark of humor. "I'm not in any rush to get there, I just…I don't want to cause you trouble because we had to stop and get me something to wear."

"The stop in Cleavestown allowed us to stock up on other provisions, as well," he said. Though they could have picked up the extra food anywhere along the road, and likely at a cheaper price, but he wasn't going to tell her that.

They set off behind the front-running Hounds, most of the pack running to the side and behind the horses. It was another hot, dry day—it was rarely anything else during the long summer months—but at least the sun was hidden behind a heavy layer of cloud, so Kai didn't have to worry about Lady Bethany's fair skin burning again. She still bore pink patches on her lower arms and the back of her neck, where she'd gathered her hair up into some sort of twisting knot.

The dress she wore was made of a thinner fabric than the borrowed clothes of Danes she'd been wearing, but already he could see the tendrils of hair at the nape were damp with sweat. She suffered in the heat, and he'd have to make sure she drank enough water. He wanted to bury his nose into the curve of that neck, draw in her scent and lick at the salt of her skin. His mouth watered at the thought, but he swallowed it back. Wasn't she proving, every hour of every day, just how special she was? And with each new miracle, she drew further and further away from Kai.

He might be her Bound, but he wasn't her equal.

Kai spotted the bird flying high in the sky when they were still an hour out from the base of the pass. It flew high and fast, capturing his attention for no reason other than it seemed to be heading unerringly in their direction. He knew it was General Tuill's newly acquitted Gryt even before it had dropped close enough to reveal its tough leathery skin and wickedly sharp beak and claws.

It was near enough that he could see the message it carried, tucked tight against its underside, before the shout went up from the first of his Hounds.

"What? What is it?" Lady Bethany asked, as the warning call echoed all around them. "What's a Gite?"

"A Gryt," Kai corrected. "It's a messenger bird."

He held his arm out to receive the Gryt, but it ignored him, flapping around Lady Bethany until she tentatively reached out a hand.

"Lady Bethany, its claws—" Kai got out, but the Gryt landed with the utmost gentleness, transferring to the pommel of her saddle and butting at her hand with its head. Looking astonished and not a little bit wary, she reached out a hand to stroke over its scaly skin, and the creature closed its eyes in bliss.

"It's tame!" she exclaimed.

"It's not," Kai assured her. "If any of us tried that, it would rip our hands off."

Though Tuill's Gryt had come to him through the gate, the birds did actually exist in the wild, making their home in the vast forests far to the south. They were deadly, strong enough to take a man's life if they were hungry enough, or in defense of a nest. And here was this one, practically in Lady Bethany's lap, looking as harmless as a kitten.

"Can you retrieve the message?" he asked.

"I'm not sure," she replied quietly. "Will he let me?"

As soon as she spoke, the Gryt lifted up on its feet, spreading its wings and exposing its vulnerable underbelly. With fingers that shook slightly, Lady Bethany tugged the tightly rolled scrap of paper free.

"Thank you," she murmured to the bird, which immediately nestled back down, as close as it could get. "Here."

When she reached out toward Kai with the tiny scroll, their fingers touched for the space of an instant. Kai tried not to show how much that fleeting contact affected him. He was as pathetic as the Gryt, which was posturing now, trying to get Lady Bethany to pet him once more.

Trying not to be jealous of a god's bedamned bird—because she *was* stroking it, running her fingers down its back, and the fucking thing was trilling—Kai unraveled the scroll. He recognized the General's jagged penmanship, evidence that the man had worked his way up from a lowly soldier and hadn't had the benefit of a fancy education to get him to where he was.

I'll meet you at the base of Hogan's Pass and escort you to the palace.

Kai's face was thoughtful as he rolled the paper back up and tucked it into his tunic. His first question was how the general had known they'd be taking Hoban's Pass instead of the more direct route, but perhaps that could be accounted for by the bird basking in Lady Bethany's attention. He'd seen no sign that the Gryt was trailing them, hadn't noticed it in the sky before it made its approach with the message, but it wasn't a normal Gryt, was it? It had come through the Ether, for all Kai knew it could become invisible if it chose.

The second, more worrying question, was why was General Tuill arranging to meet them? It certainly wasn't to socialize. Kai's instinct for trouble was screaming warnings in his head. Something was going on, but there were no more clues to be gleaned from the note. He'd have to hold his curiosity until they reached the pass.

It took longer than Kai expected for Brannon to appear and ask about the message. When his Second finally emerged, he was dusty and sweat-covered, his breathing ragged and uneven.

"You scouted ahead?" Kai asked.

Brannon nodded. "There's a whole squadron of soldiers encamped at the entrance to the pass."

"They flying Tuill's colors?"

Brannon nodded, his eyes curious and darting between his First and the Gryt. Without warning, the thing took off, startling a cry from Lady Bethany. Kai watched it lift into the sky, searching for any hint that it was able to disappear at will. It remained a solid blur against the layer of cloud, though it moved at an astonishing speed as it returned to its master.

"The general's message said he was going to escort us through the pass."

Brannon frowned, raking the damp strands of his hair back so they didn't impede his eyes.

"What does he need to do that for? What's going on?"

"I guess we'll find out," Kai murmured, his voice dropping down to almost subvocal level because now the Gryt had disappeared, Lady Bethany was taking a much more active interest in their conversation.

"Is everything all right?" she asked.

"Fine," Kai replied, which was what he'd have said whether it was true or not. There was no definite threat in sight yet, however, so it wasn't really a lie. "We'll be meeting some soldiers at the pass, king's men."

"Are they friendly?" Uncertainty widened her eyes slightly, made her fingers tighten on the reins in her hands.

Brannon snorted quietly, earning himself a jab from Kai's boot when he saw how the sound made Lady Bethany bite her lip with worry.

"General Tuill is a good man and I trust him," he told her.

"But?"

"Hounds and soldiers don't tend to mix very well, let's leave it at that."

"I see," Lady Bethany replied. "Why is he meeting us?"

Kai tried hard to keep the grimace off his face. She kept asking questions he didn't want to answer. "We'll find that out when we get there, I presume." He felt the need to be honest with her where he could. "General Tuill was at the temple. He's Bound to the Gryt that brought the message."

"I remember," she said quietly. "I saw it go through to one of the men. Why—" She paused, pressing her lips together as if she wasn't sure she should continue. "Why did some of the men not receive...I don't know what to call them. Spirits?"

"They were barren."

"Barren?"

Kai nodded and Lady Bethany's eyebrows pulled together in confusion.

"Well, what does that mean?"

"It means the spirits deemed them not worthy. Why didn't *you* reach for them?"

Why didn't she? Kai watched her intently, keen to hear the answer. She wrinkled her nose and gave a little shrug.

"They just...I don't know. They repulsed me. Something about them made everything in me draw back."

"Unworthy," Kai agreed.

"But I didn't think any of the others were worthy, either."

"*You* didn't," he replied. "Other spirits did."

"But why?"

He shrugged. "Different things will call to different spirits. What was it about me that drew you?"

Lady Bethany didn't answer straight away. Her cheeks took on a pink hue even stronger than the sunburn which still lingered on her skin, and she turned her face away.

"I don't know," she said. "I told you before. I was just...drawn to you."

"Well," Kai said, pride warring with disappointment, "I am glad you found me worthy."

The smile she turned on him was dazzling, and Kai knew then that he was going to burn in the afterlife because he was utterly lost. She'd made him her slave with nothing more than eyes that actually saw him.

16

General Tuill didn't go in for shields and standard-bearers and all the rest of the fancy shit the nobles used to announce themselves. When he rode out from his encampment to greet them, his newly acquired Gryt perched on his shoulder, he came with only a squire and two soldiers on horseback. It showed balls, because as soon as the base of the pass had come into sight—along with the squadron of soldiers waiting there—Kai's Hounds had gathered around Lady Bethany in a protective shield. Aggression sparked in the air around them, and Kai had said not a word to temper it.

He trusted Tuill as far as he trusted any man, but if this was some sort of trick, he wanted them on edge and ready to draw blood at a moment's notice.

The Hounds parted to let the general and his escorts advance until he stood in front of Kai and Lady Bethany, Brannon, and her primary guard encircling her on all sides. The squire looked extremely uncomfortable about the narrow funnel the Hounds had maneuvered them down, his fear exciting the pack until one of them snapped playfully at his heels. Well, mostly playfully. The little squeal of terror he emitted certainly sent a ripple of laughter through the Hounds.

General Tuill, smart man that he was, merely quipped, "Grow a pair, Justin. They're on our side."

This time it was the two soldiers with Tuill who snickered while the squire, Justin, flamed red.

"Strand," Tuill said by way of a greeting, then he turned to Lady Bethany and pulled off the light helmet he was wearing by the nose guard. He gave her as deep a bow as could be afforded when on horseback and with a considerable girth around his middle. "My lady."

"Lady Bethany, this is General Tuill. General, it's my honor to present to you my Bound, the Celestial Lady Bethany."

It was as pretty a speech as Kai had ever given, one he was going to have to give a hundred times when they arrived at the palace, but he was glad that the first time was here, now, with a man he respected. If he enjoyed watching Tuill, a man he liked, gaze upon his Bound with a mixture of awe, admiration, and jealousy, he was going to fucking love it when he got to shove it down the nobles' throats. He might be Kai Strand, savage dog, but he was also Kai Strand, Bound to a Celestial, and there was not a man in the world who could make that claim.

"Hello," Lady Bethany murmured, the tight smile on her face telling Kai she was nervous and uncomfortable. He growled, an instinctive, defensive reaction, and Tuill twitched on his horse until it shuffled a step back, colliding with the squire's horse and giving a sharp kick with its back leg that made the poor wretch give another undignified squeak. Kai's Hounds of course didn't help the matter, pressing in tighter, enjoying his unease.

"Shall I escort you back to the encampment?" Tuill suggested, feeling the rising tension and wisely deciding retreat was the best course of action. He smiled kindly at Lady Bethany. "I'm getting old, and I like my comforts. I've a tent back at camp with furs and cushions I'd be pleased to offer you to rest in."

Lady Bethany waited to nod until she'd glanced at Kai and received his approval, something that didn't pass by Tuill and didn't displease Kai. Let the old man know that Lady Bethany valued his opinion and let herself be led by his guidance. Besides, the general was full of shit. Getting old he might be, but he'd always traveled with no more luxury than he afforded his men, sleeping on a rough pallet on the ground, often beneath the stars or rain, whatever fortune offered from the heavens. He'd brought the tent and fancy furnishings for Lady Bethany. Had the gift of comfort come from any other—even Prince Faron, who held Kai's esteem—Kai would have seen it as a slight to the Hounds, a subtle play to try and lure Lady Bethany away from him, but he believed in the general's honesty. Tuill had brought it to honor Kai's Bound.

They returned to Tuill's squadron at a trot, the pack keeping in much closer quarters now that there were a hundred men in proximity to their Celestial, each of them a possible threat. Kai was pleased to see that the tent Tuill had set up was on the edges of the camp, allowing his Hounds to fan out around it and ensuring Lady Bethany wouldn't be encircled by men, by strangers.

He saw her dismounted and settled in the tent—Tuill had gone all out, there was even a leather bath on a collapsible frame, a bucket and pot furnace ready to heat water—then left her in the capable hands of her primary guard. That was hard. He wanted to stay with her, every moment of every day if he was honest with himself, but also because he was feeling the same stress as the rest of his Hounds. There were too many men, too close to his Bound. His instincts demanded he position himself in front of her, claws unsheathed, ready for the danger to reveal itself. But she had four exceptionally skilled Hound guards to do that, and the meaningful look General Tuill gave him when he invited Kai to dine with him around his fire told Kai that he'd better protect Lady Bethany tonight by listening to what the general had to say.

That didn't mean he had to like it.

Tuill's squire served them a meal under the gaze of the Gryt, watchful on a block perch behind Tuill's stool. He slapped Kai's meal into his hands in a manner that told him the boy was still upset over the way the Hounds had embarrassed him in front of the general and worse, the two accompanying soldiers who, Kai was sure, would be delighting the rest of the squadron with the story to mortify him. His mood didn't improve any when he went to take a seat at the fire and was sent packing with a sharp jerk of the head from Tuill.

"He's a proud one," the older man mused as his squire stomped away. "Youngest son of Lord Deston and used to being pampered and run after. He's not enjoying being bottom of the rung, but he'll learn. The boys might give him an easier time if he'd take the stick out of his ass."

"I don't know much about Lord Deston."

"He's not one for the palace. Prefers to stick to his lands where he's king. Which explains the son."

"How'd you get landed with him?"

"Keep your friends close…" the general replied with a tight-lipped smile.

"He's an enemy?" Kai asked cautiously.

"Deston? Not necessarily. Like I said, he doesn't like to get involved, but his lands border Lord Yule and they're on very friendly terms."

"I see."

"I hope you do," Tuill said. "Lord Yule is a proud man, too—"

"He's a noble," Kai interjected, drawing a small chuckle from the general.

"They're not all bad. Most of them, but not all. Anyway, Yule came away from that temple with nothing but humiliation, and you came out with a Celestial."

"That's not how it works," Kai disagreed. "The Ether chooses."

"You think Yule cares about that? Bad enough that he was labeled one of the barren, but when, forgive me, someone he thinks of as little more than a beast walks away with such a prize, well, the man's a walking wound, and he's not the type to let that lie."

"You've heard he's planning something?"

Tuill shook his head. "Nothing so well defined. Just that his pride is sorely stung, and he'll be looking for an opportunity to repay you for that."

Kai snorted. "He's a fool. He's no one to blame for his humiliation other than himself. Lady Bethany was repulsed when he stood before the Ether. She and the rest of the spirits saw exactly what he was."

"She told you that?" Tuill asked, his eyes alight with curiosity. Kai nodded. "I wondered, you know, what the spirits knew of what was happening. Of course, I cannot ask Swift." He gestured behind him, to where the Gryt sat, eyes closed and looking for all the world like it was asleep. Kai knew it for a ruse, though, one predator to another.

The general was hoping Kai would elaborate, he could tell, but he was strangely reluctant to reveal any of what Lady Bethany had told him, how she hadn't really understood what was happening, what it meant to be Bound. She *had* chosen him, that was all that mattered.

"Lord Yule," he said instead. "That is who think I should watch out for?"

Tuill snorted. "I think you should watch out for all of them. You're suddenly extremely powerful, and there's none of them won't take it from you if they can."

"Even the prince?"

"Perhaps not the prince, but he's young and an idealist. His father won't have any such compunction. Luckily for you, the man's not here. He sailed off to Trellium two days before the Solar Convection. He'll be kicking himself when he gets back and hears there was a Celestial up for grabs."

"You're assuming she'd have come to him," Kai replied, trying to rein in the jealousy that surged even at the thought that Lady Bethany might have preferred the king as Bound.

"I doubt she would have," Tuill soothed, "But the king won't think that."

"You believe he'll try to take her from me?"

"I believe it would be best if the bond between the two

of you was strong enough for it to be obvious to all that you cannot be separated."

"Our bond is strong," Kai shot back.

"Well then," Tuill smiled placatingly. His eyes remained cautious, though. "You should know that the priests have been called from White Mountain Temple. There is already a contingent in situ, and more have been sent for, including a high priest."

"They never leave the temple," Kai said. "They've dedicated their whole lives to worshipping there."

"They go where the king—and in this instance, the king's closest advisors—command. Lord Kenwick instigated this particular move, I believe." Tuill paused, making sure he had Kai's complete attention. "They are watching for any slip, any excuse, to take her from you. If they can't find one, they'll make one, and then the priests will have her Bound to another before your blood's stopped pumping."

"It'll have to be before my blood's stopped pumping," Kai retorted, "or she'll be whisked back to the Ether, and they'll be empty-handed."

"You know what I mean," Tuill said, his words heavy with warning. "Be careful, Kai."

Tuill had nothing further to add so he and Kai passed the rest of the meal exchanging idle chitchat about the recent battle against the Badari and the small band of terrorists hiding in the hills, preventing Janis from effectively concluding his takeover of the lands in the way he'd like.

"It's pissing him off," Tuill added, a smirk on his lips.

"He keeps hinting that he's going to pull my men back out there, but I told him I've had enough of that swamp. Flies and mud and a sun that feels ten times hotter."

"You've spoken with him?" Kai asked, confused.

Tuill gestured over his head. "Swift. He's astonishingly fast and damned clever. Would have made my life a lot easier of I'd had him twenty years ago."

Kai quirked an eyebrow. "What was it you said to me once? You get your gifts when you're ready to receive them?"

"Did I say that?" Tuill asked, laughing. "I must have been drunk. Wise words, though." He glanced pointedly at the tent. "You sure you're ready for yours?"

Kai looked towards the tent, too, and found himself standing involuntarily. He'd been away from her for too long.

"I don't think you're ever ready for a gift like that," he murmured. "Doesn't mean you don't hang onto it with both hands."

He walked away from Tuill without another word, ignoring the general's chuckled call of "Goodnight, Strand!"

Dane and Jay were sprawled outside the tent flaps, looking relaxed and at ease, but their loose limbs and lazily closed eyes were as much a subterfuge as the sleeping Gryt. Kai could see the narrow gleam of Jay's gaze as he kept a close watch on the soldiers camped nearest the general's tent. Miller and Bex, he bet, would be on the other side of the tent, making sure no one attempted to sneak beneath its pegged-down edges and take Lady Bethany's primary guard by surprise.

When he pushed inside, the members of that guard

were positioned around the outer edges of the spacious shelter, incongruously facing the leather walls. That gave Kai a moment's pause, before he realized why. The low tinkle of dripping water preceded a quiet gasp, Lady Bethany snatching up a drying cloth to cover her body as she stepped from the still gently steaming water of her bath.

"Kai!" she exclaimed, eyes going wide at the sight of him.

He whirled around to face back the way he'd come, but not before his eyes took in the length of her, pale and glowing wetly in the light from the oil lamps brightening up the dim interior.

"My apologies, my lady," he ground out, "I didn't realize you were bathing."

Dane and Jay would both have known, but neither of the bastards had bothered to warn him. He could have smelled the water himself, heard the gentle sounds of it moving against her body, if he hadn't been in such a rush to get back to her side.

"It's all right, just give me a second."

He listened to her hastily rub at her skin with the drying cloth then there was a silence during which he could only imagine her naked body wriggling into her clothing.

"There," she said, several long moments later. "I'm decent. You can turn around now."

She gave Kai a bashful smile when he slowly pivoted to face her, her guard making the same maneuver in discreet corners of the space. Her eyes were only for him, though, and he sought to hold that gaze, keep it on her face. That didn't mean that he didn't note the fact that she'd dried herself too quickly and with not enough care in her haste to cover herself, and her still damp skin was sticking to the thin nightdress, outlining every curve. He'd seen her naked before, of course. She'd fallen into his arms in nothing but her skin, but shock and awe had stolen the details of that moment from him. This was an opportunity to learn them anew, and he was struggling to resist the temptation.

The fact that her primary guard had been here, in the tent with her, while she'd been unclothed and relaxing in the water, was enough to make his blood boil—and he didn't give a shit that they'd been facing the wall—but he'd have been equally pissed if they'd given her privacy and left her unprotected. If that made him a fucking hypocrite, so be it.

"Did you enjoy your bath?" he managed, wincing when his voice came out rough and grating. His eyes flicked to her guard; if one of them so much as smirked he'd eviscerate them.

"Yes, thank you." She still clutched the now damp drying cloth in front of her like a shield. Not that it did much to hide her. She had a woman's figure, lush and curved, and right now Kai's body was screaming at him that she was flushed and warm and strokable. It would be nothing to dismiss her guard and tumble her back onto the sumptuous bed of blankets and furs laid out just a few feet behind her. Bedding her would be nothing like being with the gutter wenches and whores who were the only females in the world of men who'd look at him with anything other than disdain.

Look, he told himself firmly, but don't even think about touching.

"We'll be leaving early in the morning," he told her. "You should rest, enjoy General Tuill's comforts."

"All right," she murmured softly. Then she turned and looked at that bed, and back at Kai, who left before he could convince himself there was a hint of invitation there in the softness of her gaze and angle of her body.

17

When Kai said palace, I'd expected something, well, I suppose something like the Disney logo, all tall towers and turrets. Something beautiful and screaming of riches. As we approached the capital—which was a lot smaller than I imagined, its growth stunted by the restrictive city wall that wound around it—from the height of the pass road, I saw that it was more like a fortress. The walls were thick and looked like they could withstand an atomic bomb, never mind a siege, the windows narrow and dotted only here and there. In fact, the more I looked, the more I thought they were probably arrow slits, meant for defense rather than standing and staring out at the view. It was big enough, certainly, taking up almost a quarter of the available space within the encircling boundary, but it was ugly and severe and imposing.

It didn't make me feel any better about entering the thing.

It had been a strange three days, marching with General Tuill's men. And it had been a march, his soldiers walking in a rigid formation of rows of four—as many as could fit across the narrow road—their steps pounding out a rhythm. It was a marked difference from the way the Hounds traveled, ranging out and running in a fluid group that took into consideration the constantly evolving landscape and the vulnerable element in the middle that needed protecting—me.

There was a definite tension between the two groups, too. The Hounds were on edge, growls and snarls a lot more frequent than they had been before, teeth flashing at every imagined slight, and the soldiers, though they maintained their military discipline, gave off a definite air of aloofness, disparagement even. They weren't fooling me, and they definitely weren't fooling the Hounds; it was clear they were unnerved by their new companions.

All in all, it was a relief when we finally got out of the steep mountain road and began the short journey round to the front of the town, where the only entrance bigger than a garden gate was. Before long, though, I became aware of a kerfuffle near the front, Kai arguing with General Tuill.

"What's going on?" I whispered to Tor, who was riding beside me with Ferris once more.

Tor frowned and gave a little shrug. "I don't know, I can't hear."

I bit my lip. "Can you go and find out?"

The look he turned on me was less respectful and more fatherly disapproval. "And leave an opening in your guard?"

I huffed a disappointed sigh and saw Ferris' lips twitch. Though most of the Hounds still saw me as some sort of priceless glass statue, to be gawked at but not touched by their rude hands, the ones who had the dubious honor of spending much more time with me—my two sets of guards and Brannon—had started to warm up, treating me more like a person and less like some magical, mystical creature. I was winning them over with my ordinariness.

Then there was Kai. I couldn't really put my finger on

what the relationship between us was. It was a complicated, tentative thing that I was afraid to examine too closely.

"What's going to happen when we get to the palace?" I asked, for at least the fifth time. This time Ferris smiled outright.

"I'm not sure, my lady," Tor replied, as he had the other four times I'd asked.

I humphed, watching as Kai tugged at the reins of his horse and turned it back away from General Tuill. He began to ride towards us, forcing the marching soldiers to get out of the way or risk being trampled. From the angry look on his face, I rather thought he was hoping one or two of them might refuse to move.

He reached us without incident, however, maneuvering until he was able to edge Ferris out of the way and ride next to me.

"Is everything all right?" I asked, eyeing the scowl on his face.

"Of course," he replied. Liar. I could feel the unhappiness pulsing inside him. I pursed my lips, debating calling him on it versus keeping my mouth shut. I was a stranger here, after all, even if Kai had made it clear that I was a very welcome stranger.

He gave a sharp whistle that was obviously a call sign of some sort because Brannon, who had been running in and out of the pack, weaving some pattern I couldn't see, suddenly popped up out of nowhere.

"What is it?" he asked.

I tried not to feel slighted when he immediately gave Brannon the truth.

"The Hounds won't be able to enter the city gate. Tell Kert he's going to be in charge; I want you with me. Don't have him take the pack to the usual place, have him keep them in sight of the wall. The citizens won't like it, but I don't give a fuck. I want the Hounds on constant watch for a signal. They should be able to get to the palace within moments if we need them."

Whatever Brannon thought about Kai's words, he kept it off his face except for a slight lift of his eyebrows.

"I'll tell him," he replied, disappearing once more into the mass of bodies.

I waited a beat for Kai to turn and explain to me what was going on, but when he just stared ahead, anger pressing in on me, I decided to simply ask.

"The Hounds aren't allowed inside the city?"

"No." He shook his head scornfully. "They're frightened of us. They want to use us to strike fear into the hearts of their enemies, but that doesn't mean they should have to endure us in their inns or their shops, let us mingle with their women and children."

"Why were you arguing with General Tuill?" I asked cautiously.

His face closed over and he shrugged. "I don't like the idea of you being so unprotected. Tuill's right, though. There'd be a revolt if we tried to take the full pack inside the walls."

"You'll be with me though, won't you?" I asked, my stomach muscles clenching at the thought of being abandoned inside the hulking monolith.

When Kai turned to reply, his eyes were blazing. "I am your Bound. I won't leave you, not even for a second."

"Well then," I tried to smile, to soothe over his ragged surge of emotion. "I'll be safe, won't I?"

My words mollified Kai slightly, and he jerked his head at the Hounds walking and riding beside us. "Your primary guard will be with you also." A twitch of a smile. "And Brannon will be hanging about, he's hard to get rid of."

I meant what I said. I felt safe with Kai, knowing he'd protect me, but I definitely felt it when the majority of the pack peeled off as we approached the main gate. It was an arched opening in the thick city wall, with doors a foot thick and an honest-to-God portcullis hanging above the opening, set to squish anyone stupid enough to try and duck beneath it if it started to drop. Though nothing had really changed—Kai was still riding by my side, my primary guard were still right there, forming a protective ring around me— there was a clear shift in the atmosphere. It felt like were outnumbered now, our position suddenly precarious. I didn't imagine the stiffness in Kai's shoulders, or the way my guard tightened around me, just a fraction. They felt it, too.

Though the gate guards eyed us curiously as we approached, no one tried to stop us. Of course, that was likely because General Tuill led the way, sitting upright and proud in the saddle, his odd little bird swaying slightly on his shoulder. The noise of the soldiers' booted feet intensified as we entered the arch, the sound echoing around us and getting even louder as the clatter of our horses' hooves joined in. It was almost loud enough to drown out the sound of a hocking throat, but I caught the movement out of the corner of my eye as one of the gate guards shifted forwards a step and spat right at Rye's foot as he walked past.

I held my breath, waiting for a response from Rye, for him to explode, but he didn't even turn his head to look at the gate guard, though I know he noticed. He just kept on walking, head high. The only reaction I could see was a slight tightening of the hands that held onto the lead rope of my horse.

I still held the reins, though, and I yanked the poor beast to a halt, causing a stir as the fifty or so of Tuill's squadron behind me had to halt or risk falling over like dominoes. My primary guard stopped, too, heads whipping around as they looked for the reason behind my move.

"Lady Bethany?" Kai murmured beside me. "Is something wrong?"

I didn't answer him, I stared down at the gate guard, who was slow to realize that he was the object of my—and therefore very quickly everyone else's—attention.

"What did you just do?" I asked him quietly. A low burn of rage was smoldering in my gut; I couldn't tell if it came from me, Kai or Rye, I only knew it was deserved.

The gate guard suddenly didn't know where to look, what to do. He tried to turn away from me in embarrassment and I just felt something…snap. I don't know how I did it, or what even made me try, but I reached out with my mind and grabbed him, yanking him back around to face me. He was up on his tiptoes without me having any idea that I'd done it. I could lift him higher, though, I suddenly knew. I could lift him up so that he and I were eye to eye.

"What did you just do?" I asked again.

The gate guard was panicking now. His eyes were wild and there was a sheen of sweat on his forehead, his skin a sickly pale shade. I was dimly aware of gasps and mutterings around me, a tidal wave of astonishment and surprise, and even fear, but it didn't touch me in the eye of the storm, my concentration fixed on the guard.

"I...nothing," he stammered. "He's an animal, my lady."

"He's a what?" I asked, my voice in that low, dangerous tone that had made even my most unruly of pupils shut up and pay attention.

My pupils were obviously smarter than the gate guard, though, because he just repeated his answer, albeit in a tighter and higher voice. "An animal, my lady."

Disgusted, I released my mental hold on him. He fell to the mud-coated flagstones, his legs useless.

"He is a Hound," I said hotly. "And he is my Hound, so show him some respect."

I didn't pause to see if the gate guard nodded at my words, or if he was going to be more inclined to spit at me, too, now. My anger drained as quickly as it had come and I was horribly aware of having caused a scene, drawn attention to myself. I nudged the horse into a walk—probably a little too hard, because it tried to take off at a trot before Rye could steady it—and attempted to control the rush of red I felt taking over my face.

"I'm sorry," I said to Kai, once we were far enough away

from the gate guards for them not to overhear. "I don't know what came over me."

Kai didn't scold me. Instead, though his face remained unsmiling, I felt a rush of pride and satisfaction blazing from him, a feeling which doubled when he reached across and gently lifted one of my hands from the reins. I watched as he brought it to his lips and kissed the back of my fingers, eyes glowing coals, before he released me again and turned to face the wide thoroughfare we were traveling along.

Okay, then. I guessed I wasn't in trouble.

I looked across at Tor, and the oldest—and most severe—of my primary guard astonished me by giving me a wink and a quick grin, there and gone again before I could really register it. Rye didn't look at me at all, and I felt too awkward to apologize to him directly. Perhaps he'd have preferred just to pretend the whole thing didn't happen; if so, I'd made it a lot worse.

The town leading up to the palace passed by in a blur. I tried to take in the houses, the market stalls, the people all craning their necks to see what the commotion was, but my heart was thumping hard in anticipation of arriving at the palace, and it didn't help that the huge imposing edifice was right there, getting improbably bigger as we approached.

There was a welcoming committee waiting on the platform in front of the palace, a dozen or so steps raising them up above our level. I skimmed faces, wondering if I perhaps recognized one or two from the temple, but I couldn't be sure. I heard Ferris hiss beside me and wrenched my gaze away.

"The prince himself has come out to greet her?" he said, sounding incredulous.

"She's a Celestial," Kai replied, his voice deliberately mild. "What did you expect?"

"A prince?" I squeaked. "I don't know how to address a prince. Am I supposed to curtsey? I don't know how to curtsey, either!"

"My lady," Kai said, in that same calm tone, "You're a Celestial. He bows to you."

I laughed, then. I couldn't help it; the idea was so preposterous.

As we got closer, I thought I could tell which one the prince was. He wasn't wearing a crown or anything helpful like that, but there was only one man, standing right in the middle and a step forward from the rest, who wasn't grey-haired with age. He was also the only one not scowling. At his feet sat the odd dog-cat creature I'd seen him draw from the Ether.

"Who are the rest?" I asked, eyes scanning the rest of the group.

"Nobles," Kai spat. "The two in grey robes are priests from the temple."

I saw the two he was talking about, standing slightly off to the side, their faces half covered by cowls.

"They're from the temple with the gateway to the Ether?" I asked. "Why are they here?"

"Because they're hoping for an opportunity," Kai replied.

That sounded horribly ominous to me—and I didn't really understand what he meant by it, either—but there was no more time to ask questions. We were at the base of the steps, the soldiers in front of us lining up in orderly rows to the left and right and creating a small space that framed our entrance. There was nowhere to go except up to face the welcoming committee.

18

My instinct was to get off my horse as fast as I could, hide myself from view behind the gelding's bulk, but a murmured word from Tor had me lingering, high and highly visible in the saddle, while Kai dismounted and made a big deal of coming to my side, helping me down. I clutched at his fingers, my hands cold and clammy, and he paused, smiling down at me.

"It will be fine, Bethany." I forgot my worries momentarily, struck by the fact he'd called me by my name for the first time, dropping the title that made me feel like a fraud every time I heard it.

"That would be a little more convincing if you believed it too," I said, patting his chest and reminding him that I had a hotline straight to his emotional core. I looked over his shoulder, took in the line of expectant faces. "I'm afraid I'm going to embarrass you, Kai. I'm really out of my depth."

I felt his incredulity a moment before he laughed.

"I promise you do not have to worry about that," he told me. Then he sighed. "Come on, let's go and introduce you to the prince."

General Tuill accompanied us up the steps but drew back as we reached the top, allowing Kai and me to take center stage, my guard a few steps behind. The prince came forward to meet us, a welcoming smile on his face. I did recognize him, I realized. He had been the first to approach the Ether and had cut the throat of the old man.

"Your Highness," I heard Kai say, his voice sounding distant as I revisited the memory. "I have the honor to present my Bound, the Celestial Lady Bethany."

The prince moved forward and took my hand, radiating wonder. He was a handsome man, standing here in the sunlight, smiling warmly at me, but down in that underground room he'd been pale-faced, horrified but resolute.

"It is my honor," he replied smoothly.

It was my turn to speak, and everyone was looking at me. My mind was blank, though, only one thought front and center.

You murdered that man.

I couldn't say that. Even in my paralyzed state, I understood that. I pasted a smile on my face and bobbed the world's most pathetic attempt at a courtesy.

"Your Highness," I parroted the title Kai had given him.

"Faron, please," he offered. His courtly demeanor evaporated and the look he gave me was impish. "I confess, I am feeling awe-struck. Never did I imagine welcoming a Celestial to the palace. My father will be furious to have missed this."

"It's not a position I imagined myself in either," I told him ruefully.

I had, in fact, been to a palace. Buckingham Palace. It had been grand and sweeping, filled with priceless bits of furniture and portraits of very important people. I'd shuffled along with the rest of the tourists, keeping on the right side of the ropes, mindful of the blinking lights of the motion detectors and alarms, ready to bring armed security if any of us put so much as a toe out of line.

This was not like that. Prince Faron led me inside, his hand cupping my fingers in a light grip that I could have pulled away from at any time. I wanted to. I wanted to reach for Kai, keeping close on my other side, and grip his hand tight, use it to anchor myself and stop my panic from rising any further, but I was aware of eyes following my every move. The other nobles, loitering around; the priests standing silently in judgment; and other gazes that I couldn't pinpoint, but that I could feel. Ominous and malevolent.

That feeling grew as we walked through the huge double doors—easily three times my height—and the gloomy shadows swallowed me.

I listened politely as Prince Faron proudly told me how old the palace was, and how long his family had held it for. How it had withstood every siege that had been mounted against it during its long history. All the while, his Bound creature padded at his other side. I was curious about it, my fingers itching to reach out and see if its fur was as soft as it looked.

Aren't you a pretty thing, I thought.

Without warning, the creature changed track, darting behind the prince, and getting in between the two of us. Its head reached up, mouth open to reveal a row of razor-sharp teeth, and Prince Faron had a moment to bark, "Daith, no!", panic on his face, before the creature used its nose to force our hands apart and then...

Slicked its tongue along the length of my palm.

I jerked my hand away, because it left a cold, wet trail across my skin, but also because I'd thought I was about to lose my fingers.

"Are you alright, my lady?" Prince Faron asked, his features drawn and skin ashen. "Did Daith hurt you?"

Daith was currently butting its head hard against my hip in what was a clear demand for attention.

"I'm fine," I said. "He just wants to say hello."

I put my hand back out and the creature ducked under it, encouraging me to pet his head. I obliged, unable to get out of my mind the thought that I was stroking what was, for all intents and purposes, a tiger. It was a surreal moment, broken when Kai shifted beside me, unhappy at my prolonged proximity to those sharp teeth and powerful claws. The creature, Daith, growled low in its throat, drawing its teeth back in menace.

"No," I said firmly, as if I was talking to a neighborhood dog instead of a deadly predator. "He's mine."

No one was more surprised than me when Daith responded to my admonishment, ducking its head and pressing into me, seeking forgiveness. Prince Faron audibly gasped.

"I have never seen him behave like this," he confessed.

"General Tuill's Gryt was the same," Kai said quietly beside me. "It sat with her on her horse, demanding to be petted."

Prince Faron chuckled. "Clearly they understand just how blessed they are to be in your presence, my lady."

"I hope the nobles understand the same," Kai muttered.

I was watching Prince Faron when Kai spoke, so I

caught the flicker of a grimace that crossed his face before he could hide it. He chose not to respond, pretending he hadn't heard, and gesturing to me to continue on.

Okay, then.

"I hope you are well rested, my lady," Prince Faron said, ushering me towards a double door, two liveried servants standing to attention outside. Or maybe they were soldiers. Did servants wear swords at their sides? "I have taken the liberty of arranging a small reception in your honor."

Another few steps and I was able to glimpse inside the door. My heart dropped. Prince Faron's idea of a small reception and mine were markedly different. The room before me was enormous, and it was filled to the brim with important-looking people.

I did not want to go in there. I could tell by the unease and unhappiness radiating from Kai at my side that he didn't want to, either. I also knew what he'd agreed to, the promise he'd made on my behalf. There wasn't much of a choice.

"Wonderful," I said. My voice sounded breathy and strange.

Prince Faron wasn't stupid, he picked up on my reticence. "You are the first Celestial to walk among us in a millennium," he said sheepishly. "Everyone wanted to meet you."

"It's fine," I told him.

He looked relieved. A glimmer of an image floated into my head: him, walking into the room, me on his arm. It hadn't come from me, I didn't think, and the wistfulness that cocooned it made me positive it hadn't come from Kai either. It was Prince Faron's hope, and I didn't like the implication of it at all.

Before he could summon up the courage to act on it, I turned to Kai and slid my arm around his, resting my fingertips on his wrist the way I'd seen myself in Prince Faron's vision when Kai lifted his arm in response.

"Are you ready to present me?" I asked him.

Touching skin to skin, I felt his emotions like gongs rattling my bones. Surprise, then a fierce rush of satisfaction. His arm firmed up under mine and then we were moving forward: the same image but a different man by my side.

Not a man, a Hound.

"Do you know any of these people?" I hissed to him as Prince Faron hurried to recover, getting a step ahead of us so he was first to enter the room, my guard moving up so that they surrounded me from the rear in a close semi-circle.

"Nobles," Kai muttered back, his lip curling slightly. "I know almost all of them."

"Do you like any of them?" I asked.

No answer, which was answer enough. I felt anxiety clench in my stomach. I was useless in social situations like this, my working-class background not exactly preparing me for mingling with the nobility.

"Don't leave me alone," I begged him.

Kai's eyes glittered, the amber glowing a molten gold. "You're safe," he promised. "I will protect you."

That wasn't exactly what I meant, but there was no time to correct him. As soon as the prince stepped fully through the doorway into what I was guessing was a ballroom, a trumpeter tooted out of nowhere, making me jump and Kai growl, and every pair of eyes—which was a hundred of them, at least—turned in our direction.

Silence fell. Thankfully Prince Faron didn't draw the moment out, moving forward into a pocket of space and spreading his arms wide to address the crowd. He looked supremely confident in the spotlight, but then, he outranked everyone here.

I thought of Kai telling me that Prince Faron should bow to me. Theoretically, *I* was the most important person in the room. Right then, I felt like the pupil who had snuck into the staff room to find a teacher and ask a question. Small, awkward, and totally out of place.

"Lords and Ladies, your attention." He already had it but still, he paused to make sure every single person had their focus on him. Well, him and me. "It is my very great honor to welcome to the palace Lady Bethany, the first Celestial to walk among us in a thousand years."

The look he turned on me was shining. Kai was right, I thought, Prince Faron did seem to be a good man. Honest and genuine. The rest of the room, however...

I could feel it, crawling over me. Cloying and thick, like tar. Ambition, greed. Ruthlessness. There was not a one of them looking at me as anything other than a thing to be coveted. Something valuable to be acquired, by whatever means. At the back of the room, I saw a couple of the men in robes, the priests from the temple, watching me with shrewd eyes.

These were not people I needed to impress, I realized suddenly. These were snakes in the grass, obstacles to be navigated. Enemies. I couldn't tell if it was me thinking that, or Kai, but if the thoughts were his, I agreed with them.

Everyone seemed to be holding their breath, waiting for something. It took me a moment to understand that they were waiting for me to say something. To respond to the prince's glowing introduction. Just like when Kai had presented me to the Hounds, everyone was waiting for me to do something, say something wondrous. Be...Celestial. I'd been paralyzed with nerves then, paralyzed by the situation. Now...okay, now I was just as nervous. Maybe even more so. But I was also a little angry, feeding off the edginess and guardedness of Kai.

I lifted my chin, putting on my most haughty expression, and inclined my head in a short nod. I even managed to glow, pules of energy just flashing in my peripheral vision, and heard a ripple of murmurs and gasps. Good. I didn't know why, but I felt a serious need for these people to be wary of me. To see me as something Other.

Something to be feared.

I'd never been one for instincts, but I was having one now, so I decided to just go with it.

"If you will, Lady Bethany, there is someone I would like to introduce you to." Prince Faron was smiling at me, but even he seemed a little more hesitant now, approaching cautiously, like I might zap him or something.

"They're remembering the cavern beneath the temple," Kai murmured to me.

"Cavern?" I muttered out of the side of my mouth. I

didn't have his skill for pitching my voice to reach the ears of my intended and no one else.

"Where you let out a pulse that sent them all to their knees," he reminded me.

Oh yes.

My memories of that moment were chaotic, and I didn't remember at all feeling the burst come from me. I had no idea how to make it happen again, either, but they didn't need to know that.

I gave Prince Faron an encouraging smile, which gave him the courage to close the final distance between us, then regretted it immediately when he led me through the crowd—which parted to create a path for us with nods and smiles and calculating looks—until we stopped in front of an extremely stuffy looking older gentleman. He was dressed in a scarlet suit that clashed horribly with his complexion and strained to constrain a seriously rounded belly. He looked like a likely candidate for a heart attack.

"My lady, this is my uncle, Lord Rothsenberg. After the king, he is the largest landowner in the kingdom."

"My lady." Lord Rothsenberg inclined his head in a nod that was so subtle it could have been a twitch.

"Since when?" Kai barked at my side.

"Since his highness granted me the lands reclaimed from the Badari," Lord Rothsenberg replied. He had a snooty tone to suit the snooty look on his face.

"Reclaimed?" Kai asked, a dangerous edge to his tone.

The two eyed each other, Lord Rothsenberg with disdain and Kai with undisguised dislike. I had no clue what they were talking about or who the Badari were.

"Strand," Prince Faron said quietly. It was a remonstration and Kai subsided, ripping his gaze away to glare across the room.

"There's a reason your kind are kept in kennels, Strand," Lord Rothsenberg ground out. "You've no idea how to behave in civilized society."

A flush of red stained Kai's cheeks and he clenched his jaw so hard I imagined I heard those razor-sharp teeth cracking. Shame and embarrassment ran in a cold river through my veins. Not mine, his.

Oh, hell no.

Indignation rose up in me in a swift, hard rush. That, and anger that was all mine. I tugged my arm out of Kai's and drew myself up to my full height, which admittedly didn't put me nearly on a par with even Prince Faron, the shortest of the three.

"You weren't at the ceremony," I said. Like with the pulse of violent energy I'd apparently unleashed, my memories of the men who'd come to stand before the Ether were vague and unclear. It didn't matter though, because it wasn't my memories I was seeing all of a sudden. I had a crystal-clear image of standing in front of Prince Faron, the deeds to my new lands in my hand.

"What do you mean, I haven't been chosen? I'm the king's brother!"

Not my voice, not my eyes, not my hand, crushing the thick, creamy vellum in my fist. It was Lord Rothsenberg's memory, and he was still seething over it. Even more so now that a dog—a *dog*, damn it—was being paraded before him with a Celestial on his arm.

A beat of silence followed my words. Prince Faron blanched slightly, and I felt Kai's prickles of anger morph into bubbles of amusement. That was such an odd sensation that I rubbed my side surreptitiously, though the feeling was inside my skin. Lord Rothsenberg was my target, though, and it was with immense satisfaction that I saw his eyes bug and his grip on his dainty little wine glass tighten to the point the crystal threatened to shatter.

I went for the kill.

"It's a rare opportunity, I understand. A once in a lifetime kind of shot. Although—" I put on my best ingratiating smile, the one I reserved for the most troublesome parents at school. "Perhaps it's for the best. I imagine it would be crushingly disappointing to return one of the barren."

As a final flourish, I reached down and stroked my hands over Daith's glorious fur.

We left Lord Rothsenberg quickly after that. I hadn't won any friends there, I didn't think, but I was too angry to think about whether that was a bad thing. My anger didn't last, however. Prince Faron introduced me to noble after noble, and while there were no more fireworks, there was also one indisputable similarity between each excruciating little vignette of polite conversation: the way the nobles treated Kai.

They dismissed him.

They sneered at him.

They treated him like he was simple or stupid.

Some even attempted to pretend he wasn't there which,

given that I, the person they'd actually come to see, was his Bound and was clinging to his arm, was some feat.

The worst of the bunch was a man called Lord Kenwick. He was a tall, thin man with sallow skin and dark eyes, one of the few I'd met with facial hair, a thin mustache perched on his upper lip. He was one of the men who'd been at the ceremony in the temple. I didn't remember him, but he had a Bound. It was…well, I wasn't sure what it was. It was like a tiny fire sprite. It didn't have a body as such, but the flames were able to twist in odd ways to give it arms or legs, then it would blob back into looking like a tiny, contained fire again. It sat on his shoulder like a parrot when first he was brought over and introduced, but when he smiled at me during Prince Faron's introduction, he called it down his arm to land in his palm, and then he played with it, rolling it over the back of his hand and then into the cradle of his palm again, sliding it through his fingers.

I wanted to touch it, to see if it would burn or tickle, but as much as the Bound spirit drew me, its owner repulsed me.

"My lady," he crooned at me. He reached to take my hand with his free one, but I drew it back. He felt oily and slick to me, and I had the weirdest feeling that if we touched, it would slide over my skin and choke me.

"Lord Kenwick." I'd stopped giving the polite refrain of *It's nice to meet you* several introductions ago. So far, with the exception of Prince Faron, it hadn't been nice to meet any of them.

He didn't seem to pick up on my avoidance of his touch, or my less-than-warm response to him.

"What a marvelous thing you are," he told me.

A…thing?

"A thing?" Kai growled, echoing my thoughts.

Lord Kenwick waved Kai's words away with a derisive sweep of his hand. His eyes skated over me one more time, then he turned to Prince Faron.

"I have been studying the texts regarding Celestials in the palace archives. The potential applications are staggering. I would be happy to advise you." An ingratiating smile that I was pleased to see the prince replied to with a non-committal grunt.

"I'd like to see these texts," I said, turning to Kai. It would be helpful, I thought, to read about Celestials that had come before me. To see what they could do…and to see how they'd been used. Because Lord Kenwick's words were a warning gong in my head, a reminder that Kai had promised I would serve the kingdom and its king, a man I knew nothing about. Perhaps he was like his son, who seemed earnest and forthright, and perhaps he was like the nobles, who seemed…what was it Kai had called them? A nest of scheming bastards. Yeah, that seemed about right.

"I'll take you," he promised.

"Dogs aren't allowed in the archives," Lord Kenwick cut in. "We wouldn't want them pissing on the furniture, slobbering all over the texts. Besides, there's no point given your kind aren't even educated enough to read."

"I can read," Kai shot back. That red was back in his cheeks, murderous rage glittering in his eyes. I tightened my grip on his arm, a flash of him going for Lord Kenwick's throat bursting into my mind.

"We will of course make the texts available to you," Prince Faron told me, smoothing over the moment. It didn't escape me that he spoke to me, eyes and body language not including Kai. That inkling intensified when he added, "I would be delighted to take you myself."

"Perhaps," I replied.

I needed to escape. I wasn't equipped to deal with the politics and calculating, manipulative moves that were going on all around me. The pointed comments I caught but didn't understand, and the subtle, conniving little slights they kept throwing at Kai that were death by a thousand cuts. On top of all that, I had his tension pushing at me. His anger and embarrassment and humiliation. I felt like a pressure cooker about to explode.

"Kai," I murmured, ignoring whatever Lord Kenwick was saying to Prince Faron. "I need to get out of here."

He didn't ask what was wrong. He didn't ask me to hold on just a little longer. He didn't even wait until Lord Kenwick was finished speaking. He cut right over the top of him, addressing Prince Faron. "Your Highness, I am taking Lady Bethany to rest."

"Oh." Prince Faron looked at me, disappointment written all over his face, and I fought the urge to say that I was fine. That we could stay. "Yes, of course. I'm sure it's been quite a day. I'll have a servant show you to your rooms."

He reached out and clicked his fingers and a man appeared at his side instantly. He must have been hovering close enough to listen, because he didn't need any further instructions, giving me a low bow and gesturing with his arm that I should precede him from the room.

"Thank you for the warm welcome," I said to Prince Faron. He, at least, hadn't been an asshole. "I look forward to speaking with you again."

Oops. Too far. The prince positively beamed at me.

I took the time to pet his Bound and then gave Lord Kenwick's odd little fire creature a final, wistful look before walking with Kai out of the ballroom, into the cool quiet of the main palace corridor.

"This way, please," the servant said politely, taking the lead and guiding us towards a grand staircase. I expected Kai's tension to ease now that we were away from the sneering gazes of the nobles, but if anything, it got worse. By the time we were shown to the rooms that had been set aside for me, he was all but vibrating with it.

It was a sumptuous suite. There was a living room filled with fancy furnishings, fainting couches and ornate tables, flowers overflowing vases and scenting the room with their perfume, and through a half-open door I could see a bedroom with a giant four-poster bed draped in gauzy fabric. It was the swankiest guestroom I'd ever been in, but I barely noticed the opulence of my surroundings. My focus was all on Kai. My guard, too, who had slunk in behind us and taken positions around the room, were watching him warily.

"Are you all right?" I asked.

He didn't answer me. He didn't even look at me, his gaze directed firmly out of the large picture window. It was an incredible view: the town all laid out before us, the rolling countryside beyond, but I very much doubted that was why he was so fixated on it.

"Kai?"

Still nothing, except his jaw clenched a little tighter and his shoulders crept a little higher. He was such a proud man—Hound—and he'd had to stand there and be dismissed time and time again while those same nobles fawned over me. *His* Bound.

He thought I'd judge him for it, I realized suddenly. He thought I'd see him the same way they did now.

It broke my heart. I was across the room before I was aware of consciously having made the choice to move, wrapping my arms around him from the back and pressing my face into the dip between his shoulder blades.

"We came and presented ourselves," I said, my words slightly mumbled by the thick fabric of his tunic. "Can we leave now?"

Someone snorted—I thought probably Conlon or Rye—but Kai remained still as stone under my hands, which had reached around to press against his stomach. Abs. I tried not to notice but the muscles beneath my hands were rock solid. He smelled incredible, too. Like wildness.

"I don't like it here," I whispered, trying to pitch my voice for him alone. "And I don't like the nobles. You were right, they are all snakes." I paused, not sure if I should say the next bit. "I hated the way they treated you. They don't see you, none of them. They don't understand what you are. They're fools."

Kai moved, but it was only to drop his head so that he could stare at the floor instead of out of the window. He was listening, though.

"I chose you," I reminded him. "I didn't want any of the

rest. Seeing them today, talking to them, getting to know them as people, well, it just tells me how right I was."

"You are too kind, Lady Bethany," Kai murmured, eyes still fixed on the floor.

"I'm not kind at all," I retorted. "You should have heard some of the thoughts I was having about those condescending idiots."

I felt Kai shift and loosened my grip so that he could turn in my arms. I probably should have stepped back, but it felt nice, being close to him. I thought he needed a little holding onto, too.

When he finally met my gaze, his eyes were glittery, his mouth twisted in a grimace of a smile.

"I think I might like to hear some of these thoughts," he told me.

19

Kai sat with his back to the wall, watching the light breeze flowing through the open window ruffle the gauzy curtains that surrounded Lady Bethany's bed. She lay within, sleeping peacefully, no sign of the nightmares that had plagued her at the inn. It would be dawn soon, and in the short time he'd known Lady Bethany, he knew she'd rise with its first rays. He'd have to move, retreat to the living room of the fancy suite Prince Faron had provided for her.

A subtle power play that said: look what I can offer you.

Kai couldn't compete, not even close. He didn't have a home, never mind a castle. What use would there be in it, when he spent his life running with the Hounds, going where he was needed?

Going where he was told. Might as well be honest about that.

Mouth set in an unhappy grimace, he levered himself up off the floor, his muscles stiff from spending the night on unnecessary watch. He'd pay for it today, could already feel tiredness dragging at his limbs, burning in his eyes, but he hadn't been able to tear himself away. They'd been in the palace less than a day and already he could feel her slipping through his fingers.

"First," Miller murmured from his position by the door. He kept his head down, avoiding looking at Kai, like he'd done all night.

Out in the living room, he felt the silent stares of Bex

and Jay, two others in Lady Bethany's secondary guard. They could feel his agitation but, like Miller, they wisely said nothing about it.

The main door to the suite opened and all three heads swiveled in that direction, Bex coming to his feet and Jay shifting to a ready crouch. It was murky in the living room, the candles deliberately extinguished to put any would-be human attackers at a disadvantage, but Kai was still able to easily make out Dane's youthful features when he popped his head around the door.

"Barret is here," he said.

"It's the middle of the night," Kai threw back, though dawn was all but breaking the horizon. "Lady Bethany is sleeping. What does he want?"

"He wants to speak to you," Dane replied.

Kai gave Bex and Jay meaningful looks to be sure they knew to be on high alert in case this was some sort of ploy. Perhaps it was paranoia, but he trusted no one here. They both gave him short, sharp nods in return.

Barret waited in the corridor, a servant a step behind holding a torch to illuminate the gloomy passageway. Barret had positioned himself as far from Dane as it was possible to get in the narrow space, his tense body language giving away his discomfort, but he didn't have the sneer on his face that the nobles adopted when they were forced to interact with the Hounds. Barret was a soldier, one who'd risen higher than his birth would have suggested.

"What is it?" Kai asked, dispensing with the pleasantries.

Barret didn't bat an eyelid at his abruptness. "Sir Janis is here. He wants to speak with you."

"Now?"

"Now."

Panic flared in Kai's chest, but he swallowed it down. He had expected this, knew that he wouldn't be able to hover at Lady Bethany's shoulder every moment they were in the palace, but the thought of leaving her…

She has a guard, he told himself. She will be fine.

No, it wasn't enough.

"Wake her primary guard," he told Dane. In all likelihood, they'd be awake already. "I want both sets on duty. You don't sleep until I return, understood."

"First." Dane gave a nod and then vanished, disappearing into the shadows before he'd taken more than three steps. Kai watched with approving eyes, then turned to Barret. The soldier was looking after Dane, too, his eyebrows furrowed with consternation.

Good. Let him see what the Hounds could do.

"Shall we?" he asked. The sooner they left, the sooner he could return to Lady Bethany's side.

Barret started walking with no further comment, his strides long and quick. They made their way out of the guest wing of the palace and down into the lower floors, where the corridors were tighter and the walls devoid of opulent touches. Barret seemed perfectly content with the silence, but something was bugging Kai.

"Janis is here?" he asked. "I thought he wasn't coming back until the Badari resistance was quashed."

Barret gave him a sidelong glance. "Change of tactics."

"What do you mean?"

Barret didn't reply and Kai didn't bother asking again. He'd get his answers from Janis. But it could be no coincidence that Janis had returned to the palace where Kai and his Hounds were. Where Lady Bethany was.

Kai had been in the room that Barret escorted him to, many times. It was a tight, closed-off little space comprising of nothing more than stone walls and an enormous table. A single shaft of the window let in enough light to illuminate the map Janis had spread out across the wooden tabletop. He was glowering down at it when Kai entered, the fingers of one hand combing through the short goatee that hid his slightly weak chin. He didn't look up as Kai entered, his focus absolute.

"You sent for me?" Kai commented, stepping up to the table. A quick glance down confirmed that map was of the Badari lands, newly acquired by the king. Mostly.

There was a quiet click behind him as Barret closed the door. Kai didn't have to turn around to know that soldier had stayed inside the room, was now leaning up against the door. If it was a tactic designed to prevent Kai from leaving, it wouldn't work. Barret looked strong and capable, but he couldn't take on a Hound.

It got the point across, though: Janis wanted Kai for something, and he probably wasn't going to like it.

Well, that wasn't unusual.

"Hmm," Janis murmured. "I did."

He didn't expand, just heaved a sigh and rounded the table until he could reach down to tap a gnarled finger against a section of map. Kai didn't know the Badari region much more than the vicious swamp the two armies had chosen to line up against each other in, but he had enough experience staring at Janis' maps to understand that it was a mountainous region.

That was where the last vestiges of the Badari resistance were holed up, then.

"I'm surprised to see you here," Kai remarked. "I thought you'd be plucking Baradi warriors from behind rocks with your bare hands."

Janis snorted. "We did try that. Kept getting shot by poisoned arrows."

"They can't have been very good shots, then. You're still standing."

Janis lifted his eyes from the map for a moment and raised one grey, bushy eyebrow. "You should know by now that it would take more than poison to do away with me." A short pause. "Is it wise to prick at the man who decides where you go and what you do?"

"Probably not," Kai replied, smiling slightly, "But you've already decided, so it's not going to make any difference now."

"This is true," Janis said, nodding slowly, a quirk of amusement on his lips. Then he shifted into campaign mode, the change so marked even Barret would have caught it. "What we're doing is not working. We're suffering too many losses and making pitiful progress. Time is stretching on, and all the while the Badari people are watching. If we mean to rule them, peacefully, without civil protests popping up every five bloody minutes, we need to get this sorted. Decisively."

"All right," Kai said cautiously. He was waiting to see where he came in. Thankfully, Janis didn't beat about the bush.

"I want your Hounds." He pierced Kai with eyes that had witnessed hundreds of battles, dozens of campaigns. "I want them to flush these resistance fighters out of their hiding places. It's ideal terrain for them, perfect for the way they hunt."

"And the poison arrows?" Kai asked.

Janis gave a small shrug. "Don't let them know you're coming. I know just how silently your pack of Hounds can move when they want to."

That was true. And Janis was right, this sort of assignment was perfect for the Hounds because of their special skills. He still didn't like it—he didn't ever like sending them into danger—but he had agreed to this, had pledged their allegiance to the crown. Though they weren't recognized as such by the rest of the army, they were the King's soldiers.

"All right," he said. "As soon as Prince Faron releases Lady Bethany, we will go."

"No."

"No?" Kai felt his hackles rise, had to swallow back a soft growl that wanted to rise in his throat.

"This can't wait. I want your Hounds on their way today, before noon."

"I cannot. I won't leave Lady Bethany."

"You don't have to," Janis threw back. "You can send Brannon, he is more than capable."

"You expect me to leave my Bound vulnerable?"

"She'll have you," Janis replied, his tone taking on a razor edge. "She has two guards and she's within this fortress of a palace. How much more protection does she need?"

"It's the bastards within this place I'm concerned about!"

"Careful, Strand," Janis said quietly. "I think it is you they would call the bastard."

The barb hit home, but Kai gritted his teeth and held firm. His every instinct told him this was a bad idea, that it was the first step in an elaborate game to steal Lady Bethany from him. Never mind that Janis didn't usually enjoin himself in such games. He was the King's man through and through, he would do what was best for the crown.

"I said we'll go," he ground out. "I'll speak to Prince Faron."

Though, there was no way, now that the prince had got a look at Lady Bethany, that he'd want to let her go.

"Not good enough, Kai. Your Hounds go today. You'll remember what you agreed to. Your word was given as First Hound." Janis grimaced, uncomfortable, but being uncomfortable had never stopped him from saying what needed to be said. "If I am forced to report to the crown that you refused to follow orders, you know what they'll do. They'll cage your males and use them for sport; they'll hunt down wherever you're stashing your females, and you can hope that the worst that they do is slaughter them."

As a threat, it was effective, not least of all because Kai knew it was not just a threat. Janis would make the report, and Prince Faron would not be able to stand against the full ranks of the nobles, who would all demand the same retribution. If he even bothered to try.

Outmaneuvered, all he could do was give a tight, angry nod.

Janis accepted his agreement with a quiet grunt, ignoring Kai's glower and his hands tensed into fists. It wasn't personal, Janis was doing what he always did: what was in the best interests of the crown and kingdom. That didn't make it burn any less.

Understanding that he was dismissed when Janis went back to the map and started muttering to himself, Kai stalked out of the room. Barret stepped hastily to the side, getting out of the way. Smart move.

Kai wasn't surprised to see Brannon outside the door waiting for him. Too agitated to stand still, he kept going, moving at a quick clip, forcing himself not to run. He wanted to return to Lady Bethany's suite and stand in front of her like a snarling guard dog, but the weight of responsibility forced him out into the watery, early morning sunshine.

Brannon waited to speak until they were well away from the many listening ears lingering on the palace grounds. Even then, he pitched his voice low enough not to be heard by the sleepy workers starting to crowd the streets.

"What did Janis want?"

"He wants me to send the Hounds to deal with the Badari problem." The words were like acid on Kai's tongue.

Brannon considered that, eyeing his First cautiously. "That's not all that unsurprising, is it?" Then he caught on to the key word. "Send?"

"He wants the pack to leave today."

"But you can't leave," Brannon replied. "You've only just arrived. The prince and the nobles have only had a glance at Lady Bethany, there's no way they'll consent to you disappearing so fast."

"Correct," Kai ground out.

Brannon frowned. "Lady Bethany will be more vulnerable without the threat of the Hounds, waiting just outside the town walls."

Did he think Kai didn't know that?

"Yes," Kai hissed.

"But you're going to send them anyway?"

Kai whirled on Brannon, the tension inside him seeking an outlet. The sheer force of will stopped him from grabbing his Second by the throat. Shaking him.

"Janis made it clear there was no choice."

"To hell with Janis! What could be more important than protecting Lady Bethany?"

"What do you think?" Kai threw back at him.

It took a moment, but Brannon got there. Hadn't he said the same thing to Kai, the night Lady Bethany had dropped through the Ether into Kai's arms? *If we disappear, they'll just target the females and the young. They'll publicly execute them one at a time, until we slink out of hiding.*

Brannon's head dropped, a heavy sigh making his shoulders lift and fall.

"You'll lead them?" Kai asked.

That jerked Brannon's head back up. "You will need me here," he argued.

"I will, but I can't have you in two places at once, and I

think these Badari might be cleverer than even Janis anticipates. I want the whole pack to return to me. This is too much for Kert, he has not the cunning mind for an adversary like this."

"We could split the pack," Brannon offered. "I'll take half, and the rest can remain here."

Kai was shaking his head before Brannon had even finished speaking. "Janis will not be satisfied with that. We can't endanger the commune, and we can't give the nobles any excuse to take Lady Bethany from us."

"If we take the whole pack away, what's to stop them from taking her anyway?" Brannon burst out angrily.

"Me," Kai growled. "I am her Bound, I am her protector."

Brannon flinched, dropping his eyes and tilting his neck. Kai hauled in a deep breath, forcing his tone back to something more controlled.

"She has both her guards and," Kai gave a tiny smile, "I would not discount Lady Bethany herself. She is a force to be reckoned with."

"All right," Brannon replied. "We'll go, and we'll be back as soon as possible." He slapped Kai on the arm affectionately. "Try not to do anything stupid till I get back."

"I will do nothing to endanger Lady Bethany," Kai promised.

"Well, don't endanger yourself, either. I've no desire to be First Hound."

Brannon gave Kai a quick grin and a wink, then started jogging towards the front gate, heading for the grasslands beyond where the pack were camped. Kai watched him go, trying to ignore the rising panic in him that told him he'd made the wrong decision.

20

Kai wasn't there when I woke up. I searched for him, reaching out instinctively, but I couldn't feel him anywhere in the suite of rooms. Rye was there, standing respectfully just inside the door, averting his eyes when I sat up and the covers dropped into my lap, even though I was perfectly respectably dressed in a white nightgown.

"Is everything all right?" I asked.

He seemed tense and uncomfortable, slightly agitated. There were small tells, like the tight clench of his jaws and his hands, curled into fists, but it was more a feeling in the air. As soon as I spoke, it lessened, though, as if he'd locked down his emotions.

Oh dear. My thoughts immediately went to the scene I'd created at the gate. Had I embarrassed him, then?

"Everything is fine, my lady."

Right.

I slithered out of bed and padded over towards him. He shifted slightly, moving to give me more room to move through to the living room, but that wasn't my destination. I stopped right in front of him and reached out to place a hand on the rock-solid curve of his bicep. The tension amplified tenfold.

"Are you unhappy with me?" I asked.

He gaped at me, looking slightly horrified and not a little bit confused. "My lady?"

"Yesterday, at the gate. I...well, I thought I was doing

the right thing but now I'm wondering if all I really did was draw attention to you, and that you might not have liked that. So, I'm sorry, really. I was just so *angry*—" A rogue breeze whooshed through the room, whipping the gauzy curtains around my bed into a frenzy. "The way people treat you, it's just…" I bit my lip and stopped myself from going further. "But it wasn't my place to intervene, so I apologize."

The confusion Was gone, and so was the horror, mostly. He stared at me, astonished.

"My lady, it is your place to intervene anywhere you wish to," he said slowly.

I grimaced, beginning to wish I'd never brought the whole thing up. "I feel like I embarrassed you."

"You honored me," he replied, sincerity radiating up my arm.

"Well, that's one way to look at it," I said, giving an uncomfortable little laugh. "I just thought, well, that maybe you wouldn't want me to let everyone know what he did, how he insulted you."

Rye gave a tiny shudder and I felt emotion well inside me. Joy, pride, awe. My eyes pricked with the strength of it, and when I glanced up, I saw his were shining slightly, too.

"I would take a thousand such insults to have you claim me as yours again."

He meant it, absolutely. I didn't know what to do with that, so I smiled brightly, angled for a little humor.

"Well, let's hope it doesn't come to that." Perhaps a change of subject was in order. "Where's Kai?"

And tension.

Oh. My guess before had been way off the mark; this was what Rye was worried about.

"He was called away to speak with Sir Janis, my lady."

"Who's Sir Janis?"

"He's one of the king's advisors."

"A noble?" I asked, wrinkling my nose.

"A soldier," Rye corrected. "He is in charge of the king's armies."

"So, he's in charge of the Hounds?" I asked.

"Kai is in charge of the Hounds." Ferris appeared from nowhere, as he tended to do. He was scowling, but then, he was always scowling. I didn't miss the hint of censure in his tone, though.

"Kai promised the Hounds would serve the king though, didn't he? So, Sir Janis can tell Kai what to do. No?"

The scowl got more pronounced but not, I thought, because of me.

"You should come and eat, my lady. Breakfast has been delivered."

He gestured me out to the living room where a veritable feast had been laid out on the coffee table. There were breads and pastries, a steaming bowl of porridge, a large platter with what I was guessing passed for a fry up here. It all looked amazing, but everything was just slightly different than I was used to, like approaching the breakfast buffet in a hotel on holiday in a foreign country. What I really wanted was a bowl of Cheerios.

I sat down and tried to decide where to start, and realized I was the only one doing so.

"This is far too much for just me," I complained,

waving my arms to encourage them forwards. Unsurprisingly, no one moved.

"When you're satisfied, we'll eat," Tor said.

I didn't bother arguing, I just tucked in, throwing all my old life rules out of the window and having cake for breakfast. I noticed, as I tore into something that looked a bit like a Chelsea bun, that there was already a tiny bite taken out of it. The loaf of nutty bread, too, had a divot missing, and the surface of the bowl of porridge looked like it had been disturbed.

"It looks like mice have been at my breakfast," I joked, shooting my guard a small smile.

Nobody smiled back.

"You can rest assured, it has all been tested, my lady," Tor said. "Otherwise, we'd not have let you sit down to it."

"Tested?" I asked, blinking stupidly.

"For poison," he clarified.

I stared at him, my mouth hanging open, the bit of bun I'd been about to put it in stalled halfway to my lips.

"Poison?"

"Yes, my lady."

"Who would want to poison me?" I paused, thinking. "Can you even poison a Celestial?"

It was weird, to think of myself as something other than just a person, something more. Still, this seemed an important question for my future good health.

"We don't know," Tor said unhelpfully. "But as to who…anyone. Or perhaps they were only hoping to poison us, knowing we would check your food."

I contemplated the idea that someone in the palace

might try to poison me and decided that was just a step too far to handle at breakfast, so I concentrated on the other thing Tor said.

"So, you *can* poison a Hound?"

"We handle toxins a little better than ordinary men, but yes."

"And who had the dubious honor of tasting my breakfast?" asked.

Conlon gave me a little wave, flashing teeth as he grinned.

"Well—"

"We're going to do it, with your approval or without," Tor said, anticipating the edict I'd been about to make.

I pursed my lips, debated arguing further, then stuffed the bun in my mouth. It was delicious, and I soothed my stung pride at Tor's gentle admonishment by eating the whole thing.

"Do you know when Kai will be back?" I asked, eyeing the remaining bun in the basket and deliberating whether the stress of my whole situation was enough to justify stuffing it in my mouth—and how horrified my guard would be if I did it.

"I don't," Tor replied.

"Do we just stay in here until he returns?" Please tell me we do, I thought. I knew my guard would keep me safe, but I relied on Kai to prop me up. Help me navigate the nest of snakes, as he called it.

"That would be best." Tor gave me an indulgent smile. "I assure you; Kai will return to you as soon as possible."

I eschewed the second bun after one more forlorn look

and went to get dressed. My outfits had all been cleaned and placed into an enormous, ornate armoire, along with a host of other clothes. I doubted Kai or any of the Hounds had been on shopping sprees since we arrived, so these had to be gifts. They were hideous, all garish frills and poufy skirts, but I wouldn't have chosen to wear them anyway. I didn't know why, but I felt a rebellion against wearing anything that hadn't come from Kai. Feeling petulant against whoever had had the nerve to fill my wardrobe without asking me, I picked the trouser jumpsuit, knowing full well it was the one that went the most against the current fashion for women here.

When I came back through to the living room, my guard were all still situated at their posts, but the enormous breakfast had been decimated. Including the bun. Trying not to feel put out about that—if I'd even given so much of a hint that I wanted it, it would still be on the plate, waiting for me—I turned to Tor.

"I've had a thought," I said.

I'd be thinking about the day before, when I'd had that glimpse into Lord Rothsenberg's mind, seen through his eyes as Prince Faron told him he hadn't been chosen to go to the temple for the Solar Convection. The picture had just come to me, in a flash of anger, but I was wondering if I could do it deliberately. Pluck a memory directly from someone's mind. Of course, I had no idea *how* to do that, but one problem at a time.

I'd no opportunity to float my idea, though—and ask for guinea pigs—because a knock came at the door. I was apparently the only one surprised that someone was outside.

Given their instant reaction, though, bodies shifting defensively, expressions sharpening, they hadn't expected whoever it was to stop at my door.

Ferris moved to answer it, Rye covering him, while Tor and Conlon converged on me.

"Who is it?" I whispered to Tor. Ferris had opened the door, but only a hair, his big body filling the gap, shielding me but also hiding whoever was outside from view.

I don't know how I expected him to know, when I couldn't see or hear anything that was going on, but the reaction of my guards was making me nervous. I felt the absence of Kai keenly.

Tor didn't answer, shaking his head, mouth drawn into a thin line as he watched the back of Ferris' head, but Conlon did.

"It's Lord Kenwick," he murmured.

"What does he want?" I asked. Nothing good, I was willing to bet.

Conlon shrugged. "Can't hear. We'll find out."

A moment later, Ferris shut the door, but when he turned back to us, he didn't look happy. He had something in his hand, a thick sheaf of creamy paper.

"Wait here, my lady," Tor said, then he stalked across the room.

Oh, hell no. I scurried after him, Conlon at my side.

"It's a summons," I caught Ferris saying, handing the piece of paper to Tor. "From Sir Janis, with the prince's stamp on it."

"A summons for what?" Tor's question mirrored my thoughts.

"For Lady Bethany," Ferris replied, eyes darting over my face before returning to Tor, who seemed to have assumed authority in Kai's absence. He was the oldest, I supposed.

"Well, Sir Janis will have to wait for Kai to get back," Tor spat. He glowered down at the note, gaze shifting over the page in a way that made me think he couldn't actually read what was written there. He kept returning to the one spot that even I could recognize—the splodge of stamped blue wax that I was willing to bet my one and only trouser suit was Prince Faron's seal.

"According to Lord Kenwick, that's not an option," Ferris growled.

"Fuck Lord Kenwick."

"Normally, I'd be happy to agree with you," Ferris replied, "But we have to be careful." He glanced at me then looked back at Tor meaningfully.

"What does he actually want with me?" I asked.

"Your assistance with a task," Ferris said, his voice morphing into a disdainful clip that told me he was quoting Lord Kenwick directly.

"Can this Sir Janis be trusted?"

It was Tor who answered. "Sir Janis, yes. Lord Kenwick? Absolutely not."

"But it's Sir Janis who's asking for me. And isn't he with Kai, anyway?"

That decided it. Though he didn't look happy about it, Tor organized the rest of my guard and then we left— walking right into Lord Kenwick who was waiting, impatiently by the expression on his face, just outside my door, a bevy of soldiers with him. My guard immediately surrounded me, and he changed his mind about offering me his arm as we walked. I saw the thought flicker in his head then felt a jolt of anger as he saw my guard move to make it impossible. I didn't see his Bound, the little flame, but I felt a flash of heat and wondered if, somehow, he'd taken it inside him. Was that possible?

Who knew anymore.

We made a noisy convoy as we moved through the palace. My heels clipped on the flagstones and Lord Kenwick's shoes made a similar sound, making me wonder if he was giving himself a little extra height. Even so, my guard of Hounds towered over him, their tread silent, but the soldiers behind stomped in rhythm. They'd know we were coming, at any rate.

I'd lost all sense of where I was in the building, one fancy corridor looking very much like the next and almost all the doors closed against my prying eyes. I knew when we were approaching our final destination, however, because there was a soldier standing guard outside it and when he saw us approaching, he moved to open the door so we could sweep right in.

It was a large, bright room, less fancy than the suite I'd been given, perhaps, but still sumptuously decorated. There were dainty little chairs and ornately carved tables, a dresser against the back stocked with bottles of what I presumed were wines and spirits, along with elegant crystal glasses. It looked like a games room, the center space left open for more physical shenanigans.

What didn't seem to fit was the creature hobbled there,

on his knees. Two soldiers stood over him, looking ready to spring to attack if he made any move, but they needn't have bothered. He looked like he could barely raise his head. He was clothed in a mix of fur and leather, his hair thick and curly on his head, a dark beard hiding much of his face, but everywhere I could see skin, it looked bloody and bruised.

What the fuck was going on?

Where was Kai?

"Where's Sir Janis?" Tor growled, narrowed grey eyes turning to fix Lord Kenwick with a look. That was another good question. Neither of the two men standing over the unfortunate creature looked like a Sir anything.

"He is detained," Lord Kenwick replied smarmily. "He's left me to act in his stead. My lady—" Lord Kenwick smiled at me in a way that made eels slide around in my insides. "I have a task that requires your special skills."

I looked from Lord Kenwick to the wretch on the ground and back again. Whatever the task was, I didn't think I was going to like it.

21

"Which skills would those be?" I asked. I heard the wobble in my voice, but hopefully, no one else noticed.

"Like I said yesterday, I have made a study of the palace archives, the journals of previous men who have been so fortunate as to call a Celestial."

"Only the men?" I asked.

Lord Kenwick's answering smirk was amused. "Only men are permitted to enter the temple chamber when the Ether comes to life."

What a surprise.

"Right," I replied through gritted teeth.

"Of course, each Celestial is different, but there are some abilities you all appear to have in common."

"What are those?" I asked coolly. Or at least, I was aiming for coolly. The ice felt very thin beneath my feet.

"The ability to wield their energy as a weapon, something you demonstrated so adeptly at the temple." An oily smile. "Empathic abilities, prophesy…telepathy."

"I can't read minds," I said quickly. "I have no idea what you're thinking right now."

"You can't read minds *yet*," he threw back at me. "A Celestial's power increases exponentially as they age. What you are now is but a shadow of what you will become. Still," he paused and eyed me intently. "You have already begun to experiment with your abilities, have you not?"

"What?" I asked blankly.

He tilted his head, eyes twinkling. I had the feeling he was playing with me, and I did not like it.

"Something you will need to learn, there are eyes and ears everywhere in the palace."

"I don't know what you mean," I replied.

I had a feeling I did, though. A moment later, Lord Kenwick confirmed it.

"Your conversation with Lord Rothsenberg. You knew he had been denied an invite to the temple during the Solar Convexion. And you knew he was angry about it." He raised a single eyebrow. "Did you not?"

Lie, I thought. Deny it. But I was a terrible liar, and an even worse poker player. My face was already flaming, giving me away.

Tor moved to my left. Just a slight shifting of his weight, but I'd quickly learned that the Hounds could keep their predatory stillness for hours. I glanced at him, and he shook his head ever so slightly, his mouth pressed into a tight line.

Right, of course. Silence was golden.

I stared at Lord Kenwick, a small smile on my face. He stared back and I felt it, the need to push me. To poke and prod until I admitted what he already knew. He seemed to mull it for several long moments, then he looked away from me and took a few steps towards the poor battered man on the floor.

The release was almost physical. I felt myself wilt with relief and had to quickly pull myself together before Lord Kenwick turned to address me again.

"Do you know what this is?" he asked me. He loomed

over the kneeling figure, nose wrinkled like he'd stepped in something deeply unpleasant.

"A person?" I asked. We were back to playing. Kenwick was the cat, but I wasn't sure whether it was me or the kneeling man who was the mouse.

Both of us perhaps.

"Just barely," Lord Kenwick replied. The man ignored the slight, staring deliberately down at the floor. Annoyed by his lack of reaction, Lord Kenwick kicked out at him, using enough force to rock the man's whole body, but still, he kept his eyes down. "Do you know where he is from?"

"Is he one of the Badari?" I guessed. I had no idea who they were, and had only vaguely heard the word spat between Kai and Lord Rothsenberg. Apparently, I was right. Lord Kenwick gave me an approving nod.

"Very good." His praise fell like a viscous net over my skin; I had to resist the urge to rub at my arm and wipe it away. "The Badari lands have recently been acquired by the crown but…you know how these things go." A smug little lift of one shoulder. "Sometimes people don't know when they are conquered."

I really, really disliked this man. His words were for me, but I knew they were a dagger in the side for the man hunched over at his feet. So did Lord Kenwick, and he was enjoying that fact immensely.

"Our victory is inevitable; they have already lost. But they seem unable to grasp this simple fact. This thing—" another little kick, another indignity for the Badari man to endure, "is part of an irritating little band of resisters who are hiding like cowards in the mountains. They're making quite a nuisance of themselves, and they are making the Badari populace...disobedient." Another pause. "You'll be aware, I presume, that the Hounds have been dispatched to deal with the remnants of this rabble."

I was not aware of that at all.

I looked to my four protectors, caught off guard. Tor's face was carefully expressionless, and Ferris looked like he wasn't even listening, his attention moving about the room, watching for threats. I thought I saw hints of surprise and alarm cross the features of Conlon and Rye, though. Good. I didn't want to have been the only person not in the know.

"I still don't see why you require me," I commented.

"Yes, of course." He dipped his head in a short, ingratiating nod. "It will be a dangerous mission. Perfectly suited to the beast soldiers, with their special...skillset. But still, there will be casualties. How many Hounds are left?"

Lord Kenwick looked over my shoulder as he spoke, addressing the question to Tor.

I turned to stare at the oldest member of my guard. A muscle shifted in his jaw, the only outward sign that the question unsettled him.

"Two hundred," he ground out.

"So few," Lord Kenwick murmured. His eyes went back to me. "It would be a shame to lose any more of them. They are so helpful in a fight."

I tried to rein in my temper. It was hard, with the anger of the four Hounds in my guard pulsing inside me, too. If Lord Kenwick didn't get on with it and spit out what the hell he wanted, I thought I might throttle him.

"Again, Lord Kenwick, I don't see how I can help. I am not useful at all in a fight."

"Yet," he repeated, punctuating the word with a little wink. "There will come a point, Lady Bethany, when you will be worth an entire army all on your own."

"Not today, though," I replied, working hard to keep my tone even.

"Not today," he agreed. "Today, I am hoping to put your telepathic skills to use."

"I told you; I can't read minds." I glanced down at the Badari man once more. He'd been ignoring us, had shown no reaction to the conversation so far—not even when Lord Kenwick had told me about the resistance fighters—but now he'd given up all pretense of not listening, was staring hard at me. His face was so battered it wasn't easy to read his expression, but I was feeling a building sense of panic in my gut.

He was scared of me and what I might do.

"Lady Bethany," Lord Kenwick broke in, and I tore my eyes away from the frightened gaze of the Badari man, "Your Bound pledged your services to the kingdom. I do not ask you to do anything that is beyond you. I merely want you to try."

His tone was entirely reasonable, his expression mild, but I didn't need to be empathic to read the threat hidden between the lines.

I reached out to my guard instinctively, seeking to anchor myself. It didn't help. They were anxious: reluctant to allow me to do this, aware that they didn't have the power to intervene. I felt no sympathy for the Badari man and his situation in their thoughts, only a concern for the threat he might pose to me. Mostly what I felt from them, was a desire for Kai to turn up and take control.

Them and me both.

I took a hesitant step towards the Badari man and two things happened at once. He twitched on the ground, getting his feet beneath him as if preparing to spring, and my entire guard jumped forward in defense, surrounding me until I couldn't even see him and filling my senses with heady aggression. The air was full of shouts and snarls, all of it overwhelming. I put my hands up to my head, feeling a pressure building there. My skin was pulsing hard with light. I shut my eyes so I wouldn't have to look at it and concentrated on shoving every feeling, every whisper of intention that wasn't mine, out of my mind.

Silence. Blissful silence and calm. Just for an instant, then I felt a hand drop tentatively on my arm and worry flooded my senses.

"My lady?" I opened my eyes to see Rye gazing at me uncertainly. "Are you all right?"

"It was too loud," I told him.

I looked around and realized my mini meltdown must have lasted longer than the brief moment it felt like. The Badari man had moved across the room and only three of my guard now circled me. Tor was a few feet away, toe to toe with Lord Kenwick.

"I will not allow you to place Lady Bethany at risk," Tor was saying. Well, growling.

"Watch your tone," Lord Kenwick snapped back. "I could have you flogged."

Tor opened his mouth, and though I couldn't read the words I could sense the intent behind them. He was going to say something to seal his fate. I didn't know where it came from, maybe Tor or maybe Lord Kenwick, or perhaps just my own imagination, but I got a flash of a back, arms tied up between two posts, and flesh cut and torn into ribbons.

Tor's mouth snapped shut, and it was a moment later before I realized I'd done it.

"I will do it," I said, moving out of the protective triangle of Rye, Conlon, and Ferris, until I was in front of Tor and Lord Fenwick, close enough to dart in between them if need be.

And wouldn't my guard love that.

"It is not safe, my lady," Tor argued.

"Perhaps I can help with that?" Lord Kenwick suggested.

The next moment, light and heat flared just to my left as his little fire sprite appeared out of nowhere, nestled suddenly in his palm. Living flame, Kai had told me it was called. Again, I felt a burning need to touch it, but I kept my hands by my side.

Lord Kenwick lifted his hand slightly, like he was encouraging a bird to take flight, and the fire hopped free from him, floating across the room to land beside the Badari man, where it immediately exploded into a circle of fire, surrounding him on the floor. He gave a startled yelp and drew all his limbs in, recoiling from the heat.

Which is how a sensible person responds to fire.

Still, I couldn't shake the feeling that *this* fire wouldn't burn *me*. That it wanted me to touch it.

"You are quite safe now, Lady Bethany," Lord Kenwick crooned, gesturing to the prisoner. "He will not move."

I bet he wouldn't. Just as I bet doing this had occurred to Lord Kenwick earlier, but he'd held back on offering it, hoping, perhaps, to create a scene and push some buttons. I gave him my best unimpressed teacher look, then walked towards the Badari prisoner. This time he stayed put, even when I was close enough to crouch right in front of him, the warmth from the flames tickling my skin.

I looked into his eyes and imagined pushing past them, reaching into his mind. I waited for something, anything to appear, but all I saw were dark brown eyes narrowed in anger and the beginnings of resentment.

It was hard to look at him, with the evidence of his mistreatment written all over his face. Cuts, bruises. He curled one lip at me, and I saw at least two teeth missing, the evidence of their recent extraction smeared across his mouth.

"What did they do to you?" I murmured, quietly enough for only him to hear.

A flash: his hands tied to the wall while three soldiers set about him with sticks and booted feet. I gasped as pain— his pain—radiated through me, but a moment later it was gone.

It didn't go unnoticed, though.

"Are you well, my lady?" Ferris asked.

I flicked my eyes to my right and saw that he was crouched there, not two feet away. I'd not heard him approach, I'd not seen him squat down beside me. He really was a silent assassin.

"I'm fine." I looked back to the Badari man, who was eyeing me suspiciously.

How did you get here? I thought. I tried pushing it into his mind, and at first, I thought it hadn't worked, but then I saw. Soldiers' bodies littered the ground as another two, one of them wounded and bloodied but still on his feet, hauled the Badari man out from behind a rock. Some sort of crossbow dropped from his fingers when a heavy blow from a club fractured his arm.

I looked down at that same arm and realized for the first time that he was favoring it, holding it a little closer to his body. He followed the direction of my gaze and then wrenched his eyes back up to mine.

Yes, he was definitely frightened now.

It swamped me, like being doused in cold water.

Where are the rest of the fighters hiding? I asked.

Nothing. I knew my question went in because his entire face closed down, but I didn't get any images. Any flickers of memory.

"Where are the rest of the fighters hiding?" I said it aloud, wondering if that might make a difference.

Nothing.

"I won't allow you to hurt my Hounds," I told him. I felt it, a swell of possessiveness over them, a responsibility for every single life. If Lord Kenwick was telling the truth and they had been sent to deal with the band of rebels…

I couldn't stand the idea that some of them might die because I couldn't get a handle on these strange new abilities

I had. I felt that panic, that gripping urgency, and pushed it at the Badari man.

Instantly, I was hit with a flood of images. Him galloping across a wide meadow on a horse. In the heat of battle, swinging a weapon, the euphoria of the fight upon him. Sharpening a knife by firelight. Nothing that was useful. Was he throwing things at me to try and put me off?

Annoyed and feeling the expectant pressure of the room, the pressure inside me, I shoved harder.

There they were, all of them, hidden in caves. The Badari soldier's memory opened up wide enough for me to rush through the tunnel with him, peer out onto a ledge that gave a perfect bird's eye view of the king's soldiers, painstakingly climbing the steep, rocky ground below.

I drew in a relieved breath, prepared to pull back and report what I'd seen, when I caught just a ghost of something else.

Panic. Desperation. Distraction.

"You're hiding something," I said.

The panic flared hard. I was dimly aware of the Badari man trying to scramble backward, but there was nowhere to go, the fire surrounded him on all sides. His pain rocketed about in my head as his flesh burned, and it broke his concentration just long enough for a blast of something to come through.

A second cave, this one filled not with soldiers but with wives and children, belongings packed in about them, fear on all their faces. An entrance, completely invisible to someone who hadn't been shown that it was there.

A weakness.

I gasped and the Badari man locked gazes with me. He knew, he knew what I'd seen. The next moment he flung himself at me, trying to launch himself over the fire. The living flame erupted between us, creating a liquid wall of vibrant oranges, and firm hands wrapped themselves around my rib cage as Ferris pulled me away. A frustrated wail came from behind the fire and the Badari man started shouting at me in a language I didn't understand. Lord Kenwick snapped out a command and the living flame shifted shape and became a solid cage around the man, muting his words.

Startled, I shook off Ferris' hold and whirled to face Lord Kenwick. His gaze was on the flames, and the Badari man hidden inside, but a moment later it latched onto me.

"He showed you something, didn't he, Lady Bethany?"

Too shaken by the last few moments to even think about denying it, I nodded shakily.

Lord Kenwick stepped closer, expression intent. "What did you see?"

Starting to get my wits back about me, I bit my lip. I might be naïve and a serious fish out of water, but I wasn't stupid. If I told Lord Kenwick about what I'd seen, he wasn't going to use the information to send them baskets of muffins.

But...

I looked to my guard. They were angled about the room, trying to protect me from potential threats from Lord Kenwick, the watching soldiers, and the living flame. I could tell the fire spirit unnerved them. I couldn't blame them, it was certainly unnerving, continually twisting and arcing in the shape of an oversized, old-fashioned birdcage.

Fire just should not do that. But then, it wasn't really fire, was it?

The Hounds, though, they were four of only two hundred. Almost the entirety of the rest of the pack was apparently en route to try and deal with the Badari rebels. Sent, presumably, because the ordinary soldiers were struggling.

How many would die, trying to pick the Badari out of their hills?

How many could I save, with the information in my head?

"My lady?" Lord Kenwick prompted. "What did you see?"

"I know where the Badari are hiding," I told him. I thought of the bird's eye view I'd had, peering down the cliff. "And how they're finding out exactly when and where your soldiers plan to attack."

Lord Kenwick's mouth unfurled into a delighted smile, then he cocked his head and peered at me, considering.

"There's something more?"

Damnit, why hadn't I learned how to hold a poker face?

I licked my lips. "There is," I said.

"What is it?"

I looked to my guard again. To Tor, Ferris, Conlon, and Rye. They were where my loyalty lay. And with Kai, who felt responsible for the life of each and every Hound. God, where was Kai?

"He showed me where they are hiding their wives and children."

"Oh, you are worth your weight in diamonds," Lord

Kenwick breathed. He clicked his fingers at one of the soldiers. "Bring me a map."

"I can't do that," I said hurriedly. "I can't point it out on a map. I'd have to try to show, attempt to put the image into your head."

I thought I could do that. At the very least, I could describe it in detail.

Lord Kenwick thought about it for a moment, then nodded. "Very well."

He gestured for me to come towards him, but I hesitated.

"What will you do with the information?"

"My lady?" He frowned slightly.

"If I show you where the women and children are, what will you do with that knowledge." I swallowed. "They're not soldiers, they're innocents."

"Ah, I see." He gave me a patronizing look. "You worry for them, fear the Hounds might rage in and tear them to pieces?"

"I...what? No." I hadn't thought about the Hounds hurting them at all. It was soldiers I imagined, hacking at limbs, tearing clothes from bodies...

"You needn't worry, my lady. In fact, the information you hold will probably save lives. All we need do is threaten their families and the Badari soldiers may well surrender. We mean to rule then, not crush them."

That all sounded very rational, but I didn't trust it. Not from Lord Kenwick's lips.

What choice was there, though? I couldn't hold the lives of strangers over the Hounds. I wouldn't.

Taking a deep breath, I pulled the images I'd received from the Badari man and tried to push them out of my mind and into Lord Kenwick's. Almost immediately, he inhaled sharply, and I knew I had succeeded.

"Oh, that is wondrous. What a marvel you are." Lord Kenwick gave me a nod that was as close as I thought he came to a bow. "I thank you for your service to the crown, Lady Bethany."

I didn't say anything back. The only words I had were pleas for the lives I'd just handed him, and Lord Kenwick wasn't the type to listen to pleas.

He turned to leave the room then paused and turned back to us. "Oh yes, one more thing to take care of."

He looked to his living flame and made a sharp gesture with his hand. There was a whoosh and the fire folded in on itself, became a tiny flicker that swam along the floor until it could climb up Lord Kenwick's body to rest on his shoulder.

There was no sign of the Badari man who had been enveloped within its fiery embrace, just some black ash on the rug and a stink in the air, burnt flesh and bitter ash. Lord Kenwick's heels clicked on the wooden floor as he walked away.

22

She wasn't in the suite of rooms, and neither was her guard. Where was she? Where *the fuck* was she? Kai paced the small square of open space in the living area and fought not to panic. He was panicking, though. He'd left his Bound sleeping and returned to an empty suite.

No Lady Bethany, no Hounds, no sign of a struggle. Nothing to explain where they'd gone.

There were a million innocent reasons why she might have left her rooms, but Kai's mind skipped right over those and went to the nightmare ones. The ones that tormented him in his sleep. Lady Bethany in shackles while priests stood chanting over her, dissolving his Binding and handing her to someone else.

In his very worst nightmares, she wasn't even struggling; she wanted to go.

He looked again at the undisturbed pillows on the chaise, the dainty chairs still standing on all four legs. The long, thin lamp standing right by the door. Everything was as it should be, which meant she'd left this room of her own volition.

Was she already bound to Prince Faron? Would he even feel it when their link was dissolved? He felt a crushing tightness in his chest, his heart fighting to beat through its unyielding grip. He—

The door opened.

He whirled and watched as Ferris slid inside, eyes

searching the room and hunting for threats before he widened it to allow Lady Bethany and the rest of her guard to enter. They locked eyes and, as usual, Ferris' expression gave nothing away. He moved into the room, taking up position at the weakest point, back to the window, and watched Lady Bethany enter.

If Ferris's face was a blank mask, Lady Bethany's was a picture. She looked pale, drawn, and agitated. When she caught Kai, standing waiting for her, she stopped dead and her eyes welled up with tears.

"You're here," she said, lower lip trembling.

Kai stared at her in horror. She was unhurt, as far as he could see, but obviously distraught about something. He had almost no experience dealing with crying women. Screaming in anger, yes. Sometimes even screaming in pleasure. But tears unnerved him—and tears from Lady Bethany made him feel like his insides were being ripped out.

He looked to the rest of her guard helplessly.

"What happened?"

His voice seemed to be the thing to break Lady Bethany's sudden paralysis. She stumbled across the room and curled into his chest. Kai wrapped his arms around her, feeling the tension in her shoulders, her shaky, uneven breaths. He fixed Tor with a look.

"Where were you?"

"Lord Kenwick appeared with a summons from Janis bearing the prince's seal."

"And you went, without waiting for me?"

"Lord Kenwick was not inclined to delay. The letter

bore Prince Faron's mark," Tor reminded him, before Kai could snarl that he didn't give a fuck about Lord Kenwick's schedule. "And besides, we thought you were with Janis."

"I was," Kai snapped.

"And we realized that when we arrived, neither you nor Sir Janis were in sight." Tor kept his voice deliberately even, not rising to Kai's aggression. Conlon and Rye were avoiding his gaze, eyes resolutely on the floor, while Ferris watched calmly.

"What did he do to her?" Kai demanded.

Lady Bethany pressed closer into him for a moment, then pulled back and lifted her head so that she could look up at Kai. She was still pale, but her eyes had lost their sheen.

"He had a Badari man there, a prisoner. He wanted me to get information about the rebels from him."

Kai's jaw clenched so tight he thought his teeth might break. "He had no right to ask you to do that."

"Doesn't he?" Lady Bethany asked. "I thought you promised that I would serve the crown?"

He had. He had promised that. But that had been when he was grasping at straws to hold onto Lady Bethany. Now that he was here, facing the reality of his choices, it was a different matter entirely.

"Were you able to get the information Kenwick wanted?"

She nodded. "I was able to see his memories, and I showed Lord Kenwick where they were hiding and...and where they were keeping their families, to keep them safe."

Her lower lip wobbled. Guilt flooded Kai's body from the tiny press of her fingertips against his stomach.

"Lord Kenwick said he would only use that information to threaten them. Do you think he was telling the truth?"

There was not a chance Kenwick would hold to that. He claimed to be a man of his word, but his word changed with the wind. That was not what Lady Bethany wanted to hear, though. He didn't need a direct line to her emotions to understand that, even a blind man could have read it on her face.

"The threat may be enough to encourage the Badari rebels to surrender."

Then Kenwick would send soldiers in to kill the Badari women. Or maybe he'd just set whatever cave they were hiding in on fire, force the Badari soldiers to watch the smoke and listen to the screams.

He tried to keep that knowledge from sounding in his mind, but with Lady Bethany in his arms, her anxiety flooding him, it was impossible. He knew he had failed when the tears in her eyes spilled over and fell down her cheeks.

"Oh God." A hand crept up and pressed over her mouth. "I didn't know what to do, and you weren't there." She paused. "Why weren't you there?"

As accusations went, it lacked any kind of venom, but that didn't matter. It still hit Kai like a sword to the gut. Striking hard then twisting viciously.

"I'm sorry," he murmured.

"I needed you," she said, swiping at her cheeks. Her

eyes sharpened on him, though her eyes were still drawn in anguish. "I needed you and you weren't there!"

She tried to pull back and Kai instinctively tightened his arms. He forgot that she was a Celestial, forgot that, as a lowly Hound, he'd no right to put his hands on her, never mind try to keep her anywhere she didn't want to be. He only knew that she was hurting and angry. That he'd failed her, and he needed to fix it, or he'd never be able to breathe again.

"Bethany, please—"

"Let go!" she wriggled harder, putting more strength into getting away from him, but her energy stayed muted under her skin. She could have blasted him with it if she'd wanted, thrown him into the wall and broken every bone in his body. She didn't.

Instead, she lifted both hands and started slapping at his chest, her face screwed up with angry tears.

"Why weren't you there for me? I hate this place! And I hate these people! I don't want to be here anymore."

The slapping hands turned into tiny fists, but Kai barely felt their impact. It was her horror at what she'd done, her desperate need for comfort, that was shredding him.

"Get out," Kai growled.

Lady Bethany paused, staring up at him in confusion, but it wasn't her Kai was talking to. He lifted his head and pierced Tor with a look, sweeping his eyes across the rest of her guard. "Out. Now."

Conlon and Rye made to move immediately, but Ferris stayed put, his gaze on Tor. Who stepped closer instead of heading for the door.

"Kai—"

"I said get out." The words were almost undecipherable through the growl in Kai's voice, but the leader of her guard would get the message. Still, he held his ground.

"She asked you to let her go," Tor said quietly. He held himself tightly, prepared to defend, but he didn't back down.

Only the fact that Tor was acting to defend the Lady Bethany—and the fact that the Celestial herself was in his arms—prevented Kai from ripping the Hound limb from limb.

"Tor…" he rumbled warningly.

"You put me in charge of her guard, charged me with her protection," Tor said. He swallowed audibly. "That includes protecting her from you, if need be." He dropped his gaze from Kai to Lady Bethany. "Are you all right, my lady?"

Lady Bethany had lost the angry look on her face. Her cheeks were still flushed, eyelashes wet, but confusion was the dominant expression on her face as she looked from Kai to Tor, felt the charged atmosphere in the room. Her hands had stopped beating at Kai, were now pressed to his chest, fingertips of one hand resting lightly right over his heart.

She shifted her feet, as if she might pull away, and Kai braced himself to let her, loosening his grip instead of holding onto dear life like he wanted to. A moment later, everything in him relaxed when Lady Bethany moved closer to him, replacing her hands with her head, which she rested against him.

"I'm all right, thank you Tor," she said.

Tor dropped his head in a respectful nod and turned to leave. His shoulders were hunched, his discomfort at turning his back on his First right now palpable.

"Tor?" Kai called. Tor paused, turning enough to look at Kai with one guarded eye. "You did the right thing." He narrowed his eyes at the older Hound. "But don't do it again."

Tor gave a ghost of a smile, then exited, closing the door behind him and leaving Kai alone with his Bound.

"I'm sorry." The words tumbled out of his mouth. It wasn't a phrase he was accustomed to uttering, pride usually preventing him from admitting he was wrong. He had no pride when it came to Lady Bethany, though. Only a desperate desire to be worthy of her.

"It's all right," she sighed, the energy seeming to drain out of her.

"No," he disagreed. "You needed me, and I wasn't there."

"I understand why, though. It wasn't your fault. You wouldn't have done it if you could have helped it." Lady Bethany pulled back enough to look up at him. The anguish was back in her eyes, a deep unhappiness wrenching at Kai's guts. "I've killed those people, haven't I?"

"No." Kai repudiated her claim immediately, accompanying the words with a sharp shake of his head. "The rebel soldiers did that when they decided to fight instead of surrendering."

"Can you blame them?" she asked. "Who would willingly give up their home, their land. Their way of life."

"I did." Kai hauled in a breath, trying to loosen the

tightness in his chest. "I made that choice. I enslaved my people to keep them alive."

Lady Bethany lifted a hand and placed it on Kai's cheek. Sympathy washed through him. He wanted to pull away—he didn't want her pity—but he wouldn't give up her touch on his bare skin for anything. She was so close, the heat of her ran the length of his body, the smell of her filled his nostrils. He willed his dick to stand the fuck down, but she didn't help the situation when she shifted her hand to the back of his neck, fingers sliding into his hair, and urged his face down towards her, until they were touching, forehead to forehead.

"I'm sorry," she said. "I'm sorry you had to make that choice. But you did make it. You're strong enough to see what had to be done so that you and your people could survive."

Kai had told himself those same words a thousand times, but hearing it from Lady Bethany, somehow made him doubt himself all over again.

"Did I?" he asked.

He felt like a child, pathetically seeking approval, but he needed it. He needed Lady Bethany to agree that he'd made the right choice, the only choice.

"You know you did," she murmured. "Sometimes you fight by not fighting. Sometimes you fight just by surviving."

She stroked softly at his nape and Kai fought a full-body shudder. Preventing himself from tightening his arms around her and crushing her to him was almost painful.

She's a Celestial, he reminded himself. She's so far

above you it's unfathomable. Be grateful for what you have, you mangy asshole.

"How has this turned into you comforting me?" he asked, striving for humor to lighten the moment.

She chuckled softly, and Kai felt it in his dick. A bolt of lust shot through him like she'd wrapped her dainty little hands around him and stroked.

He shifted away from her, ever so slightly, so she wouldn't feel, but he forgot about her hands on his skin. He watched with dawning horror as she puffed out a shocked breath and her pupils dilated.

Fuck!

"My lady—"

He didn't get any further. Lady Bethany stopped his words by moving up on her tiptoes and covering his mouth with hers.

23

I'd never been so turned on in my life.

It flushed hot through my skin, between my legs throbbing in time with the rapid beats of my heart. A few minutes ago, I'd been sobbing, then my own anguish melted away in the face of Kai's torment. I'd wanted to comfort him. Now, I wanted to climb him like a tree.

I was aware that it wasn't normal, that it wasn't coming from just me. I knew that what I was feeling originated from Kai, but I also knew that my own body was reciprocating, amplifying it until common sense and propriety flew out the window and I just, well,

I just chucked myself at him.

I went up on my toes and melded my mouth to his, kissing him deeply and sucking lightly on that pouty lower lip. I went back for more, teeth clashing slightly as I searched for his tongue. I felt surrounded by him, his hard body all along my front and his arms steel bands around my waist. My own hands were clutching at his shoulders, tangled in his hair, as something like a frenzy took over me.

Naked, my mind whispered to me. We should be naked.

Great idea.

"Bedroom," I gasped, tilting my head back as Kai's mouth went straight for my neck. "Let's go to the bedroom."

He didn't agree or disagree. He didn't say anything. He

just reached down and grasped the back of my thighs, lifting me and parting my legs so they wrapped around his waist in one smooth movement. Jesus, I loved how strong he was.

I grabbed his jaw with both hands and pulled his mouth back to mine as we walked, distracting him so he banged into the doorframe on the way into the bedroom, catching my shoulder on the edge.

"Shit," he hissed, breaking away from me. "I'm sorry, I—"

"Don't care," I muttered, shutting him up by nipping at his earlobe. "Bed."

The next moment we were there, the sumptuous covers enveloping me as Kai pressed down on top of me, this new angle allowing for deeper kisses. My legs were still spread, knees on either side of his hips, and as he let me feel his full weight, I felt something else. Ooh. It was impossible to resist flexing my hips, driving up into the length of his cock. He felt it, and I felt his reaction to it.

Fucking hell. I almost came on the spot.

My clit twitched hard, and my eyes rolled back in my head. I made a sort of shuddering moan that I'd never done before in my life. Kai pulled back, lifting until his weight was on his elbows. His eyes were a dark gold, and he was breathing heavily.

"Are you all right?" he asked me.

Yes. Ooh, yes.

"Touch me," I begged.

I wanted more of that, more of his hands on me, and I wanted more of those lightning streaks I felt when his arousal scorched down our bond into me. I raked my nails across the back of his neck and saw the pleasure ripple over his face a moment before I felt it.

"Touch me!"

He leaned down to capture my mouth again, one hand ferreting under me until he could press the flat of his hand between my shoulder blades, urging me up as his weight bore me down, and the other crept towards my breast. I waited with breathless anticipation as he covered it, and discovered its shape with his fingertips, then I accidentally nipped at his tongue when he swiped his thumb over my nipple.

"Fuck!" he hissed, his body turning to stone above me. "I felt that. I felt how you reacted when I touched you." He swallowed. "Do you feel what you do to me?"

I rocked my hips against him again, doing it three, four times, beginning a rhythm, and we both groaned in tandem.

"Yes," I breathed. "I feel what you feel."

"That's…" he tailed off.

"Magnificent," I finished for him.

"Bethany—" It was a scrape across my nerves, the way he tried to draw back from me. He wanted to devour me—and wow, did I want to be devoured—but he was a Hound. A dog. And I was a Celestial. What the fuck was he doing, desecrating the gift he'd been given? The thoughts were clear for me to read on his face, but they also resounded through my head with the force of a gong. He'd already overstepped, just what he'd done so far was enough to…

I shut the thoughts off by dragging his head down and latching my mouth to his. His resistance crumpled as a flare of heat ignited us both. I'd never felt anything like this, not even close. It was a clawing hunger, all my nerves set alight, my nipples hard, and between my legs swollen and wet. We'd barely started foreplay and I was already ready to take him.

"Clothes off," I said, tugging at the collar of his shirt. "I want to feel you, skin to skin."

The words came out of my mouth, but I wasn't sure if it was my thought or his.

He tore his shirt off—just ripped the material from his shoulders without lifting his mouth, without pausing the kiss. I was a little disappointed that I didn't get to see, to revel in what I was pretty sure was golden, well-muscled flesh, but I could feel. I let my hands rove over his shoulders, down his arms where his muscles were clenched tight, holding him slightly above me so he wouldn't crush me with his weight. Across his back where my fingertips felt the slight furrows of old scars. I might have asked about them, but the brief shot of shame I glimpsed when he felt my surprise and curiosity had me speeding past them to the waistband of his trousers.

"These too," I said.

He had to leave me briefly to oblige, and I spent the time yanking my trouser suit off my shoulders, kicking it free of my legs and divesting myself of the flimsy, frilly underwear that was the fashion of the day.

I chucked my clothes to the floor and looked up to see that he hadn't returned to me, was standing by the side of the bed, just staring.

Oh, he was as heart-stopping as I'd imagined. Tanned, sleekly muscled and almost hairless bar a light dusting on his chest and around his groin. His cock was long and erect, bobbing slightly. His hands were clenched by his sides and his eyes were molten. He was perfect and I was…well, I was all right, but I'd never been naked with anyone who looked as good as he did before, and I felt a tendril of insecurity curl up in my belly. My fingers had started creeping towards the covers to cover my thighs, at least, when he pounced.

He took me down to the mattress with force, shocking a startled little gasp out of me. One hand took a gentle grip on my throat while the other pressed into the pillow beside my head. I reached up to kiss him again, wanting to lose myself once more in the rush of sensation, but he held himself just out of reach.

"You are perfect," he told me. His voice was low and guttural, the words distorted slightly, but there was no misunderstanding them. There was also no dispute about how deeply he felt them. His honesty, his awe, and incredulity were rippling on the surface for me to swim in. I swallowed back my denial.

"Thank you," I murmured. "So are you."

A huff of laughter, his thoughts rejecting that utterly. I had no chance to argue, though, because he went back to kissing me, his hands exploring the newly revealed territory of my body.

He molded my breasts, learning their shape free of the confines of my clothing, playing with my peaked nipples. Nails scored lightly down the sensitive skin of my sides, cupped my ass and squeezed. I parted my legs further and tilted my pelvis so that when his hand quested between us, his fingers could delve into my wetness and find my core, circle around my clit.

Fuck! His joy, the heady arousal running through his veins, it coalesced with mine and I bucked against his touch, ready to come immediately.

"Please," I whimpered, "*Please!*"

"I want to taste you," he murmured.

"No." I shook my head from side to side, strands sticking to the sweat forming on my forehead. "I need you to fuck me."

I'd never been a wild lover, preferring candles and romance, sensual touch, but right now I wanted to be screwed within an inch of my life.

"Bethany—"

I was a delicate thing. He might break me.

The thoughts whispered in my head.

To hell with that.

"Fuck. Me," I said, almost snarling.

"Bethany—"

I bit his lip. Just reached up and clamped down on it, hard. A metallic taste sprang up on my tongue and I realized I must have drawn blood. I didn't have time to apologize, though, because my action had the desired effect. He growled, a rumble that rippled through his chest to mine, and his careful cradling of my body became a vice that held me in place. He hitched my thighs higher up on his hips and then thrust, sliding into me in one firm movement.

My muscles squeezed around him, his cock sliding over nerves that had been screaming for attention; I felt both at the same time. Groaned in tandem with him as he withdrew and then plunged forward again.

"Oh," I panted. "Oh God, oh fuck."

It felt like the best orgasm I'd ever had, and I wasn't even coming yet. I clutched at him, nails raking his skin, urging him on with helpless little noises. My head tipped back as he kissed his way down my jaw and found the spot between my neck and shoulder. He sucked the skin in deep and then I felt his teeth there, biting down as he started thrusting in a rhythm.

The world turned into a white haze, only the heat of his limbs around me holding me to reality, his cock sending blooms of pleasure through me with every forward drive. I came, and came again, lost in pleasure, clinging on for dear life as my nerve endings showed me what they were really capable of.

"Come," I whispered in his ear. "Come for me, I want to feel it."

My eyes rolled back in my head as he reacted to my words, thrusting harder, his mind focused on filling me with his seed.

"Yes," I gasped, answering his unspoken desire. "I want that."

It was sexing, *fucking*, as I'd never experienced it: complete abandon to touching, to feeling. And pleasure. When his orgasm rolled through him, it surged into me like a tidal wave, consuming me. I clung to him like a limpet as he shuddered his way through it, his thrusts stuttering.

The world came back slowly, first with the sound of our intermingled pants, then the dampness of my skin, the warmth of the places we were touching. I reached up and put my hand on Kai's jaw, where he had his head buried into my shoulder.

"Wow," I said. Not very eloquent, but my brain felt like it was misfiring.

Kai did much better. "You bless me, my lady."

"Bethany," I muttered.

"My Lady Bethany." I felt him shake against me as he laughed.

What came next all happened in a blur. We were lying, curled up together beneath the blankets, his front along my back, his mouth pressed to my shoulder and his arms around me. We were quiet, just basking in the afterglow, his fingers lightly playing with mine.

There was noise, low words that I couldn't make out, but I caught the angry tone. I'd no sooner lifted my head, felt Kai's arms tighten around me, than the bedroom door opened, and Lord Rothsenberg's face appeared. He was scowling, shoulders hunched to ward off the furious figure of Tor at his back, but when he took in the two of us, lying repose in the tousled bedsheets, his expression shifted to one of shock, then horror.

More shouting. Pounding feet and slamming doors that I couldn't make sense of as Kai grabbed me around the middle and thrust me behind him, blinding me with swathes of fabric. By the time I'd unearthed myself, he and Lord Rothsenberg were face to face and the space was filled with soldiers and Hounds, each trying to outmaneuver the other. I clutched a sheet to my chest, mortifyingly aware that the room was full of men, and I was completely naked. Kai didn't seem to care, his bare backside to me as he snarled in Rothsenberg's sneering face.

I stopped caring too, when the soldiers surrounded Kai, two of them grabbing him roughly by the upper arm, and the Hounds began shifting patterns, so they were a solid wall in front of me.

Leaving Kai alone on the other side of it.

"Wait!" I stammered, finding my voice of the first time and trying to traverse my mattress strewn with pillows and tangled bedding. "What are you doing? Help him!"

More soldiers piled in, fighting their way through the doorway even though there wasn't space, cramming into my bedroom wall to wall. They outnumbered the Hounds at least two to one, and I could see more bristling with weapons in the living room, just waiting for their chance.

"What are you doing? Go and help him!" I landed on Tor as I half-fell off the bed, and he caught me automatically, righting me even as he shielded me from the soldiers in the room. I slapped his shoulder when he nudged me back, and positioned himself squarely in front of me. "Tor!"

"We protect you, my lady," he reminded me, his words muttered out of the side of his mouth as he kept his attention on the scene in front of us.

Kai was struggling, fighting against the soldiers who were trying to take him to his knees, but he wasn't trying to break free. He was snarling words at Rothsenberg that I couldn't hear, and every so often he'd glance in my direction.

Panic, that's what I felt from him. Panic and fear and… shame. Regret.

That last one was like a punch to the gut, but I ignored it, drawing myself up, trying to draw on the energy inside me. It was sputtering like a candle in the wind, though, my concentration frazzled. I couldn't just blast it out. Kai was in the room, so were my guard. I needed control, I needed—

My breath froze in my lungs as a weird lethargy stole over me. Dimly, over the raised voices, I caught the sound of chanting. It was mesmerizing and dizzying, I wanted to run towards the sound and clap my hands over my ears so I couldn't hear it.

"Priests," Conlon spat. "They've brought priests! Kai—"

I didn't know if Kai was being affected in the same way as me, but he stopped resisting the soldiers and the next moment he was on his knees, arms shackled behind his back. I uttered a little whimper at that, my hand reaching out to him, but there was an impenetrable barrier of determined Hounds in front of me, and my legs felt weak and shaky. I wasn't sure they'd hold me if I took a step.

I stood and watched as a pair of soldiers hoisted Kai out of the room.

I let them take him away.

24

"Scum." Rothsenberg's voice came from behind Kai, but a moment later, his fancy-heeled boots came into view as he circled his prey. Kai was no one's prey, but on his knees, with his hands shackled in front of him and chained to a loop in the stone floor, he supposed it looked that way.

He took a deep breath and tried to keep the rage he felt tamped down and under control.

It was cold in the room, and no one had thought to give him anything to cover himself with. Just another humiliation, another way to show the animal what he really was. He forced his body to stillness, refusing to give them the satisfaction of seeing him shiver.

"I told my nephew you weren't worthy of such a gift. To think, I was passed over so that you—*you*—could be given a chance in the temple. It's a disgrace, an outrage."

Rothsenberg stopped directly in front of Kai, breathing heavily through his nose. He stank of adrenaline and ire. Kai did his best to ignore him, staring through the space between his purple, velvet-covered calves to where a weak shaft of sunlight crawled across the flagstones.

He felt the air stir as Rothsenberg darted forward, but with his hands bound he couldn't stop the noble from grabbing a fistful of his hair and hauling his head back.

"Are you listening to me?" Rothsenberg hissed. A dribble of spit slithered down his chin.

Instead of answering, Kai drew his lips back, revealing his sharpened canines.

Rothsenberg flinched, but he quickly replaced that with a sneer, confident the heavy irons would hold Kai. Unfortunately, he was right.

"Look at you," Rothsenberg drawled. "Who could possibly think you were a man? You must have had to hold the Celestial down, force her. There's no other way she'd endure your touch."

Kai had spent his entire life being insulted, disparaged, and put down; the barbs barely registered anymore. This one, though, cut like a burning knife to the chest. The tentative hold he'd had on his temper evaporated and he snapped, growling harshly and slashing to the side with his teeth. Rothsenberg was completely unprepared for the move, and Kai tasted blood as his incisors sliced through Rothsenberg's billowing sleeves to tear flesh.

"Bastard!" Rothsenberg reacted by smashing Kai across the face with his studded leather glove. The blow was as weak as the man himself, but still, it left Kai's ears ringing.

He looked up and grinned as one of Rothsenberg's servants hurried forwards and slashed away the noble's sleeve, wrapping his bleeding forearm with a scrap of fabric.

"You'll regret that," Rothsenberg warned him.

"I doubt it," he threw back.

Rothsenberg chuckled a cold laugh, his calm demeanor back in place. "Perhaps I'll make you watch when I take your Celestial. If she'll have you, she'll certainly spread her legs for me."

"Watch your mouth!"

Rothsenberg waved his servant away irritably as the young man tried to fiddle with the knot of the makeshift bandage, then he crouched down so that he and Kai were on the same level, though he kept himself well out of reach, Kai noticed.

"No," he said. "I won't. You seem to be confused about who holds the power here. You stole what should have been mine, and now I'm going to take it back."

"Lady Bethany would never have answered your sacrifice in the temple," Kai retorted. "You'd have left one of the barren."

"Well then, it's just as well you went and got her for me then, isn't it?" Rothsenberg asked, that supercilious look back on his face.

Kai's answer was lost under the opening of the door. Harsh sunlight blinded him for a moment, so he smelled Janis before he heard him. Stress, tiredness, and the musk of the aged books and papers the older man was always consulting.

"Rothsenberg," Janis said quietly. "I wasn't expecting to see you here."

Rothsenberg had retreated as soon as Janis entered, and was now alongside the wall, all but pretending disinterest.

"Well," he said, raising a shoulder nonchalantly, "I thought it was best not to leave this one to his own devices."

"I'm sure the six soldiers in the room would have sufficed," Janis said dryly.

He and Rothsenberg locked eyes and something unspoken passed between them. Kai had seen it before, had spent enough time among the nobles to understand the code: Janis wanted Rothsenberg out of the room, but he didn't have enough authority to order it. And Rothsenberg had just reminded him that he knew it.

Normally Kai didn't give a fuck about their petty games, but he wanted Rothsenberg gone, too. Whatever happened in the room, he didn't want the cruel, vindictive nobleman to be a part of it.

Unfortunately, he had even less choice about it than Janis did.

"Strand," Janis said, his voice blank of all expression. There was a harsh, grating sound as he dragged a chair across the room until it was directly in front of where Kai knelt, then a creak of bones and a stifled moan as the old man sat down. "This is not where I expected to see you next."

There was no judgment or disgust in the words, but Kai struggled to stifle a grimace, aware of Rothsenberg, watching calculatingly from the shadows.

Unperturbed by Kai's lack of response, Janis leaned forward, resting his elbows on his knees. It put them more on a level, but it also put him within reach. He didn't fear Kai, though. He never had. He didn't need to.

"What the fuck were you thinking?" the older man asked.

Kai stared at him, unable to answer. The truth was, he hadn't been thinking. Well, he had. He'd thought it was a bad idea, and that he wasn't good enough, and that he'd be desecrating the gift he'd been given—all the things Janis was thinking right now. Then Lady Bethany had pressed herself against him and put her mouth to his, and he'd felt her arousal echoing his own. He was Kai Strand, First Hound to two hundred deadly soldiers, and he'd been helpless to do anything but take what she'd so sweetly offered. When she had commanded him to fuck her, he'd lost his mind entirely.

He'd mated her, teeth locked in her neck, every instinct in him telling him this was right and proper.

Now, kneeling on the cold floor, his rational mind once more ruling over his base instincts, he had to agree with Janis. *What the fuck had he been thinking?*

He didn't give a shit what Rothsenberg thought of him, or even Janis, though the king's war advisor held his respect as much as any man.

He had been given a gift from the gods, blessed beyond his wildest imaginings, and he hadn't appreciated it. He'd had to grasp for more. Lady Bethany was far too good for him, and just because she'd wanted him to, didn't mean he'd have any right to do it.

Was she even right now filled with regret?

He shouldn't have left her. He hadn't intended to, had been arguing with Rothsenberg, heedless of the soldiers plowing into the room. But then...one of those bastard priests had been there. Kai had heard the chanting, had ignored it, until it had grabbed him right in the chest, wrapped cold hands around his bonds, and squeezed. He'd felt a bolt of fear—possibly his, possibly Lady Bethany's— and the fight had fallen out of him. He'd felt weak, jittery. He'd allowed the soldiers to take him, a small part of him telling him he deserved this, deserved to be punished for what he'd done.

He'd left Lady Bethany safe with her guard, but now he was desperate to see her, to be sure that she was fine with his own eyes.

"Where is Lady Bethany?" he asked, ignoring Janis' question.

Janis sighed, then slowly shook his head.

"You don't get to ask that, not anymore."

Panic and frustration clawed at Kai, and he yanked at his restraints, filling the room with the clank of the chains. They held, though.

"Is she all right?" he demanded.

Pity flashed across Janis' face for a moment before he wiped it clean.

"She is a Celestial," he reminded Kai quietly. "No one in this palace will do her any harm. As far as I am aware, she is right where you left her." He paused. "It is your own neck you should be worrying about."

"Kill me and Lady Bethany winks out of existence."

Rothsenberg snorted from his position by the wall. Janis held himself to a grimace. All of a sudden, Kai knew what Janis had come to tell him.

"They're going to try and take her from me," he ground out.

"You handed them a reason," Janis replied mildly. "You put your hands on a Celestial."

"She wanted me to!" Kai argued. Rothsenberg's words from earlier were still echoing in his ears. The idea that he'd force her, take what wasn't freely given, filled him with fury, but he needed to keep his head. "I would never put my hands on her without her consent. Her desire."

He hated having to explain himself to Janis, to give any intimate details to Rothsenberg, but his pride was the least of his worries.

"You think they care whether she wanted you or not?" Janis asked quietly. "There were eyes everywhere in the palace. They knew when she ate, slept. They knew if she sneezed sniffing the damned flowers. They were watching and waiting for a reason, and you handed them one. No one wanted you to have her in the first place, and no one who matters will question this decision."

No one who matters, that was the key thing. It didn't matter if Janis agreed or disagreed, it wouldn't matter if the Hounds revolted. The nobles had been horrified when such a gift had been given to someone not in their elite little club, and they'd found a way to change that.

No, he'd gifted them a way to change that.

"She won't agree to it," he said. "She won't let the priests dissolve our binding."

He said it with confidence, ignoring the little voice at the back of his head that whispered doubts, that asked who wouldn't rather be bound to royalty over a dog.

Janis gave a little shrug. "The priests seem to think they can do it with or without her consent. That her power is undeveloped enough that she won't be able to stop them."

Rothsenberg made an unhappy noise, taking a step forward, but Janis waved his concerns away.

"What difference will it make to tell him?" he snapped at the noble.

"And me?" Kai asked, speaking through a throat suddenly made of shattered glass. "What happens to me?"

"You're to be executed," Janis said.

"You won't live to see another sunrise," Rothsenberg sneered viciously.

"Actually, he will," Janis disagreed, the pinch of his mouth betraying his annoyance. "The priests need to wait for the king's return to transfer the binding." He turned back to Kai. "You have a couple of days yet. Three at the most. Don't ask," he said, already shaking his head. "You won't be allowed to see her."

"Please," Kai hissed through gritted teeth. He was prepared to beg, blind panic gripping him. "Let me speak to Prince Faron. If I talk to him, maybe I can—"

Janis levered himself out of his chair and dropped a hand on Kai's shoulder, stemming his words.

"Who do you think signed the execution order?" he asked.

25

I lost my virginity to a boy called John on the conservatory couch in his friend's mom's house. We were caught *in flagrante*, and both our parents were called. I remembered the feeling, sitting on the couch with him, the space of the empty seat in between us and all our clothes back on, waiting for my mom and dad to come and get me, and thinking I might die of embarrassment before that happened.

This was a hundred, a thousand, times worse.

I was clothed in one of my dresses, my trouser suit lost somewhere among the mound of tangled sheets that I couldn't bear to look at, and I was sitting on the couch in my living room, my guard standing around me. We were all waiting for something to happen. The waiting was unbearable.

And still, that something happened before I was ready for it.

Dane slunk into the room. He was pale and visibly shaking, his eyes darting about the space. They landed on me, but before I had time to open my mouth and ask what he'd found out, they skated on, finally fixing on Tor.

"Uncle—" he said. Then his mouth seemed to stop working.

I wasted a moment being surprised that Tor was Dane's uncle, while the man himself strode across the room and folded Dane into an enormous hug.

"It's all right," I heard Tor murmur as I hurried over to join the pair. "Just breathe."

"What? What is it? What's happened?" I asked.

Dane turned away from me, and I felt a stab of hurt before I realized he was wiping furiously at his eyes.

"Prince Faron has sentenced Kai to death," Dane mumbled, his voice catching on the final word.

"Scheming pricks!" Rye hissed. Tor silenced him with a look.

I looked from face to face. I saw anger, resentment, and even resignation. What I didn't see was surprise.

"I don't understand," I said, shaking my head. "What has he done?"

No one answered. Conlon was staring hard at the floor and Rye became suddenly very interested in his fingernails. Even Tor avoided my gaze. Eventually, Ferris spoke from over my shoulder.

"You, my lady. He did you."

"Mind your tongue," Tor ground out.

I waved my hand at him; I didn't care what crude words were bandied about so long as I got some answers.

"I don't understand what's wrong with that!" I exclaimed. "I wanted him to. I *asked* him to!"

Even Ferris couldn't hold my gaze after that declaration.

"Oh, for goodness' sake," I snapped, fear giving way to frustration. "You're all acting like a bunch of blushing virgins! Someone speak to me!"

"You are a Celestial, my lady," Tor said carefully.

"Yes, I know that!" I spat back.

He gave a wry smile at my indignation. "The nobles have been looking for an excuse—any excuse—to try to take you from Kai."

"What does us having sex have to do with that?" I demanded.

"They called it a desecration," Dane offered quietly. "Prince Faron had you designated a holy figure, and as such, touching you is an offense." He grimaced, shifting his feet uncomfortably. "*Mating* with you—"

"Is a death sentence," Tor finished for him.

I was astounded. "Surely Celestials have slept with their Bounds before?" I asked. "We're people, we're flesh and blood!"

We have *needs*, I finished to myself.

"Previous Celestials have always been men," Tor reminded me.

"Well, that doesn't mean anything," I replied tartly.

Conlon and Rye goggled at me, while Ferris gave a tiny smirk.

"I don't understand why what we did was so bad," I said, appealing to Tor, wrapping my hand around the strength of his forearm.

His expression softened, as much as it ever did. "It wasn't," he told me. "But the nobles were hunting for an excuse, and you gave them one. Kai knew it too," he added, patting the back of my hand. "And he chose to do it anyway."

"He said Prince Faron was good," I said, still searching for understanding of how things had gone so horribly wrong. "I thought they were friends."

Tor shook his head, anger darkening his eyes. "We're Hounds, my lady. They use us when it's convenient, but never make the mistake of thinking we're anything but animals to them."

There was a moment's silence, anger reverberating around the room from all five Hounds.

"You are much more than animals to me," I said quietly.

I felt pride flicker at that, but it was quickly replaced with tension.

"What can we do?" I asked Tor. "I thought...I thought Kai's life was tied to mine. If they kill him, don't they lose me?"

I swallowed back my fear at returning to that floating nothingness. Now that I was back on terra firma, back among people, the thought of going back to the resounding silence of my mind was horrifying.

"They'll transfer the bond," Ferris said.

"Prince Faron?" Rye asked.

Tor shook his head. "He is already Bound to that creature. You cannot have two Bound. They'll wait for the king to return."

"We have time, then," Conlon muttered.

"A little," Tor agreed.

"Wait," I interrupted. "I thought I had to be willing for the priests to transfer the bond? That's what Kai told me. And I am not willing!"

Tor shrugged. "If they have signed an execution order, they must think they can do it. They'd not risk losing you."

"Tor." My grip on his arm was white-knuckled now. I

must have been hurting him, but he didn't complain. "What can we do?"

He rubbed at his forehead, and I felt the weight of responsibility on his shoulders. I was making it worse, I knew, but I couldn't help it. I'd no one else to lean on.

"I don't know," he said. "Brannon is not here, and without the pack—"

"Can we get them back?" I asked.

Tor made a face. "We could send a messenger, but there are only the eight of us here to protect you as it is."

"Send someone," I said firmly.

Tor smiled grimly. "It's not that simple, my lady. The pack moves fast, if I sent a runner, it would take them days to catch up, and then the pack has to get back to us."

"When is the king coming back?" I asked.

Tor spread his hands. "I don't know, and I doubt anyone is going to give us that information."

"General Tuill," I blurted suddenly.

Tor frowned. "He and Kai are as friendly as is possible for a ranking officer to be with a Hound, but his allegiance is with the crown. He will not help us."

"He has the bird though. The...Gryt?" I stumbled over the word. "It's fast, Kai said. It could reach the pack much more quickly. Deliver a message for us."

"It could," Tor agreed. "But like I said, General Tuill will not help us."

I lifted my chin and stared at Tor. "And what if I don't ask?"

There was a long pause. "My lady?"

I didn't answer him, scared to voice the thought I had

in case I couldn't do it. Instead, I turned my back on him and stormed through to the bedroom. I ignored the bed and the crumpled mound of sheets there, evidence of the deed that had created all this mess, and went to the window. The latch gave way easily, and then I threw both sides of the window open.

"My lady, what are you doing?" Tor asked behind me. I turned to see the four members of my primary guard and Dane, watching me cautiously. Tor even had his hands slightly extended, like he was preparing to grab me if I tried to throw myself out the window.

I turned back to the brightness of the day and drew in a deep breath. I thought of the Gryt, what its warm weight had felt like, the feel of its feathers. The sense of connectedness I felt when I touched it. Closing my eyes, I reached out my arm and called it inside my mind.

What did Tuill call it? *Swift*, I thought. *I need you.*

I felt monumentally stupid, standing there, but I tried to ignore that, focusing on projecting outwards, seeking out the bird. I thought I felt something, some sense of recognition, an answering call, but I had no idea if I was just imagining it. I kept pushing the thought out, and kept my arm outstretched even though my muscles were burning.

Come to me, I thought. *Please.*

I was just about to give up, frustrated tears pricking behind my eyes, when I heard a startled gasp.

"Is that—" Rye muttered, but someone shooshed him.

I knew it was Swift now, could feel his consciousness as he flew closer, but I kept my eyes closed until I felt the shifting of air against my face as he beat his wings for landing, the sharp sting of claws as he landed lightly on my arm.

"There you are," I sighed, opening my eyes and smiling at him.

He shifted along my arm until he was close enough to rub his head against my chest. I smiled, gently stroking his front with my free hand.

"I need your help," I told him quietly.

The bird blinked at me, and I had the feeling he understood.

"My lady," Tor rumbled quietly. "If you're thinking what I think you are, it won't work. Brannon can't read, and neither can anyone else in the pack."

Shit. I hadn't thought of that.

"Draw a picture," Conlon offered. "The pack running to the palace. Brannon will get the idea."

"We can do that," I agreed. I'd draw a damned comic strip if I had to. "And Swift will help, won't you?" The bird blinked as if agreeing. "I need you to take a message to Brannon, to the Hound pack. And I need you to make sure they come back with you." I drew in a deep breath. I was having a conversation with a bird, of all things, but I felt sure he understood. He was no ordinary bird, after all. "Your Bound will not like it," I told it. "Will you do this, for me?"

It clicked its beak, then nudged my chest again playfully.

"It's like it understands," Conlon breathed, creeping closer.

"It does," I said, stroking the Gryt's head, then tapping

its beak warningly when it hissed angrily at Conlon. "Don't do that, he's my friend."

"If we're going to do this, we need to do it now," Ferris said warningly. "Tuill won't fail to notice that his Bound is missing, and it won't be hard to work out where it might have gone."

"All right," I said, pulling the window closed and bringing the Gryt more fully into the room. "Does anyone have a pencil and paper?"

It wasn't great, what I came up with. My guard politely refused my offer for them to draw the message, looking at the pencil Ferris produced like it might bite them, and I surmised they'd probably had few opportunities to hold one. The Gryt, which might actually bite them, wobbled back and forth across the desk, its anxiousness fueling my own.

Hurry, it seemed to whisper to me. Faster.

I went as fast as I could. The message was no good if Brannon couldn't understand it. With clumsy-feeling fingers, I drew an approximation of the palace, and men I hoped Brannon would recognize as Hounds racing back to it. To add an extra sense of urgency, I drew a noose, after confirming with my guard that Brannon would recognize the symbol. Apparently, they hung criminals here too.

The thought of Kai dangling from the gallows, the rope tight around his neck, made me shudder. A dot of water blotted my picture, blurring one of my lines and I realized it was a tear. I sniffed it back and folded the piece of paper.

"This needs to go to Brannon," I told Swift firmly. "Brannon."

It hopped forwards, bouncing slightly as I tucked the

bit of paper into its messenger pouch. As soon as I had it in place, it took off and started flying about the room, as keen to get going as I was to have it leave. I raced through to the bedroom and threw open the window, standing back as the Gryt zoomed through.

"Fly," I whispered to it, even though it was already a dot in the sky and was too far away to possibly hear. "Don't fail me."

I turned to see my guard had followed me through and were also watching the Gryt soar towards the horizon.

"What happens if it doesn't work?" I asked nervously. "What if the Gryt doubles back and delivers the message to General Tuill?"

No one spoke, then Ferris shrugged. "We will be no worse off than we are right now, my lady."

Okay.

"So, what now?"

Ferris lifted one cheek in a rueful half-smile. "Now we wait."

Terrific.

26

I'd anticipated waiting alone. Pacing grooves into the floor while my guard watched on, still and silent as always.

That wasn't to be.

The Gryt had barely disappeared from sight before there was a knock at the door. My guard jumped into action, four of them surrounding me while Tor, taking the responsibility of leadership as always, moved forward to answer it.

The door opened before he could grasp the handle. I saw him tense, move to attack, then all but throw himself backward as Prince Faron stepped inside. The prince didn't even seem to realize the danger that had been an inch from mauling him; his eyes skated right over the Hound as if he wasn't there, searching until he found me, hovering awkwardly in the middle of the room.

"My Lady Bethany!" he exclaimed. He strode towards me, sympathy written all over his face. His Bound creature stalked at his side.

Prince Faron stretched his hands out towards me as he walked, and I automatically lifted my own to accept the small embrace. His grip was warm around mine, comforting and strong.

"I am so sorry to hear what happened to you," he said, brows drawn together over sorrowful eyes.

"Thank you," I replied, feeling tears prick my eyes as his sincerity washed over me.

"I just cannot believe such a thing would happen."

"It was so sudden," I agreed, my voice thick. "I didn't know what to do."

But now the prince was here, he could help me. Dane had said that Prince Faron had sentenced Kai, but he was here, now, looking to make things right. Maybe he could-

"I thought Strand was better than that. I thought...I thought he had honor. Clearly, I was wrong."

What? The hope inside me was doused as what felt like a bucket of ice water came cascading down over my skin. I ripped my hands from his.

"You must be traumatized," he went on, "and I cannot blame you. But rest assured, Strand will be severely dealt with for what he has done, and I am personally going to ensure your safety until my father returns. Come, let us remove you from these rooms. They must hold awful memories for you."

He made to reach for me once more, and I stepped to the side, avoiding his touch. A flicker of consternation crossed his face, and I covered the move by bending to his cat-like creature, who was waiting by the prince's side but staring up at me with adoring eyes. I stroked its head and it nuzzled into my palm.

"You misunderstand," I said carefully. My thoughts were racing, trying to figure out what to do. "Kai did nothing I did not want him to do. This thing, it's all been a horrible mistake."

"And of course," the prince went on, ignoring my words, "we will replace your guard. Not that anyone will hurt you here, but I shall have members from my personal escort see to your protection—"

Absolutely not.

"I don't need a new guard," I said quickly. "I am perfectly happy with the protection that I have."

There was a stillness in the air around me, a watchfulness. I didn't need the caution and agitation pulsing from each of the Hounds in the room to know they were gathering themselves to make a stand against the prince. I couldn't see how that would end well for any of us. I tried to push out a feeling of calm, made a low gesture with my hand for them to hold, wait.

"My lady, I really must insist. After what happened—"

"I insist," I said, feeling my tentative hold on the Hounds slipping. I wasn't their First, I was the person they were sworn to protect, and they were a hairbreadth from doing what they thought they needed to, to ensure my safety.

Prince Faron paused, frowning at me slightly. Then I felt his resolution harden. "No, I'm sorry, I can't allow it. These Hounds—"

"No!" I shouted. Between panic and stress, I threw energy at the word and the room rattled as furniture banged against the wall and the lights danced in their sconces.

Everyone stopped, eyeing me warily. I had meant my words for Tor, who I'd felt start to move, knowing his focus was on Prince Faron's throat, but it seemed I had grabbed everyone's attention. I could feel a sense of awe and caution emanating from Prince Faron; he had forgotten what I was, and I had just reminded him. I looked down, and saw his hand was buried in Daith's ruff. The giant cat was watching me calmly, though. Even if Prince Faron sicced him on me, I doubted he'd attack.

I decided to press my advantage.

"I will keep my guard," I told Prince Faron. "I do not need or want any others."

I was aiming for firm, but panic was still fluttering in my chest, and I felt my voice reverberating as it came out. A fine tremor ran over Prince Faron's skin and his head jerked in a sharp nod.

"As you wish, my lady." The words sounded dragged out of him, but I didn't care. I'd got what I wanted. "You will allow me to change your rooms, however."

It was said with all the assertiveness Prince Faron could muster. I debated mutinying, out of sheer bloody-mindedness, but a room was just a room. It was probably better to accommodate him where I could.

"That's fine," I said graciously.

He gave me a pleased smile and a little nod, then offered his arm. I didn't want to take it but again, it seemed stupid to antagonize him on purpose.

"We shall get you settled into your new suite," he said, giving my hand a little pat, "and then arrange some refreshments. What you need after such...events, is a little calm. I have cleared my day to stay with you. I'll have some musicians come to play for you and you can just sit and rest."

The prince had relaxed, I noticed. Something about the routine of taking me by the arm, leading me, had settled something inside him. Put him back in his comfort zone. I felt his usual self-assuredness oozing back over me.

It irked me. This was the man who'd signed Kai's death sentence and here he was, now, walking along with a smile on his face.

Heel. I sent the command out more sharply than I meant—it wasn't Daith I was angry at, after all—but it worked. The creature halted immediately, darting behind Prince Faron and reappearing at my side, pressing his head gently against my side as we walked as if to apologize.

"Daith!" Prince Faron said quickly. "Here!"

Stay. I thought it as a whisper, softly, gently, and Daith purred at me, keeping his place alongside me.

"Daith!"

The creature ignored him, prowling beside me, his tail occasionally twitching against my hand and lightly tickling my palm.

Prince Faron frowned at Daith, confused and a little troubled. Clearly, he was used to immediate obedience from his Bound.

Yes, I thought coldly, *I can do that. I can take him from you.*

Prince Faron's eye flicked up to me and I worried momentarily that I might have projected that thought, but Prince Faron gave a little shrug and seemed to dismiss the idea.

"It seems he likes you," he said.

"He's marvelous," I replied. My mind was racing. I'd commanded the Gryt who was—I hoped—on the way to get Brannon and the rest of the pack back here to help us. And now Daith had chosen to obey me instead of his

Bound. Could I do that to all the spirits who had come through from the Ether?

Thoughts of Lord Kenwick's little fire sprite burned in the back of my head. I had seen first-hand its destructive power, but though it called to me, I'd never touched it, and it was out with anything I'd experienced.

We exited the corridor where my previous room had been onto a wide upper foyer, a grand stone staircase heading down towards the main entryway, and a narrower stairway heading up. Prince Faron made to take me straight across, to the opposing wing of the palace, but I paused.

A flicker of grey out of the corner of my eye caught my attention. I looked over to see one of the priests, sandals slapping against the stone floor as he walked quickly away from us. He twisted to give us a wide-eyed look, and I realized he was very young, his face thin and features feminine, and also that his arms were full of books.

"Is that the archive?" I asked, nodding towards the large double doors he'd just exited.

"Yes," said Prince Faron. "Well, the library. The archives are held within it, though."

"I would like to see that," I replied.

"Of course! I'm sure we will be able to arrange a tour for you—"

"Not now?"

"Oh. Well…" Prince Faron frowned slightly, and I glimpsed an image from his mind where I lounged on a chaise while he handed me a slice of cake, sunlight basking the room and soft music playing in the background.

No, thank you.

I'd no desire to be courted by Prince Faron—because that was what it had looked like—while Kai was God knows where, experiencing God knows what. If I had to sit and smile and listen to lyrical bloody flutes, I thought I'd scream. And who knew, there might be something useful in the Archives. I was making new discoveries about myself every day, but time was of the essence. Lord Kenwick had implied that men who had previously Bound with Celestials had written about the experience. I wanted to know what they'd found out.

"You did promise to take me," I threw in, giving him my best attempt at a pleasant smile.

"I did, yes." He took a deep breath and the image of him feeding me cake disintegrated. "I would be delighted to show you our library, Lady Bethany." His overly bright expression faded slightly when he glanced over my shoulder to where my guard were lurking menacingly. They were keeping it together, but I knew they were agitated about what was happening to Kai.

So was I.

"What is it?" I asked.

"Your Hounds will not be able to accompany you inside," he told me.

"Why not?" I asked, an edge in my voice. "I assure you they won't cock a leg on any antique furniture."

I hadn't forgotten Lord Kenwick's insults to Kai over access to the archives. I'd been furious then and I was similarly angry now.

"Of course not," Prince Faron said, waving my words away with a laugh. "It has just ever been the case."

"Perhaps it's time to change that?" I suggested acidly. "You are the prince, after all."

The library reminded me of an old British university, with vaulted ceilings and bookshelves reaching higher than any student could hope to reach. Old-fashioned ladders were anchored into runners, allowing precarious climbs to books on the uppermost shelves. It was lit by dozens of lamps ensconced on the stone walls and every available surface, an attempt to make up for the fact that the imposing outer edifice of the palace didn't allow for much light to enter the building. It gave the place a warm, enclosing feel, even though it was a large room.

It was fairly empty of people, an old, wizened librarian behind an enormous desk and a pair of young men sat at a table, books and paper spewed in front of them, the only occupants. They all turned to stare as we came in, chairs squeaking against the floor as the boys darted to stand at Prince Faron's presence. Their eyes raked over me with disinterest—I was just some woman—then widened perceptibly when they caught Rye prowling behind me. It had been a compromise, to leave most of my Hounds guarding the only entrance, Rye gaining Prince Faron's approval because he scared him less than Tor or Ferris.

Which was silly, because Rye could have torn his head from his shoulders with relatively little effort. And would, if he thought I was in danger.

At the moment, Rye was looking around with as much interest as me, making the most of being given a brief glimpse at a world usually closed off to the Hounds. Like Dane, he was on the younger side, though he'd fully grown into himself, and the predominant expression on his face was wonder, taking in the impressive collection of knowledge. Tor, or even Ferris, I mused, would have scowled at just one more thing the noblemen kept from them.

"We have many incredible texts in here," Prince Faron was saying animatedly. "The illustrations within them are simply beautiful. Oh, and there are some wonderful old maps with exquisite detail, I'd love to show them to you."

"Which room is the archive?" I asked, ignoring his offer.

Under normal circumstances, I'd have pored over this place like an excited child in a sweet shop. The books, the paintings decorating the walls, the skill in the woodwork all around me. It was amazing, and Prince Faron was offering me unfettered access to the good stuff, things I bet the ordinary visitor never got to see. But these weren't normal circumstances, and right now I couldn't give a shit about ancient tombs with gilt-edged pictures in them. I needed information.

"Right. Of course." Prince Faron gave me a weak smile, clearly dispirited that I was robbing him of his chance to show off. I didn't feel my usual pang of regret at disappointing someone, this man signed Kai's death warrant. "This way."

We traveled the length of the library, and I allowed my eyes to glut themselves on the spectacle as we walked. Once Prince Faron approached a small door set discreetly into the back wall, though, I was all business. He clicked his fingers at the aged librarian, and the older man shuffled over as fast as his stooped body could carry him, arthritic hands fumbling at a giant ring of keys.

It took him a while to get the door open, even once he'd found the right one, a long, ornate brass key, and I felt frustration rise up in me. I wanted to grab the damned key and do it myself. Heat flushed over me in a wave...and the librarian gave a startled yelp and jumped backward, blowing at the palm of the hand that had been struggling with the lock.

I looked down to see the metal glowing white hot, and the door slightly ajar.

Oops.

"Apologies," I said, not sounding very sorry at all. Because I wasn't, I was itching to get in there.

The old man looked disgruntled—I'd burned the hell out of his hand, it seemed—but Prince Faron was looking at me like I was Jesus, just having performed a miracle.

Which, I supposed, wasn't too far off as an analogy, and wasn't that an uncomfortable thought.

"Shall we go inside?" I asked brightly.

Prince Faron gave himself a little shake and then reached for the door, pulling it wide and standing back for me to enter. I gave a small smile—I hadn't missed that he had been a little anxious about touching the handle in case I burned him, too.

A moment later, I forgot about that. The archive had none of the grandeur of the library and also, at first glance, none of the organization. It looked like the filing cabinet in my classroom—everything jammed in, and the drawer forced shut on it—only magnified a thousand. There were shelves of books, but there were also piles and piles of papers stacked randomly, chests shoved in a corner.

"Wow," I said.

It was overwhelming and disheartening. How could anyone possibly find anything in here?

"It requires some re-organization," Prince Faron said a little sheepishly. "But—" he held out an arm and guided me over towards a table all but invisible under more piles of parchment, "the librarians have been working on pulling together what we know of Celestials since, well, since you came through from the Ether, and we've amassed quite a wealth of writings."

"All of this is about Celestials?" I asked, eyeing the pile with a mixture of excitement and alarm. I reached out tentatively and picked up a very old, very yellowed sheaf that was lying on top. Ink had sunk deep into the surface, and it was written in an almost illegible scrawl, but I *could* read it, picking out the word 'the, ' 'and,' as well as, randomly, the word dragon. It seemed baffling to me that it should be written in words I could read, but honestly, it was the latest bizarre thing in an incomprehensible string of bizarre things, and I was just going to roll with it.

"Everything we could find."

"Great," I said, putting the sheet back down. "I'd like to take it all to my rooms, please."

There was way too much here for me to read, even if I stayed all day. And the archives were not exactly a comforting or welcoming environment. Already, I could feel the dust working on my nose, demanding I sneeze.

"Pardon?" Prince Faron's face fell.

"I'd like to take it back with me, to study. I have time before the king returns, after all."

How much time wasn't clear, so I wanted to make the most of it.

"Oh, I'm not sure…" Prince Faron tailed off.

The librarian, who had stayed with us, was lingering in the door, still nursing his hand, and looked apoplectic, but he wasn't the decision maker here. I looked hard at Prince Faron.

Say yes, I thought. *You want to please me.*

I waited for a long, drawn-out moment, my heart pounding in my chest, before the prince gave a reluctant nod. "I'm sure we could arrange that. They are, after all, about your kind. It's only reasonable you should want to read about their exploits."

"Wonderful," I said. I beamed at him, putting a hand on his arm. I was laying it on a bit thick, perhaps, but I didn't want him to change his mind. "Now," I said, looking around me, "where would I find information on the Hounds."

"The what?" Prince Faron asked, looking startled.

"The Hounds," I said firmly. "I'm bound to one, I want to read about their history, too."

27

There was a rat in the room. It was keeping to the shadows, understanding the threat Kai posed to it, but it was getting more and more curious, its twitching nose encouraging it to get within reach. Kai kept still as stone, head leaning back against the wall, manacled hands resting on one crooked knee, the other leg stretched out. Minutes passed, possibly hours. Eventually, the rat slunk out of its corner and darted across the floor, pausing by Kai's foot.

Still, he didn't move. Not even when the rat took an experimental bite.

Please with the docility of its prospective meal, the rat slipped along the inside of Kai's bare leg, sniffing as it went. He waited until it was uncomfortably close to his balls to strike. Hands dropping with astonishing quickness, he grabbed the rodent by its furry little body, squeezing hard. The rat gave a startled squeak, then went floppy.

"Sorry friend," Kai whispered to it, "but no one is going to feed a dead man."

As meals went, it wasn't appetizing. The rat was skinnier than he'd thought, with almost no meat on its bones, but it was better than nothing, which was what the guard standing outside his door was going to give him. Using his claw-like nails, he tore off the rat's head and made quick work of skinning it. Flinging the tattered scraps of bloody fur into the corner, where hopefully it would attract one of the rat's little friends, he tore into the under-whelming meal.

The door opened before he was finished, but he ignored the stink of perfume that announced Lord Kenwick's arrival into the room, as he'd ignored the distinctive ring of the man's heeled boots on the stone floor as he approached Kai's cell. He kept his eyes carefully staring into nothing and concentrated on gnawing tiny slivers of meat off the rat's thigh bone.

Kenwick made a noise of disgust and he ignored that, too. What did a pampered noble know about survival?

"I brought you news," Kenwick said eventually, obviously tired of being ignored. "But perhaps you don't want to hear it?"

Kai paused; the rat still poised in front of his face. This might just be another attempt by Kenwick to taunt him, but there was something in the lord's tone that made him think otherwise. A self-satisfaction, a smugness. The bastard was happy about something.

No, fucking delighted.

Dropping his hands down to rest on his thigh—the rat's body still in his clutches because he wasn't going to be goaded into wasting food—he looked up at Kenwick. The man had left the door to his back, probably to give him an easy escape if Kai so much as shifted in his seat, and the light spilling in from the torch sconce in the corridor threw him into heavy shadow. Still, Kai's eyesight was exceptional, and he could see the gleam of Kenwick's teeth as he grinned.

"Do we have to do the song and dance first?" he asked, "Or are you just going to tell me?"

"That's the problem with you dogs," Kenwick retorted. "You don't understand the value of the dance."

"Perhaps it's just the fact I don't want to dance with you," Kai replied. He shifted, chains clanking, and Kenwick flinched. "You're too skittish. I don't want you stepping on my toes in those heels."

Kenwick muttered a curse, lip curling up into a sneer. Whatever news he'd come to impart had to be good, though—or bad, from Kai's perspective—because he didn't turn on those fancy heels and stalk off. Instead, he hunkered down, taking great care to keep the tails of his coat off the floor.

"Your days of speaking out of place are numbered, dog. A messenger just arrived at the palace." Kenwick paused, licking his lips. "The king's banners have been spotted descending from the northern pass. He'll be here by the morning."

Whatever words Kenwick spoke next were drowned out by the clamoring in Kai's head. Panic and adrenaline surged, but he held himself in place, and refused to let loose the snarl building in his throat. Kenwick was watching him closely, hoping for a reaction, and he wouldn't give the bastard the satisfaction.

"How did a worthless animal like you call forth such a weapon? I can't understand it. I mean look at you, filthy, naked, eating rats. You disgust me." Apparently displeased that Kai hadn't railed or raged, Kenwick went on, his voice taking on a darker, more vicious edge. "No doubt your Celestial will be delighted to bind to the king. A man who's worthy of her. Perhaps she'll reward, him, maybe she'll suck his cock and—"

No. That was too much. Kai burst forward, clawed hands reaching to grab Kenwick by the throat, but the noble had positioned himself perfectly, and when the chains pulled tautly, Kai's fingers closed on nothing but air, Kenwick just out of reach.

"Fuck you!"

"Alas, probably not." Kenwick gave him a rueful smile, his eyes twinkling with cruel delight. "Although, you never know. Perhaps if I'm a very good boy and please the king, he'll think I deserve a reward."

"You deserved to leave the temple barren!" Kai hissed.

"And yet," Kenwick replied, lifting a hand and cupping his fingers. A flame immediately appeared there, dancing merrily in his palm. "I didn't." He looked down at the ground at Kai's feet, where the remains of the rat lay in a mangled sprawl. "Allow me to make your final meal a little more palatable."

He flicked his fingers slightly and the flame jumped to the ground, rushing across the stone at an astonishing speed. It reached the rat before Kai could move, consuming the thing until there was nothing left but blackened bone. It flared as it did so, sending a wave of heat over Kai's thighs, burning him. He jolted back, but with the wall behind him, there was nowhere to go. He bit his tongue with a hiss as he felt his hair singe and his flesh burn.

"Oh, I'm sorry, did it catch you?" Kenwick asked, opening his hand, and allowing the fire spirit to rush back to him. "Tricky to control the flames, sometimes."

He gave Kai a smile completely lacking in sincerity and closed his fingers into a fist. The flame extinguished into nothingness. He dusted off his knees, even though he'd scrupulously avoided letting any part of himself touch the floor, then stood.

"Your cell faces north. Perhaps you'll be lucky and hear the trumpets heralding the king's arrival."

He threw Kai one final smirk then turned and left. A moment later, the cell returned to near darkness as the soldier outside closed and bolted the door.

For a long moment, Kai remained there, on his knees on the cold stone floor, head bowed, breathing deeply through his nose. The skin along both thighs was burned and blistered, but he was barely aware of the pain. It was nothing compared to the pain in his heart.

He was about to lose the only blessing he'd ever been given.

Reaching down, he grabbed up the charred remains of the rat and hurled it at the opposite wall, letting loose a furious roar as he did so. Who gave a fuck if Kenwick heard it now? The bastard had won.

28

After two days of constant squinting at cramped, illegible handwriting, my head was absolutely killing me. The new quarter's Prince Faron had ensconced me in were littered with pieces of parchment, some that were helpful stacked up in organized piles, the useless ones tossed to land wherever they lay.

I'd learned next to nothing.

There was an *awful lot* about what great deeds the various nobles had done to earn, in their eyes, the privilege of calling forth a Celestial. Pages and pages about their bravery in battle, and their steadfastness in the face of…all those difficulties they must have endured, being born with a silver spoon in their mouths. They did describe some of the things their Celestial had been able to do: mind reading, creating explosions, emotional manipulation. All things I'd managed to myself, albeit ham-fistedly. There was nothing about healing, I noticed with interest, and also nothing about controlling anyone else's Bound.

What was very frustrating was there didn't seem to be any writings from the Celestials themselves. Nothing that gave their thoughts or insights, or, more helpfully, any how-to guides on how to control the powers I'd been accidentally uncovering with anything like purposeful intent.

There was also absolutely nothing about the power the priests held. The spells they used to transfer bindings, or about whatever they'd done to me to make me feel all wobbly and weak when Kai was arrested.

What I *had* found, was lots of writing about the history of the Hounds, and what I read there made me very, very angry. It seemed they'd been persecuted from the get-go. First, they were ostracized, seen as too wild, too animal, to live among "civilized men". Then, they were used for sport, like those idiots who flew to Africa in the hopes of shooting a lion, or a giraffe. It disgusted me back home, and it disgusted me here.

When the Hounds began fighting back, staging periodic attacks on settlements for the murders of females and young, sport turned into genocide. They made themselves too much trouble, and the response was simply to wipe them out. The agreement Kai had told me about, where the males promised to fight for the kingdom in exchange for the women and young being allowed to live in peace within a compound, was a relatively recent thing, a concord that had been struck out of desperation when the Hounds were all but wiped out.

My Hound guards hadn't been able to help with the research. Though Tor and Dane each had a little reading, the scrunched-up scrawl was beyond them. I shared what I discovered as I exclaimed and cursed my way through the sanctimonious bull the nobles had spouted to justify their actions but none of it was a surprise to them. Tor's jaw hardened into granite, and Ferris actually spat on the ground.

"They think we're savages," he growled. "Good for nothing but bloodshed."

"They're fools, then," I replied bluntly.

My simple statement earned me a rush of affection from all the corners of my guard, and that made me sad. I went back to reading, and it didn't take long for sadness to evolve back into anger.

"There's nothing here that helps," I said eventually, tossing the piece of parchment I'd be squinting over back down onto the table in disgust. "There's nothing to tell me how to control my powers, nothing that tells me what the priests are going to do. Nothing that gives Kai any damned rights in this place even to appeal the death sentence. It's all fucking useless!"

Silence greeted my outburst, and it took me a moment to realize that it was because they were shocked by my language. Well, if there was ever a time to swear, now was it.

I rubbed my forehead. My head was pounding, and I'd give my right arm for a bottle of ibuprofen. On one of Prince Faron's brief, awkward little visits, he'd offered to procure me a "tincture". Given that I had no idea what sort of things might be brewed into medicine here—I'd seen enough documentaries about medieval medicine to be wary—I'd declined.

"It's been nearly two days," I said. Two days that had felt like a lifetime. "How much longer do you think it will be before the pack returns?"

"It's impossible to say," Tor rumbled. He'd said the same thing the last dozen times I'd asked him, with unending patience. Unlike me, who'd had a hissy fit the third time a voice from the back of the car piped up, "Are we nearly there yet?"

I swallowed that memory back down—because I couldn't keep functioning if I let myself remember the past—and focused on Tor.

"They have to be nearly here," I said.

"If the Gryt did as you asked and took the message," Tor said, "and if it was able to find them."

"And if Brannon was able to decipher it," Conlon added.

"Decipher it?" I snapped, "That drawing was brilliant!"

He stared at me for a moment, shocked, before he realized I was joking.

"It was a masterpiece," he agreed. "If it returns with the pack, I am sure they will ask to display it in the finest gallery in the kingdom."

I gave him a wan smile then looked back to Tor. "Surely if the Gryt didn't deliver it, if it returned to General Tuill, we would have heard about it by now?"

I imagined Prince Faron storming in, waving my terrible attempt at a pictorial message in the air and shouting about treachery. Well, perhaps not Price Faron, he seemed like an eager puppy, desperate to please me. Lord Rothsenberg, though, definitely.

"Perhaps, perhaps not," Ferris said quietly. "It might suit them to keep us in the dark."

I scowled at him, annoyed that he was probably right. I'd told myself that the fact we hadn't heard anything about Swift, General Tuill's Gryt, meant that it was off delivering my message, bringing the pack back to us. Bring help. The thought that Brannon and the rest might be running on towards the Badari lands, completely oblivious, was a hard, uncomfortable stone in my gut.

"We still have time," Conlon said. He came over to stand at my shoulder, crossing his arms and glowering at Ferris, as if he was annoyed at him for upsetting me with the truth. "The king's not here yet. He might—"

"Someone's coming," Rye said, shifting from where he'd been leaning idly against the door.

"Who?" Tor barked, shifting position to get between me and the door.

"I can't tell," Rye replied, a frown on his face as he listened to noises I still couldn't hear. "Lots of people. At least six."

Six people. That wasn't Prince Faron just "popping in" to check on me, his two personal guards lingering outside. I glanced up at Tor and saw he was exchanging meaningful glances with the rest of my guard. They were radiating tension, all of them in a state of stark readiness.

Great.

"What do you think's happening?" I asked. It was a pointless question, but I couldn't help myself. My guard hadn't left my rooms in the past two days either, even though I'd pleaded with them to go and try to find out what was going on with Kai. My secondary guard had stuck by my side too, were currently crashed out on the floor of my bedroom because they'd refused to sleep in my bed, even though I wasn't in it.

"Bex," Tor snapped.

I looked to the bedroom door and saw that my

secondary guard had noted the disturbance, were already awake and alert and coming to take up positions around me. It was extremely crowded in the living room, with eight hulking Hounds taking all the available floor space, and I couldn't see the door anymore. I stood, causing a small avalanche as the parchments that had been arranged on the couch around me slid to the ground.

"Stay where you are please, my lady," Tor murmured.

Right. It was oh so tempting to hide behind all that muscle, but the fact was, given the disdain with which the Hounds were viewed, unless it came to a physical fight, I was the person in the room best placed to negotiate with whoever came through the door.

And if it came to a physical fight, eight Hounds weren't going to be able to win against a palaceful of the king's soldiers.

Ignoring Jay's muttered, "My lady!" and the hand Miller stuck out to halt me, I weaved my way through my guard until I was at the front, beside Tor. Who heaved a heavy sigh.

"I'm the Celestial," I reminded him.

"Yes, my lady," he intoned.

Despite the situation, I managed a quick grin. "You're regretting volunteering now, aren't you?"

The look he turned on me was utterly without humor. His eyes were dark, sincerity etched across his face.

"Never," he replied. "Watching over you is an incredible honor, and I will happily give my life to protect you."

"No one is giving any lives!" I shot back. I knew my

words would fall on deaf ears, knew all the Hounds in the room were willing to die for me. Had they been strangers, I'd have hated the idea, but they had become a family of sorts to me, since I'd dropped into their midst just a couple of short weeks ago. Unease churned in my stomach. I took a deep breath and turned to the door. Even I could hear the footsteps now.

Someone gave a jaunty little knock, and so I knew it would be Prince Faron before he opened the door at Tor's growl, "Come in."

None of my guard looked surprised at his appearance; they'd probably been able to smell him fifty feet down the corridor.

"Lady Bethany," Prince Faron said, smiling warmly as he saw me standing ready to greet him. His eyes flicked about the room, and I saw his jaw clench as he took in the number of Hounds present. I was able to see over his shoulder too, though. He'd come with a full accompaniment of guards. Unusual.

"To what do I owe the honor of this visit?" I asked. Best to start off pleasant, at least.

"I have wonderful news," Prince Faron said, yanking his gaze back to mine and plastering that smile back on his face. "My father has returned!"

"He's here?" I squeaked.

I'd expected more warning, expected to hear when he was close. And I'd definitely hoped for more time. I didn't dare exchange a look with Tor. There was nothing to say, anyway. The pack weren't here, even if Swift, General

Tuill's Gryt, had delivered the message, they hadn't made it back in time.

"He arrived just an hour ago," Prince Faron replied. "I wrote to him of your wonderful arrival among us, and he cut his trip short just to meet you."

"Is that so?" I said cautiously. Kai had been naïve, I thought, to ever think that the nobles would let him keep me. They would have found some excuse, no matter what. Or, perhaps, they'd just have done it without pretense. Either way, we'd been heading towards this. They really were a nest of scheming bastards.

But I refused to believe it was a fait accompli. Not when Kai's life hung in the balance.

I just had no idea what I could do.

"It is," Prince Faron said, oblivious to my mood. "He's wearied from traveling, obviously, but he simply can't wait to meet you. It would be my honor to escort you."

He held out an arm, a genial smile on his face.

Start pleasant, I reminded myself. Giving him a smile that was more of a grimace, I wound my arm through his and allowed him to lead me towards the door.

"Oh," he said, as all eight members of my two guards moved to cover me as we prepared to exit into the corridor filled with soldiers who were, I noticed, armed to the teeth, swords and knives bristling over their uniforms. "I'm afraid your Hounds won't be permitted to accompany us."

"Why not?" I asked, my own flare of panic quickly drowned out by the surge of aggression from the Hounds.

"It is forbidden, I'm afraid," Prince Faron told me, not sounding sorry at all. "The First Hound may come before the king under very special circumstances but not, well, not—"

"Not the rest of them," I finished for him, a growl in my own throat.

"It's the danger they represent, you see," Prince Faron said, finally catching on to my tone.

"Because they're animals." His thought, not mine. I could all but see the words, ringing in his head.

Prince Faron had the good grace to look embarrassed. "I'm sorry, they will have to stay here."

"No," I said.

"My lady, I really must insist. They will not be allowed into the King's receiving chamber, and if they try to accompany you, they will be executed."

"They don't have to come inside," I bit back, though I really, really wanted them to. "But they can accompany me there and wait outside."

The Hounds had excellent hearing. They'd probably be able to hear everything that was said, and if I started shouting, I knew they'd be at my side in a moment.

I glanced at Tor and saw his expression was granite. He gave me a tiny nod, though.

Ok, then.

I turned to Prince Faron, trying to feel determined and not scared.

"Take me to your leader," I said.

No one laughed.

29

We caused quite a stir as we walked through the castle. A Celestial, a prince, his Bound creature, eight Hounds and a half dozen soldiers. Everyone looked our way, and when they realized who and what they were looking at, scuttled out of our path. I noticed, as we walked, that the number of soldiers swelled until the Hounds were outnumbered two to one.

Knowing my guard as I did, those were still good odds, but there were plenty more soldiers lurking in the palace, and no more Hounds.

Prince Faron led me down towards the front doors of the palace, and then halted in a foyer before an enormous set of double doors. Four guards stood by the two doors, two on either side and two blocking our path, and then guards positioned about the place—in a corner, standing by a statue—ready to jump into action should the situation require it. It was a much more visible protective presence than I was used to seeing; you could feel a change in the palace now that the king had returned.

"This is as far as your Hounds may go," Prince Faron said to me. "If they try to enter the throne room, they will receive no mercy, no matter the reason."

"I understand," I replied. I understood that my Hounds wouldn't care about that if they thought I needed them. "No one needs to die today!"

I meant it as a joke, but as Prince Faron shifted uncomfortably on his feet, I realized what he was thinking.

He expected Kai to die today.

Well, fuck that. Not if I could help it.

"My father is very excited to meet you," he said, glossing over the awkward moment. "He never dreamed to see a Celestial walk the kingdom in his lifetime!" He moved to the door, and the two guards standing there slid to the side. "Come, let's not keep him waiting any longer."

Hounds might not be able to enter the throne room, but apparently the same didn't hold true for soldiers. The bevy of swordsmen followed us in, joining the dozen who already existed inside, lining the walls. I gave them a brief glance, then turned my attention to the room. I'd never been in here before. It was grand and imposing, all cold stone and stark angles. Most of the floor space was bare, just a single, luxurious red runner stretching out towards the back wall, where the king sat on his throne. Was it always this bare, I wondered, or had all the furniture been shifted out to create this stark effect? Was I supposed to be intimidated?

I was intimidated, but by the task that sat ahead of me, rather than the squat, chubby little man who sat on the throne. Prince Faron's mother must have been a statuesque woman, I thought, and beautiful, because I couldn't see any of the king in his son.

There were several other men in the room, nobles by their dress. They were standing around the throne, like groupies around their idol. Not that they'd much choice: there was nothing to sit on unless they wanted to pop a squat on the stone floor. I noted Lord Kenwick among the group, and Lord Rothsenberg. Another face or two seemed familiar, but their names escaped me. They all stared as Prince Faron led me up the red runner, past lines of armed, lethal-looking soldiers, but I kept my gaze on the king. He was a ruddy-faced man, his eyes scrutinizing me shrewdly. I expected him to get up to greet me, to come down off the plinth his ornate throne sat on, but he just sat there. Watching me.

"Father," Prince Faron said, once we were close enough that he didn't have to raise his voice to be heard, "It is my great honor to introduce Lady Bethany, the Celestial who was called from the Ether during the Solar Convexion."

Prince Faron made the announcement, then dropped to his knees. I wasn't ready for the movement—and I wasn't going to my knees!—so his arm ripped from mine as he dropped. I took a subtle step to the side so he wouldn't be tempted to reach for it, or worse, try to hold my hand, when he stood back up.

"My, my," the king said. He did stand up then, the movement slightly awkward given his weight and the fact his feet didn't actually touch the floor when he was sat on the throne. He clomped down towards me. We were around the same height, though he had to outweigh me by at least eighty pounds. He waited until we were face-to-face to speak again, and I had to make a conscious effort not to step back. Traveling apparently didn't leave time for things like baths. "Aren't you a wonder?" he breathed.

"Hello," I said, because it certainly wasn't nice to meet him, and I couldn't think of any other pleasantries. I felt cold all of a sudden, goose bumps breaking out across my skin. My whole body felt a little off, slightly tingly, like it wasn't working quite right, and I'd put it down to the adrenaline that was racing through my system, but the way it had amplified significantly now that the king was within arm's reach of me gave rise to other suspicions.

There were priests somewhere in the room, and they were doing something to me.

I couldn't see them, but there were drapes covering parts of the walls, particularly along the wall behind the throne, and for all I knew they were hiding alcoves.

Beside me, Prince Faron's creative gave a low growl, hackles rising. I wondered if he was feeling it, too. Prince Faron hushed it, putting a hand down to rest on the nape of its neck and it quieted.

"I couldn't believe it when my son wrote to tell me about you," the king went on, oblivious to mine and Daith's discomfort. "I immediately cut my visit short and returned to the kingdom. It has been such a long time since one of your ilk graced us—"

"A thousand years," I interjected helpfully.

"A thousand years," the king agreed. "My ancestors will be burning with envy in their graves. What a future the kingdom has, with you at my side. No one will dare stand against me."

"I am already Bound to someone," I pointed out. We were coming down to it now, my one chance to try and save Kai's life right in front of me, and my heart was hammering in my chest.

The king waved my words away with a regal sweep of

his hands. "That is no matter. The priests tell me they can correct that…little problem."

"You don't need to do that," I said quickly. "Kai has already promised that I'll work to help the kingdom."

It was as if I hadn't spoken, the king turned from me and waved at one of the nobles behind us. "Fetch the dog."

"Your highness—" I tried.

He turned back to me, his eyes alight. "I would like to see what you can do. I hear you are capable of creating an explosion? Show me."

"I—" I felt wrong-footed. I'd practiced arguing with the king in my head, but I'd envisaged an older version of Prince Faron, not this arrogant, dismissive man. He was used to wielding power and it showed.

I wasn't sure what to do, or how to change tack. The king wasn't treating me with anything like the reverence his son had. I didn't feel powerful, I felt like…a shiny new toy. The king had the expression of an eight-year-old handed a BB gun.

Feeling slightly panicked—okay, very panicked—I turned to a plinth tucked against the wall, a vase balanced on top. I sent a surge of my anxiety into the thing, and it instantly shattered, the soldiers on either side exclaiming and darting away from the barrage of shards flying towards them.

"Marvelous!" the king said, clapping his hands.

I was breathing hard, looking at the soldier who'd been directly to the right of the vase. He was holding his hand up to his temple, a trickle of blood seeping out from beneath his fingers. I hadn't meant to do that, hadn't thought about what might happen when the vase exploded. These…gifts I had; they were dangerous in the wrong hands.

And I had the feeling the king's hands were definitely the wrong ones.

"I have hurt one of your men," I said. "I would make amends. Heal him."

The king's eyes narrowed immediately. "You have healing abilities?"

"Yes." Should I have revealed that? I didn't know. I felt like I was standing on very thin ice. I didn't even have Tor's reassuring presence in the room. God, I wanted Kai here. I gestured towards the soldier. "May I?"

"He will be fine," the king said, turning away from the man. "Halfdan!"

On the king's shout, a man emerged from behind one of the drapes on the back wall. I caught a glimpse of a corridor there before the heavy material fell back into place. The mystery of what might be down there only consumed me for a moment, though. Halfdan was draped from head to toe in a thick grey robe. It had a draping hood that hid most of his face, only a braided beard and hooked nose visible. He was one of the temple priests.

"Your highness?" Halfdan enquired, bowing low.

"Bring me Birger. I want to do the ceremony now." He turned to the back of the room where the nobles were watching with great interest. "Where the hell is the Hound?"

As if on cue, the great double doors that I had entered, swung open once more. At first, all I saw were soldiers, but then I glimpsed Lord Kenwick, his fire dancing in his hand, and on the other side of him-

"Kai," I breathed.

He looked up immediately, as if he'd heard me, though I was sure my voice hadn't carried even as far as the king and Prince Faron beside me, and our eyes locked. I felt a rush of warmth, the effects of whatever the priests were doing lightening briefly. I raked my eyes over his form, which was naked bar a grotty pair of trousers, and noticed he was dirty and disheveled, but not really bruised. He didn't look like they'd hurt him.

Would I have known if they had, I wondered? Would I have felt it?

I felt his relief at seeing me, safe and well. And fear, not for his own life, but that he was about to lose me.

Not a chance, I thought, trying hard to project the words into his head. *If they kill you, they lose me.*

Kai had told me that once a Bound man died, the spirit he'd called from the Ether vanished back there. Of course, there was no way to know if that was true or not, but if it was...

The thought of returning to that void of endless nothingness made my stomach clench. The silence, the loneliness, the disorientation of having no up or down, no left or right. But if the alternative was to stay here and be the king's puppet, rain down who knew what kind of destruction?

Kai's eyes widened. I was glowing, I noticed suddenly, my breaths coming in harsh little gasps. I was on the verge of exploding, I thought.

Not yet, a little voice whispered inside my mind. *Not yet.*

I tried to see out the door as it closed behind Kai, to see if I could glimpse Tor or one of the other Hounds, but all I saw were the uniformed shoulders of the guards.

"Lord Kenwick," the king boomed beside me, making me jump. "I look to you to contain the Hound until the priests are ready."

"Of course, sire," Lord Kenwick replied oily.

He led Kai a little further into the room and then a soldier pushed Kai to his knees. A moment later, Lord Kenwick's fire sprite exploded from his hand, encircling Kai in a wall of flame.

"Please," I gasped, turning pleading eyes on the king. "You don't have to do this. Kai promised we would work for the kingdom."

"You don't leave your most precious treasure in the hands of another man and pray he looks after it," the king told me, "Never mind a dog. You belong at my side."

"I won't," I spat back. "I won't bind to you."

"Kenwick," the king said coolly.

A moment later, Kai screamed in pain. I whirled to see the fire had tightened on him and was licking at his skin.

"Stop it!" I shouted. I turned to the king, prepared to blast him the way I'd blasted the vase—he couldn't bind to me if he was splashed over the floor like a can of spilled paint—but before I had a chance to focus, Prince Faron grabbed my arm.

"Contain her!" he yelled.

I blinked, not knowing what that meant, and tugged, trying to free myself. Whatever Prince Faron's reverence and awe of me had been, now he was coolly ruthless, tightening his hold as I tore at his fingers with my free hand. His jaw was clenched and resolute, but I could feel his distress radiating up my arm. This wasn't going the way he'd hoped.

Well, it wasn't going the way I'd hoped, either!

My suspicions about what might be lurking behind the drapes around the room were confirmed a moment later when we were suddenly surrounded by a half dozen priests. Not Halfden, and the old priest—Birger?—the one I thought was in charge, was nowhere to be seen either. The priests freed their hands from their robes, and I flinched, hunting for weapons. No guns here, though. The priests themselves were the weapons. When they started chanting, I felt that cold grip wind around my heart and squeeze.

"No,' I gasped.

I pulled at Prince Faron once more, but I felt weak now, my thoughts scattered. My whole body felt like it had been whacked with a tuning fork, my cells vibrating. It was disorienting, and it rocketed my panic higher.

"Kai!" I called in desperation, though there was nothing he could do to help. Kenwick's fire had him pinned in a cage. I heard him roar in frustration, but I couldn't feel the anger. It was like whatever the priests were changing had flung up a temporary block between us.

"Please," I said, whirling back to the king. "Please!"

Please make it stop. Please don't do this. Please just leave us the hell alone.

It didn't matter which one I meant, the king ignored me, turning back to the rear of the throne room.

"Where the hell is Birger?"

"I am here, Highness." The high priest appeared between one blink and the next, an expertly performed sleight of hand. I froze, my struggles against Prince Faron pausing for an instant, then redoubled my efforts.

"I want the binding performed now!"

The high priest paused, keen eyes taking in the scene. He was the only priest without his head covered, his thin hair pulled back into a bun and a strange symbol tattooed on his forehead.

"The binding ceremony is a tricky thing to manage, Your Highness. I need time to prepare—"

"Now!" the king growled.

Birger's lips pinched, but he nodded. "As you say, Your Highness." He stepped forward. "You will need to be touching the Celestial."

The king moved towards me, meaty hand already reaching to grab at me. I tried to shy away, but Prince Faron held me in place. Trapped, I tried to reach down into the well of energy inside me, the core that I'd only made the first steps in mastering. It spurted and died, held prisoner by whatever spell the priests were chanting. Blind panic took over then.

"Help!" I screamed. "Help!"

The Hounds outside couldn't have failed to notice the commotion in the room, and with the armored presence both inside and beyond, in the foyer, there would be nothing they could do, but rational thinking had given way to sheer instinct. I'd only felt this helpless once before in my life, and I hadn't been able to stop that.

I could not handle it happening again.

The king clamped his hand on my arm, tearing at the fabric of my sleeve so we were touching, skin to skin. The high priest performed his magic trick once more and appeared suddenly beside me. He placed his hand over the king's, and I felt an immediate zing right down to my bones. The world wobbled a bit, and I dimly heard the high priest yell something to his brethren around the outskirts of the room.

The chanting they were doing changed tempo and, though it didn't seem they'd gotten any louder, the words were ringing in my ears.

"Don't lose the connection, Your Highness," I heard Birger say.

It was happening. I could feel something inside me writhing, as though my innards were being shifted about. Liquified. Birger started chanting along with the priests, and the feeling intensified.

"No," I whispered. Then, more strongly, in a voice I didn't recognize as my own, "No."

30

Daith, I called to the creature at my side. *Help me.*

It responded immediately to my call, jumping up and clamping its teeth into the king's arm. The king yowled in pain and tried to free himself, releasing me in the process.

"Daith, no!" I heard Prince Faron shout, but the creature ignored him, turning to savage at the high priest's leg, fangs sinking in deep.

Free of the king's grip, and whatever energy the high priest had been channeling, I stumbled to the side. I felt light-headed, disoriented, but I also felt like a core of something had come to life inside of me.

"Get her! Hold her down!" Not the king's voice, I didn't think, but a noble perhaps. It rang with authority, and the soldiers in the room reacted, exploding from their positions, drawing weapons. Heading towards me.

I flung out a hand and they lifted in the air, and were thrown backward to slam into the stone walls. Swiping my arm sideways, I tore the priests from their feet and threw them as hard as I could across the floor.

"Her Bound!" Prince Faron this time. I knew his voice; though I had never heard it so frightened. "Kenwick!"

Kai! I turned in horror to see Kenwick, a smile on his face, waving his hand at the fire sprite. It responded immediately, falling in on Kai and burning him alive.

"Don't kill him!" Birger shrieked. "Not yet!"

The fire wasn't killing him, but it was agony. I could

see it on Kai's face as he writhed, unable to escape the flames.

Enough, I thought it in my mind, and threw it at the fire. *Come to me.*

I knew that it would obey me. Whatever the part of me inside that had awoken it, understood my powers better than I did. The fire was mine to command, as was the cat creature, and the Gryt.

The fire zoomed towards me, twining around my body like a puppy, delighted to welcome its owner home, like it had been waiting for me to claim it. It didn't burn, only tickled my skin with warmth.

Keep them back, I thought. *Protect me.*

"To me!" Kenwick was shouting, "To me!" His hand was outstretched for the fire spirit, but it was ignoring his calls. I saw the panic on his face when he understood that he'd lost control of his Bound, that it was mine now.

Burn him to ash. The words whispered in my mind, but I didn't think they were mine. Was it the fire spirit, begging permission? I wasn't interested in killing anyone, though, I just wanted to get out there. Get Kai out of there.

Pulling hard on the energy now swirling inside me, I threw out a burst of power, knocking everyone in the room to the ground, then I dashed to Kai's side, grabbing his arm where he was struggling to get up off the floor. His flesh was bubbled and blistered from the fire.

"Are you ok?" I gasped. Stupid question, of course he wasn't. "Can you get up?"

Kai didn't answer, just groaned, bleeding and raw hands reaching for me.

I glanced up and saw the fire spirit had surrounded us in a little circle of flame. We were safe, for the moment.

"Let me help you," I murmured.

I pressed my hands against his torso, where the damage seemed to be worst, following him down to the ground when he tried to flinch away from me. Adrenaline was pounding through my system, my thoughts scattered and frantic. I couldn't remember how I'd healed Conlon, but I poured sheer desperation down into my hands, sobbing with relief when his skin started firm up before my eyes.

There wasn't time to deal with every little injury, but I pressed my hands to his face, which was weeping, one eye exposed, the eyelid burned away, and held on until the gaze that stared back at me was the Kai I knew.

"My lady," he breathed.

I let out an ugly cry, then pressed my mouth against his, kissing him hard.

"Fuck this place," I told him. "I think we should leave."

"I was wrong to bring you here," Kai agreed.

"So, we should go," I pressed.

He let out a ghost of a smile. "I do not think they are just going to let us walk out, my lady."

"You let me worry about that," I told him. "Can you stand?"

He got to his feet with some heavy support from me, then looked about. It was only then he noticed the fire shield, Daith prowling around the edges of it.

"What is happening?" he asked.

"I've borrowed Lord Kenwick's fire sprite," I panted, shoving my shoulder under Kai's armpit so he wouldn't undo all our hard work and crash to the ground. "And Prince Faron's creature. They're coming with us."

"What?" Kai asked, blinking. He was going to pass out, I thought. A sheen of sweat beaded on his forehead. I couldn't feel any heat from the fire sprite, but Kai obviously could.

"I'll explain later. Let's go."

I looked behind me, the soldiers were getting to their feet, the nobles crowded around the king, who was still on the floor with his son. They'd been closest to me when I'd slammed everyone with my power. The priests, too, were regrouping. Under Birger's urgent encouragement, they'd started chanting again. I felt whatever spell it was they were wielding try to slide over me, sticky and clinging like a spider's web. It couldn't get a grip on me, though. Whatever rage had propelled me into action was burning hot enough to make me impervious to their sorcery. Or maybe it was the fire spirit, blazing between me and them.

Keep them back, I instructed the fire spirit, and it spread out, creating a shield from wall to wall, preventing the priests, the soldiers, anyone from stopping us from shuffling towards the door.

"Daith," I said to the creature beside me, "Be ready."

I needed to give the same advice to myself. I was planning to blast the soldiers outside with energy, and give us a chance to escape, but I was shaking all over, was struggling just to keep Kai on his feet.

I reached out with my mind and grabbed the door handles, wrenched the thing open with my mind and—

Instead of the line of armed palace guards I was

expecting, came face to face with my guard, bloodied, battered, but standing amid a floor littered with groaning bodies.

They look as surprised to see me as I was to see them.

"We need to go," I stated. There would be time for explanations on both sides later.

Jay and Bex rushed forward to take Kai from me, handling his weight much better than I had. Without him to prop me up, though, I wobbled.

"My lady," Tor was at my side in an instant, a hand winding around my waist.

"If you don't start calling me Bethany, I'm going to burn you alive with my new fire spirit," I gasped.

"With your—" He turned and looked at the wall of flame, paled.

"It's coming with us," I said. "Get everyone in close."

Tor did as I said, barking out orders, and as soon as all the Hounds were gathered in close, I called to the fire sprite.

I give you a choice. Stay with your Bound, or come with me.

Jesus, I hoped it came with me, or my plans to get us out of there were scuppered, but I also wasn't Lord Kenwick to command and enslave.

I needn't have worried. The fire sprite rushed towards me like a small child afraid of being left behind. It wrapped around us, and several Hounds shouted out shocked exclamations.

"It's all right," I promised. "It won't hurt us."

Daith butted my hip with his head, as if reminding me that he was there.

"You are coming too?" I asked him. "You don't have to."

He yowled and butted me again, which I took as a yes. All right, then.

I slammed the doors of the throne room behind us with my mind, mangling the locks so they couldn't be opened again. Then we started heading towards the main door of the palace. The fire sprite obscured much of the world around us, but I could hear the yells of the soldiers. No one tried to fight their way through the flame; I couldn't blame them. It was no ordinary fire; I'd seen it consume a man in moments.

I hadn't been outside in days, and my eyes had become accustomed to the yellow warmth the countless sconces in the palace put out. When we made it to the front door, the light was absolutely blinding. Tears streamed from my eyes, and it took me a moment to realize why we'd stopped, why the Hounds around me were muttering quietly.

The guards hadn't tried to stop us in the tight corridors of the palace. In fact, they'd been guiding us outside to the wide space in front of the palace...where it seemed an army had gathered to greet us.

Shit.

The fire sprite continued to burn around us, apparently unperturbed by the move from inside to outside, and none of the soldiers waiting for us made a move to try and penetrate the shield. I had a feeling, though, that they weren't going to move aside for us. Which meant... stalemate.

Could the fire spirit mow a path through them, burning men to ash? Was it powerful enough for that?

And was I willing to order it to try? How many men would die if I did?

They weren't fighting for a Celestial. They were just here because they'd been ordered to be.

"I can't," I whispered.

I wouldn't.

"My lady?" Tor asked. Then, "Bethany?"

"I don't know what to do," I confessed. "We can't fight our way through, and I can't, I can't—"

My voice choked. I was at the very end of my strength, the end of my ability to cope. I was about to be the worst heroine in history and burst into tears at the eleventh hour.

"Incoming!" The shout went out from one of my guard.

I jerked, looking to the army of soldiers, but they hadn't moved.

"Arrow!" someone else shouted. "Arrow!"

I turned to the sky, and caught something speeding towards us through the blue. I didn't have time to focus on it. Ferris grabbed my shoulder and pulled me into a bent-over position, his chest lying across my back, protecting me.

"Wait," Tor rumbled. "It's not an arrow."

Ferris relaxed his grip and I wiggled free, just in time to see a giant bird plummeting out of the sky. The Gryt. It was General Tuill's Gryt.

I threw my arm up for it to land on, bracing for a hard landing, but the bird decelerated with astonishing skill, landing with delicate claws on my forearm.

"Do you have a message," I asked, ferreting about at the

feathers on the bird's front, but there was no tiny piece of parchment tucked away. Instead, the bird ducked and weaved, doing a little dance to try and catch my eye. I stared at it, confused, and an image bloomed in my mind. The pack, seen from high above, from a bird's eye view, right outside the town gates.

"The pack," I gasped. "The pack is here."

"What?" Tor asked. "Where?"

"They're outside the gates," I told him. "The Gryt showed me."

"That's where they'll stay if the gates are barred," Ferris muttered. "This place is designed to withstand a siege."

"We need to go to them," Tor agreed.

"Right," I said. "Right. There's just the little matter of—" I gestured to the lines of soldiers standing in front of us, "them."

"Can you keep the fire spirit around us as we walk?" Tor asked.

"I can," I replied dubiously, "But I don't think they'll move."

A hint of a smirk flitted on Tor's lips. "You are a Celestial, my lady," he reminded me. "Move them."

Right, move them. My muscles trembled at the very thought, but the pack's arrival had buoyed me. Help was here if we could only get to them. I looked over to Kai, struggling to stand. I knew if I didn't get us out of this moment, he would die and I'd either be given to the king as his personal havoc wreaker or disappear back to the silence of the Ether.

No thank you.

I took a deep breath and turned back to the soldiers in front of us. I imagined a line right down the middle of them, and threw my thoughts in that direction, shoving aside anything that stood in my way. Bodies tumbled to the side and cries of alarm rent the air. A small wall I hadn't noticed exploded under the force of my mind, filling the air with choking dust.

The path was clear, though. For a moment at least.

"Let's go," I gasped.

Feeling a bit like Moses after he'd parted the Red Sea, I scurried down the tunnel I'd made, moving with a lot less dignity than the biblical figure probably had. The wall of fire flamed around us, preventing any of the recovering soldiers, or those who had been stood outside of the blast radius, from grabbing at us. Perhaps it was because we were outside, or because I was spreading it wider than I had before, but it seemed to me that the fire was more transparent than it had been previously, the world beyond visible like I was peering through rippling water.

I hoped it wasn't running out of steam, like I felt I was, or we were all screwed.

We were moving as fast as we could, with Kai half propped up and me a stumbling mess, but the town gate seemed to take an eternity to appear. Every second I expected the fire wall to fail, for us to be fallen upon and restrained by the soldiers, stalking us as we carved a way through the town. When the gate finally came into sight, I was so relieved I almost dropped. The fire spirit wobbled around me, shocking me back to my senses. The pack were there, I reminded myself. Right there.

In fact, I could feel them, the warm pulsing mass of them waiting just on the other side of the wall. Aggression, anxiety, anger; it was thick in the air.

Brannon, I thought, envisaging him in my mind, right at the front of the throng, teeth bared in threat. *If you can hear this, we're coming. We need to get out of here. Fast.*

I had no idea if he could hear me, and silence rang in my head afterward, nothing coming back, but I forged ahead anyway.

"The gate, my lady," Tor murmured beside me. "Can you?"

"No," I told him honestly. "I can't. I'm sorry."

I was spent, clinging onto the control I still had by my fingertips.

"It's all right," Tor said. "Time for us to look after you now."

The fire spirit took us right up to the gate, but try as I might, I couldn't push it out to encapsulate the little guard huts where the controls to open the siege gates were kept.

"Can you move the fire," Ferris asked, "so it's keeping the soldiers back?"

I nodded. "I think so. But the gate guards—"

Ferris gave me a wink and a grin, deliberately exposing those wicked sharp canines.

Oh. Right.

I did as he asked, unwrapping the fire from around us and sending it backward, to flare out as an impenetrable wall. Immediately, we were under attack. The gate guards fell on us, steel flashing in the weak sunlight. They didn't get near me, though, my guard exploding to meet the threat head-on. Daith, too, joined the melee, sinking teeth into a gate guard's leg, then going for the throat when the man dropped.

Time seemed to stand still as violence rang out around me, but even so, it felt like just a few, frightened heartbeats later that Jay and Dane had their hands on the gate wheels, were turning them with long, hard pulls, and the town gates groaned open.

There, standing on the other side, were Brannon and the rest of the pack. A wall of strength. Just seeing it, made mine give out.

"You're here," I gasped. Then everything gave way.

31

Seeing Lady Bethany drop made everything in Kai turn to ice. His body had betrayed him, and he'd not have made it down to the gates without the help of the Hounds, but seeing her legs give way beneath her, her eyes roll back into her head, he forgot his own weakness.

He caught her before she hit the ground, shoving Rye out of the way when her guard member moved to do the same thing.

"Bethany?" His voice was tight and panicked in a way he'd not heard before. She was warm in his arms, but the glow that always pulsed beneath her skin had retreated so deep it was almost invisible.

Prince Faron's terrifying Bound creature was with them still, and it shoved its nose into her palm, whuffing like a worried pet.

He and Kai both.

"What in the fuck is going on?" Brannon appeared at his shoulder, worried eyes staring down at Lady Bethany, whose eyes were fluttering as she tried and failed to regain consciousness. "I was only gone a couple of days!"

"It's been a very bad couple of days," Kai replied. "We need to move, fast. Tell me you have a horse?"

Brannon, who had been eyeing the firewall with a mixture of awe and fear, jerked his head back to his First and nodded.

Thank the gods for small mercies.

"Get it."

"Kai, what the hell is going on?"

"I'll tell you once we're far from here."

It took almost no time to get a horse front and center. Kai scrambled up, his body protesting its recent abuses, and Brannon and Tor carefully passed Lady Bethany up to him. She nestled against him, slurred nonsense babbling from her lips, her eyes still closed.

"What do we do about that?" Tor asked, jerking his head towards the fire sprite.

"We hope it stays put long enough for us to get a head start," Kai replied.

"And the creature?" Tor glanced at Daith, who was prowling around the horse's legs.

"The creature is free to stay or go." It would come with them, Kai knew. It was as enamored with Lady Bethany as he was.

Well, perhaps not quite as enamored, but Kai would bet his left arm that the creature would go wherever Lady Bethany did. Prince Faron would not be pleased with that, but Kai had had about enough of dealing with the palace. The accords he'd struck for the Hounds were over, they had to be.

There would be fallout from that, but he couldn't think of the consequences right now.

In honesty, it was amazing the peace had lasted as long as it had.

"Let's move." He kicked the horse into motion and emerged from the shadow of the gated archway, out into the midst of the pack. The Hounds were disciplined, seasoned fighters, but they crowded the horse and its burdens like mother hens, trying to get a look at their Celestial. He could understand their concern—they'd no idea why they'd been called back and now their angel, their salvation, had emerged unconscious and wan—but now wasn't the time or the place.

"To the pass," he barked out.

A shiver slid over the pack as the Hounds reveled in having their First back in charge, then the mood changed between one heartbeat and the next. They ranged out, taking up position. The front runners streaked across the flat expanse of land that separated the fortified palace down from the foothills and the pass that would give them some measure of protection, and the rest of the pack gathered at the rear, forming a wall between Lady Bethany and the royal soldiers, ready for the moment when the firewall failed.

Kai expected a barrage of arrows to rain down on them as they fled, but the skies stayed empty bar General Tuill's Gryt, soaring above their heads.

"We need to deal with that bird," he warned Tor, who was running at his side, with the rest of Lady Bethany's guard. "He'll relay our position straight back to the general."

"I wouldn't be so sure about that," Tor panted, the pace hard for the older Hound. Not that he'd ever admit it. "That Gryt is Lady Bethany's now. Why do you think the pack is here? I don't know how they got here so fast, still. It must have guided them a shorter route home."

How the pack got there was a very good question Kai hadn't bothered to ask, he'd just thanked his lucky fucking stars. There would be all sorts of questions to answer once they were far enough away for his heart to stop clamoring in his chest at the imminent threat of danger.

When the firewall eventually gave way, it did so with a whoosh that sent a frisson over Kai's skin. He looked back to see a streak of fire zooming towards them at an astonishing speed, covering the ground they'd managed to place between themselves and the town in seconds. Frightened shouts went up from the Hounds at the rear, some of them turning to face what they perceived as a threat. Kai knew better. Like the creature Daith, like the Gryt, the fire sprite was Lady Bethany's now.

"Let it through," he shouted. "Don't engage."

Any Hound that tried to engage with the fire was likely to be incinerated at any rate.

His Hounds sprang out of the way and the fire sprite whizzed through the ranks. Even though Kai had given the order to leave it, he couldn't help but wince and round his shoulders protectively as the flame shot straight for them. It circled around him, close enough for him to feel the heat singe the hairs curling around his right ear, then settled in Lady Bethany's lap. A moment later, it vanished, as if it had sunk into her.

Lady Bethany groaned.

"What happened?" Tor asked, eyes narrowing on the space where the fire sprite had disappeared. "Where did it go?"

"I don't know," Kai replied, teeth gritted at the whole fucking situation. "Let's just get somewhere safe."

He glanced behind, expecting to see soldiers streaking out of the town gates now that the fire spirit was no longer holding them at bay, but other than a small group clustered around the gated entrance, there was no one to be seen.

They weren't being followed.

"They're not chasing us," Conlon commented, his words coming in gasps, a sign of the hard pace the pack were setting. "Why aren't they chasing us?"

"I don't know," Kai said. He didn't trust it.

"It's her," Ferris said. "Lady Bethany."

"Lady Bethany is in no shape to fight anyone," Conlon argued.

"Do they know that?" Ferris shot back. "She has the full pack and now three other Bound creatures under her control."

"I can't believe they'd just let her leave, though," Conlon said.

"What choice do they have?" Tor said, siding with Ferris. "The fire spirit alone is enough to consume the town. It won't be over," he warned, lifting his gaze to Kai. "The king wants her."

"Well, he can't have her," Kai growled. "She's mine."

"He'll lick his wounds, then he'll try again," Ferris said. "He'll find a way to exploit your weaknesses."

The commune, that was what Ferris was referring to. The females and young. The reason Kai has been drawn into bringing Lady Bethany to the palace in the first place.

"We'll have to make sure we have no weaknesses, then," Kai replied.

A brief moment of quiet. "And how do you plan to do that?" Tor asked.

That was the trouble, Kai didn't know.

"Let's just get the hell out of here first," he said. "Then we'll sort out the rest."

They ran hard all the way to the pass, the horse lathered in sweat by the time Kai pulled it to a walk so that it could pick its way gingerly over the rocky, narrow path. The ground sloped up steeply, pushing Lady Bethany back into his chest. She still hadn't woken, and that worried him, but they needed to get further into the mountains before he dared to call for a stop.

As the higher ground swallowed them, he felt a little of the pressure ease in his chest. The pack ranged out, clambering over rocks with ease and allowing Kai and Lady Bethany's guard to take the narrow path. This was where the Hounds held the clear advantage and were able to move much more quickly than the regimented soldiers who were weighed down with their armor, weapons, and ungainly limbs.

It was why Janis had sent them to deal with the Badari problem, after all.

Though they were hampered slightly by the horse, whose delicate legs and shod feet struggled with the uneven ground, they had still made enough progress after an hour or so of climbing for Kai to feel comfortable agreeing with Brannon when his second suggested a small widening in the path was a good place to take a breath and regroup.

It was Brannon that Kai passed Lady Bethany off to, watching as his Second laid her out on the most comfort a traveling pack could scrounge together: a handful of grubby-looking blankets. He slid off his horse and had no choice but to join her when his knees buckled.

"You look like shit," Brannon said, eyeing him shrewdly.

"That's a fairly accurate assessment," Kai replied, reaching for Lady Bethany's hand. She was out of it still, her eyes closed as her head rested against a rolled-up spare jerkin that was serving as a pillow, but her skin was warm, the pulse from her core a little stronger, he fancied.

Or maybe he just hoped.

At any rate, he felt a need to touch her constantly, and after the ordeal they'd both just endured, he wasn't going to question it.

"What the hell happened?" Brannon pressed, crouched down on Lady Bethany's other side. "We were halfway to the mountains when General Tuill's damned bird descended on us and nearly pecked the lift out of me, trying to deliver your message."

"It wasn't my message," Kai disagreed. He glanced up at Tor.

"Lady Bethany sent for the pack as soon as you were taken," Tor confirmed. He, too, looked exhausted, the stresses of leading Lady Bethany's guard wearing on him. He was one of Kai's most experienced Hounds, but that came with a price. He was almost to an age when a Hound was allowed to retire back to the commune, something that very rarely happened because Hounds just weren't allowed to live that long, but Kai knew he'd never go now. He'd stay and protect Lady Bethany if it killed him.

un Until it killed him.

Kai understood there was no point arguing. Besides,

there soon might not be a commune for Tor to retire to anyway.

"You were taken?" Brannon asked.

"The king wanted Lady Bethany," Kai said. "He was going to force bind her."

"I thought the Celestial had to be willing to transfer the binding?"

"Apparently the priests found a way around it. They have spells we didn't know about. They were able to grab at our bond, strangle it. How do you think they got me out of her room?"

There was a heavy beat of silence.

"They took you from her bedroom?" Brannon asked quietly.

Kai looked over at his second and saw the real question in Brannon's eyes.

"She invited me," Kai croaked out. "I'm hers to do with as she pleases."

"You...you fucked her?" Brannon's voice seemed torn between horror and awe.

"You would have refused her?" Kai shot back.

Brannon looked down at Lady Bethany. "I could not," he admitted.

Kai swallowed back the urge to kill his Second for daring to even contemplate such an honor—he'd asked the question, after all—and went on with the debriefing.

"Prince Faron signed an execution warrant, but they had to wait for the king to return before it was exacted, to transfer the binding. Otherwise, I'd be food for the Gryts."

"You seemed to have things fairly well in hand by the

time I saw you," Brannon said, a small smirk on his lips. "How did you get away from the priests? And why the hell do we have a Gryt and whatever that damned creature is, following us."

"And a fire spirit," Dane chipped in helpfully from where he was untacking the horse.

"And a fire spirit," Brannon agreed, even though said fire spirit was currently nowhere to be seen.

"I am...honestly not certain," Kai admitted. "I was surrounded by Kenwick's wall of fire, waiting to die."

"Lady Bethany," Tor said quietly. "She was... incredible."

"She's amazing," Brannon agreed.

She was, Kai thought. She absolutely fucking was. She was also awakening.

32

My head was pounding like a thousand tiny miners had taken to digging for gold inside my skull. I cracked my eyes open and immediately regretted it when the sunlight blinded me, bouncing gaily off an encircling wall of light sandstone rocks. It was warm, too. Or rather...I was warm. I could feel heat bubbling in my chest, but my hands and feet felt the chill of the air around me.

The fire spirit, I realized suddenly. The fire spirit was *in me*. I felt a moment's panic, images from the film Alien flashing in my mind, but when I turned my hand palm up and asked the fire spirit to move there, it did so without hesitation, appearing as a little flame, dancing merrily.

Someone gasped and I followed the sound and saw Brannon watching the flame with astonishment.

"Brannon," I croaked, "Where are we? Where's Kai?"

"Here." Kai's equally rusty voice came from beside me. He was sprawled out on the same pallet of small blankets that was trying valiantly to protect my aching body from the hard ground—and failing miserably. I hadn't even realized he was there, or that my guard were standing just a pace away, watching and waiting. The rest of the Hounds were there, too. All of them crammed into a small clearing in what I was now beginning to recognize as the pass we'd taken to come to the palace.

Everything was slow to come to me, though. I felt like

I was drunk, piecing the world together at half the speed I normally did.

I needed to get it together.

I tried to sit up, and Kai's arms immediately came around me, keeping me still.

"Just rest," he said. "Just rest a minute. You've exhausted yourself, my lady."

I glowered at him, annoyed at my own weakness and that he was right. Just trying to lift my torso off the ground had shown me that my muscles were jelly.

"Would you just call me Bethany?" I snapped petulantly, picking on the only thing left to argue about. "I've saved your life, you've saved mine. You've been inside me, for goodness' sake! Will you please just call me by my name? *Sans title!*"

Someone sucked in a breath, and I remembered just how surrounded we were. Oops.

Get it together, Bethany!

"Bethany," he growled at me, and I was pretty sure I was about to get a lecture in over-exerting myself again, but wow...the way he said my name. All growly and low like that. Places twitched and a flush ran right through me.

I wasn't thinking clearly, obviously, because I should be asking where we were and where we were going and if any soldiers were chasing us. Those were all important questions. Very important questions. Instead, I was thinking about Kai's hands being all over me, his cock...well, like I said. Inside me.

That had been the most erotic experience of my life,

like I was drowning in desire, every touch a tiny flame of pleasure.

"*Fuck me,*" Kai muttered beside me.

Precisely what I was thinking, I shot back.

It was a fleeting thought, and I was embarrassed as soon as I finished it, cheeks flushing red, but I also meant it. I didn't have to ask if Kai heard the words, his jaw turned to stone...and so did something else. I could feel it against my hip as he lay beside me.

"Brannon," he ground out. "Split the pack. I want half of them to scout ahead, check there are no surprises. Send the rest back, make sure we aren't being followed."

"It'll be night soon," Brannon argued. "Janis wouldn't be stupid enough to send troops into this kind of terrain in the dark. Not against us."

"Just do it," Kai spat.

"All right." Brannon looked from Kai to me and back to Kai again. He inhaled and his eyes widened, flashing back to me. I watched him blush crimson and it would have been amusing if I wasn't coloring to match. "I should...take myself away as well then, First?"

"You should," Kai agreed. Then, "Not too far. Just...out of earshot. Take her guard with you."

"Yes, First." Brannon nodded at Kai, avoiding looking at me. When he turned and walked away and started shouting orders to the Hounds, though, he was smirking.

In an inordinately short length of time, the tight, rocky clearing was empty except for the two of us, and the Bound creatures, Swift and Daith. I watched Kai eye them, clearly wondering if he could order them away, too. Well, he could try. I knew they wouldn't listen—to him anyway.

Go, I thought. *Just for a little while.*

The Gryt flew off immediately, soaring up to the higher ground. Daith took a lot longer, throwing Kai a long look before hauling his large cat-like body off the ground and padding away.

"I don't think that thing likes me," Kai muttered.

Daith paused and his tail twitched.

Daith, I thought warningly.

He waited a moment longer, then resumed his dignified retreat.

"Definitely doesn't like me," Kai said, once Daith's long tail had disappeared around the rock wall and out of sight.

"He helped save your life," I pointed out.

"I doubt that was for me," Kai replied dryly.

"Well," I said, giving a little shrug, "I like you."

I shifted around so that I was on my side facing him, rather than reclined on my back. The rocky ground dug hard into my hip in this position, but the reward, lying flush against the length of Kai's body, was worth it.

I rested my fingertips on his tunic, stroking lightly at his stomach muscles through the light material.

"My Lady Bethany," he corrected.

"Are you going to refuse me?" I asked, smiling slightly. "You don't want to refuse me."

It wasn't just his erection that was telling me that. He was radiating arousal, along with a heady possessiveness that should have been a red flag to me, but which really made me want to press into him, rub my body against his.

"You're a Celestial," he said, leaning back to put an inch of space between us. "It's a desecration."

"That sounds filthy," I murmured. "Desecrate me."

"Bethany, please—"

"That supposed to be my line."

I pushed into him, closing the small distance he'd put between us, and, when he went to re-establish it, I leaned with him, until he fell onto his back, my torso draped over him. I shifted so that I was high enough to reach his mouth, pressing my lips to his and straddling his thigh, rocking against him. I was turned on already, and I groaned as I felt the pressure against my clit.

Hands clamped on my ass, encouraging me to keep rocking. I did so, rotating my pelvis in tiny circles, and we both moaned.

"I love feeling your pleasure," Kai whispered, pulling away from my mouth and kissing his way across my cheek until he found that sensitive skin under my jaw.

"Our pleasure," I countered. I ground against him again and both of us shuddered. I ran my hands over his shoulders and down his sides. He made a noise of pleasure at my touch, but I also didn't miss the tiny spike of pain he tried to conceal from me. "Are you all right?" I asked.

"I'm fine," came the immediate response.

"Hmm," I said. "I would see for myself."

I sat up, putting a hand on his chest when he went to follow, ensuring he lay sprawled beneath me. My hands went to the ties at the top of his tunic, loosening them to reveal the upper portion of his chest. Bruises and the shiny red of burn marks marred the skin.

"I'm fine," he repeated.

I ignored him, encouraging him to lift just enough so that I could tug the tunic off him. It was awkward, with him lying beneath me, and though he tried very hard to hide it, I could tell that one shoulder was stiff and paining him.

"You don't have to pretend with me," I said. "I feel how much it hurts you, and I have eyes." I pressed my fingertips lightly to his abdomen, which was a canvas of blue, purple and yellow bruising.

Kai set his mouth mulishly. "You are exhausted, I don't want you to waste your energy healing me. I am fine."

"I believe I told you I wouldn't be dictated to over who I chose to heal," I murmured, trying to keep my tone light. I quirked my mouth in a smirk. "But if you really are fine—"

"I am."

My smirk widened. "Then perhaps I'll just waste my energy on other endeavors. Besides," I added, leaning down until my mouth hovered over Kai's chest. He watched me with avid eyes. "Kisses have magical healing properties, too."

I dropped a kiss on a small, fingerprint-sized burn on his left pectoral, then moved across to the next bruise, and the next. I could feel Kai's gaze on me, but I kept my focus on my task, kissing better every single tiny hurt he'd endured because of me. When I'd finished with his chest, I moved down to his stomach, chasing the marbled pattern of bruises with the tip of my tongue. Kai groaned, his stomach muscles tightening and his erection pressing harder against his trousers. I could feel it, nestled in between my breasts.

I wouldn't be rushed though; I was determined to attend to each injury, even shifting over so that I could press soft, open-mouthed kisses to the sensitive skin on his side. Kai twitched and shifted; my touch as ticklish as it was pleasurable.

"Hold still," I instructed him. "I'm doctoring."

"Are you sure you aren't torturing me some more?" he asked, flexing his hips slightly in a silent plea.

"Let me guess," I said, shifting onto my knees and slipping back a bit. I put a hand to the fastening of his trousers, his cock rigid beneath the tough material. "This is where it hurts?"

"It is," Kai agreed, a mischievous gleam in his eye.

"I suppose I'd better have a look then," I replied, just as mischievously.

I made short work of unfastening his trousers and sliding them down and off. As soon as he was naked, Kai tried to sit up and reach for me, but I planted my hand back in his chest and shoved.

"You're being a very bad patient," I admonished him.

"I have heard that before," he grinned.

"Lie back and let me see!" I commanded. Then, more softly, "Lie back and let me tend to you."

It wasn't in his nature to do so, to submit and let me explore, but after a moment's hesitation, Kai did as I asked, lifting his good arm so he could rest a hand behind his head, and create a pillow so that he could watch me.

And he was watching me, eyes hot. I felt a surge of hesitation, of shyness, but he wanted me, I could feel that with absolute certainty. I swallowed my inhibition, concentrating on what I was doing. I ran my fingertips up his inner thigh and then along the hard length of him. I circled the head with my fingertips, gathering a glistening drop of precum and smearing it around his tip. He bobbed beneath my touch, obviously wanting more, but I hadn't much chance to explore him last time, and I was determined to make up for it.

He had a very pretty cock.

I continued my torture of him a little longer, tracing a vein that ran down his shaft and caressing the soft skin of his balls, then I let my mouth follow the same path, swirling my tongue around the head and then kissing my way down to the base. I was about to be mean, leave his cock entirely and smatter kisses across his hips and thighs, but a hand in my hair made me pause, even though his grip was gentle.

"Bethany," he murmured.

I glanced up to see his eyes were slits, his features suffused with pleasure and mounting frustration.

Oh, all right then. It wasn't as though it was a hardship.

I engulfed him in my mouth, wrapping my fingers around the thickness at the base of his cock and starting a slow rhythm, sliding up and down, coating him with my saliva.

I gasped. I could tell that Kai was enjoying my ministrations. He was panting lightly, and his hand had tightened slightly in my hair. Out of the corner of my eye, I could see he'd given up using his free hand as a pillow and was now clawing at the ground with it, trying to stop himself from grabbing me and taking over.

That was enough in itself, especially when I glanced up

and saw he'd thrown his head back, mouth open in ecstasy, but also…I could feel it, what I was doing to him, pulsing hard in my clit. I liked giving oral, liked showing my partner pleasure, but with this link between us, it was almost like he was licking me as I was sucking him.

Wow.

I tried to concentrate on what I was doing, tried to keep the images of Kai and me, locked in a '69' position out of my head, but I wasn't succeeding.

"Oh, yes!" I heard Kai hiss the words and then the next thing I was in motion, hands tearing at my clothes. I landed on the pallet on my back and hands spread my thighs apart, a hot mouth delving between my legs. My eyes rolled back in my head at the sharp pleasure of it and I tried to close my legs. It was too much.

"No," Kai growled. "Let me."

Trying to distract myself, I reached for Kai's cock. He'd read my mind and had positioned himself just as I'd imagined, hovering over me in the soixante-neufe position. I drew him into my mouth, taking him as deep as I could, hollowing my cheeks as I sucked and licked. He growled in response, redoubling his efforts and it was just…pleasure upon pleasure. Vibrating and growing as we fed it back to each other.

"Oh God," I gasped, pulling my mouth away so I could haul in quick, agitated breaths. "God, I'm going to cum."

I felt Kai's clawed fingers dig into my thigh where he had my leg held in a firm grip. He drew my clit into his mouth and flicked his tongue over the sensitive nub in a series of rapid flutters and that was it, I exploded.

The world went white for an endless moment. I clutched at Kai's legs, trying to hold on as convulsions rippled through my lower abdomen.

"Again," he said, lifting up for a moment to kiss my inner thighs.

What?

"I can't," I panted. "Please, fuck me."

"Again," he repeated.

He dropped his head back down, strong hands holding me in place when I tried to shift away, my clit too sensitive for even the gentlest touch. I couldn't go back to pleasuring him, could only press my head against the long length of his thigh as he forced my body to give him what he wanted.

It was ecstasy and agony, too much and yet I wanted it, to reach the peak again and feel that rush run through me. I shook against him, my nerves overstretched and sweat beading on my skin. This time when I came, I cried out, the sound echoing off the rocks around me. I heard a crack, the ground beneath me vibrating slightly, and the hiss of what sounded like slipping gravel, but I didn't have a chance to look and see what was happening. Kai was on top of me, inside of me, surrounding me. I felt his heat as his body covered mine, tasted myself on his lips as his tongue delved in to play with mine. I felt his desire rocketing down our connection and my core, which had decided it couldn't possibly take any more, suddenly fired up, ready to go again.

I wrapped my limbs around Kai and did my best to hold on for the ride as he drew back and plunged forward, drew back and plunged forward, moving agonizingly slowly at first then faster and faster until I couldn't catch my breath, couldn't separate the surges of pleasure from each thrust. It was like one continuous orgasm, my head thrown back just as his had been moments ago, my nails digging hard into his skin. I was aware that I was jabbering nonsense, a litany of, "Oh God, oh please, oh yes," dribbling from my lips, but I couldn't stop it and I didn't care. I was lost in abandon, simply feeling as Kai pounded his way to an orgasm that tore through us both, scraping over my nerves like a jagged lightning streak.

I definitely heard a crack this time. I opened my eyes as Kai dropped his weight down onto me, burying his face into my neck, and saw puffs of dust in the air.

"What's happening?" I asked. "Earthquake?"

I hoped not, because I couldn't move. I felt like jelly, my body utterly spent.

Kai laughed; the puff of hot air ticklish against my sweaty skin.

"No earthquake," he promised. "It was you. You release energy with your pleasure."

I tried to digest that. I could crack rocks with my orgasms? It sounded laughable, but I'd learned to stop throwing around the word impossible.

"Are we safe?" I asked instead.

Kai lifted his head and looked around us. The dust had settled quickly; all was quiet and calm again.

"We are," he said. He looked down at me, laughter in his eyes. "If you want to bring the mountain down on us, we'll have to try again."

"Maybe in a minute," I suggested, smiling. A moment

later, though, the humor fell from my face. "Are we safe, Kai?"

A different question this time, and Kai understood. He grimaced, then detangled his limbs from mine and held out my tunic for me to slide into. I did so, my body objecting to being asked to move, then I watched him gingerly fight his way into his own clothes with dread sinking slowly into my stomach.

If we had to be dressed for this conversation, I already had my answer.

"What's going to happen?" I asked. "Where are we going to go?"

Kai sighed. "I broke my word to the king. I promised you would serve the kingdom and then—"

"And then he tried to steal me from you anyway," I interjected heatedly. I wasn't letting Kai take the blame for what had happened. It had been the machinations of the nobles that had made everything go wrong.

"I gave them an opportunity," Kai reminded me.

I waved that away. "They would have found one anyway. It was me that took you from the palace," I pointed out. "I'm the one who really broke your word."

Kai made a face. "It doesn't matter now," he said. "What's done is done."

"So, what are we going to do?" I asked. "The king will react, won't he?"

"He will," Kai agreed. "But he won't come at us, not with you here. And the three Bound creatures you've taken from his nobles."

I nodded soberly. I wasn't really sure how I'd ended up

with a fire sprite, a Gryt, and whatever the heck Daith was, but I was grateful to have them along.

"What will he do, do you think?"

"He'll strike at the commune."

"The commune? Where your women and children are? Kai—"

"We'll move them," he agreed. "I'll send half the Hounds there, have them pack everything up and escort everyone to the Badari mountains."

"The Badari mountains?" I asked, frowning. "Isn't that where…? I don't understand."

"It's perfect," Kai said. "They have the high ground with limited access, and they've riddled those hills with tunnels. Their resistance fighters were right to hole up there."

"But—" I didn't follow. "Weren't you and the pack a big part of the reason that they lost their lands in the first place? Surely they won't let you just move in?" I blanched. "You aren't planning to finish the job the king started, are you? Take it from them?"

"No." Kai shook his head firmly. "Not that." He made a face. "It might take some negotiating, but alone neither of us can stand against the kingdom, not for long. Together, we might have a chance."

"Do you think the Baradri will go for that?" I asked.

Kai gave me a wan smile. "There is only one way to find out. I do have one trick up my sleeve."

I reached out and plucked at the torn and filthy sleeve of Kai's tunic. "This sleeve?"

He chuckled and showed me the other arm, where the material had been torn off at the elbow. "This one."

"What is it?" I asked, then I realized. "It's me, isn't it."

"It's you," Kai agreed. "The Badari are very religious people. And I am bringing them an angel."

An angel. Though I knew what he meant, I couldn't help but envisage a heavenly being, good and pure, with brilliant white wings and a glowing halo.

"I am not much of an angel," I said softly. The idea of the Hounds' safe haven being dependent on me and my budding but inconsistent powers, my now indisputable status as a Celestial, was frightening to contemplate.

"Yes, you are," he disagreed. "You are perfect. An angel among dogs."

"You are not dogs," I disagreed, scowling.

"We are," Kai replied. "And you are our salvation. You'll see."

Right. Okay. The fate of the whole species, resting on my shoulders.

Terrific.

About the Author

Charli Mac writes Erotic Romance, often with a Fantasy or Science-Fiction twist. She's the author of the *His Mate* series as well as the RH sci-fi novel *Seven Stars*.

Originally from the lowlands of Scotland, she moved to Colorado in December 2019 (so she still has the accent…) for the sunshine and gorgeous Rocky Mountains.

Also from Dreamsphere Books

Dragon's Breath: Black Flame
Kenla Nelson

Nihility the Harbinger feels a flicker of danger, a sense of impending doom. She is the black dragoness, Empath, and Weaver of the Dreaming.

Destined the Farseer has been too long away from his body in a place called the Between. He is Nihility's mate, bonded eternally through their heart of hearts. Known as the prophet, and Walker, he now finds himself at the center of an old danger.

The demons known as the Prem threaten their homeworld. Hurrying to her mate's aid, Nihility calls on Destined's other mate, the Watcher, Endrir the Broken. All must unite, and overcome their differences—even if it means Endrir must expose the secrets he has tried to keep from Nihility—for the three dragons face more than just the seven great demons who seek their freedom. Jezzar, the once great dragoness, leads the forces of darkness, and Nihility will need her strength to face her, as only she can.

For she is the wielder of the Black Flame, their only hope.

Also from Dreamsphere Books

Realms of Valeron
Alison Cybe

When Roka joined the Realms of Valeron, he was a fledgling elven cleric with only a minor healing spell and a dingy brown robe to his name. But that was just fine, since it was the hottest fantasy MMORPG, with over a million players, and Roka could not resist the allure of this rich, bright fantasy world, eccentric NPCs, and ravenous monsters.

And best of all, he met his friends—a wild and eccentric band of misfits who would change his life forever!

Join Roka and his newfound guild as they face devastating Razor-Squirrels, confront the Labyrinths of Ancient Storylines, and rush to max level in order to take part in end-game content (while probably not reading any of the quest text as they go!). But the real treasure that they find isn't the Bejewelled Anklets of Monster-Commanding or even the mythical Pointy Stick—it's the friendship they make along the way.

Enter the Realms of Valeron, a tale of high humor and eager adventuring like nothing before!

Available now in paperback and ebook

Also from Dreamsphere Books

Immortal Whispers
Kon Blacke

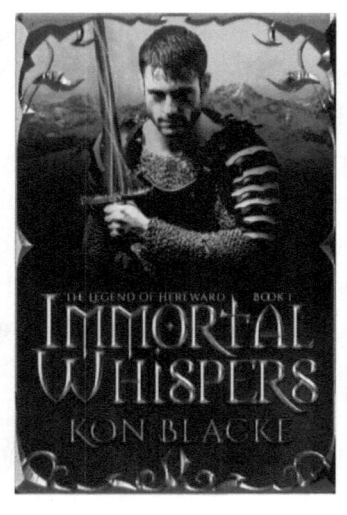

The Whispering Monks have foretold change to the world, and it's fast approaching. They also speak of the mortals who'll be involved.

Hereward, a lord knight who only worships the steel at his side, as the mad magician Ealdræd has taken away everyone he had ever loved. Wymond, an oblate determined to find his true self, even if it means turning away from everything he has ever known. Beornræd, a powerful magician who fears to love again after the cruelties of his past. Kieron, a stable hand with dragon blood flowing through his veins and is the rightful heir to a realm of unimaginable beauty.

All four will travel their own paths, to destroy their pasts and rebuild their future, as they thwart the evil plans of Ealdræd and his conduit, the immortal Abbot Hosho.

The whisperings continue through epic battles, both on the ground and in the sky.

The whisperings shall continue beyond the aftermath.

As it has been foretold.

Available now in paperback and ebook